LEGACY: THE REVELATION

LIZA MALLOY

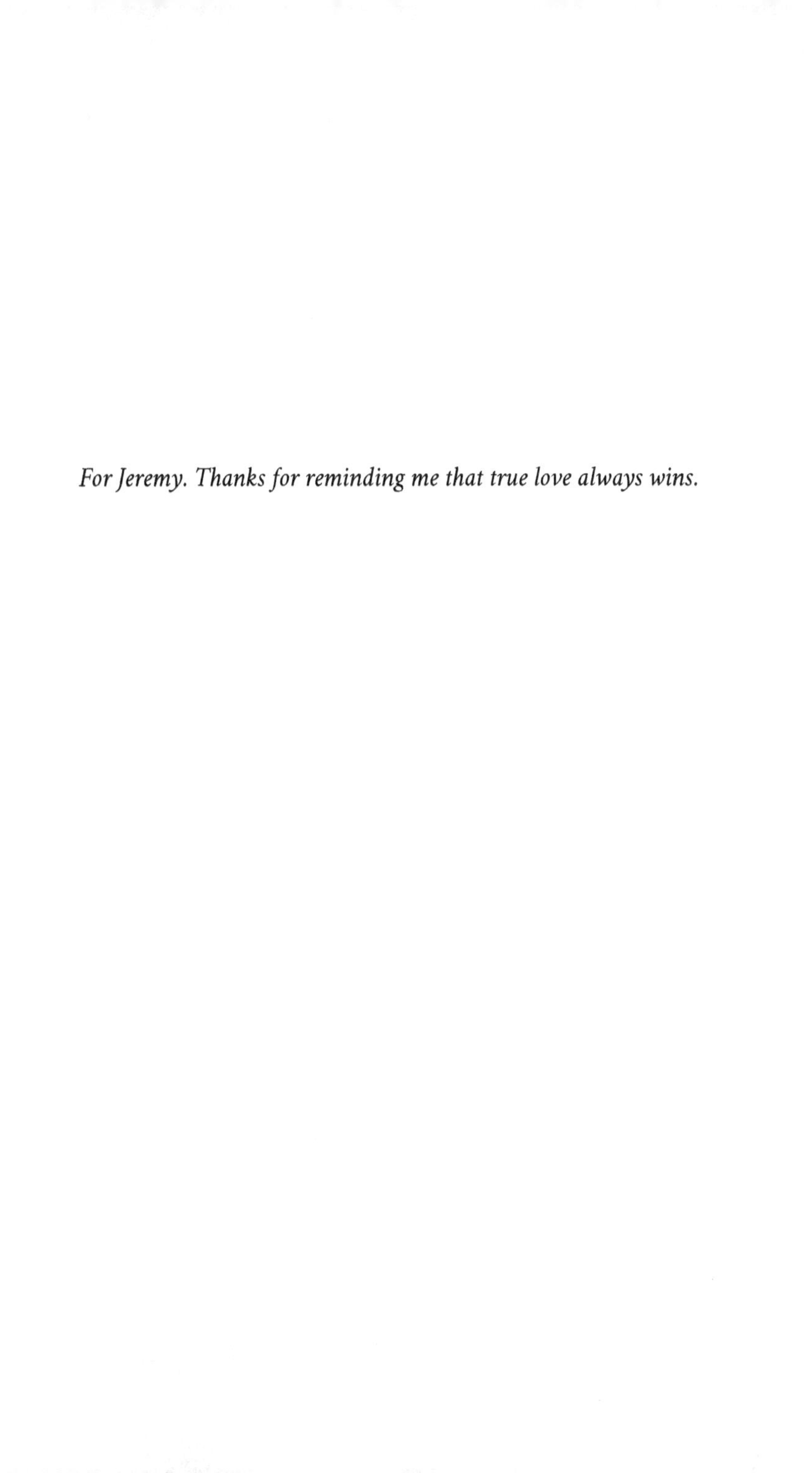

For Jeremy. Thanks for reminding me that true love always wins.

CHAPTER ONE

JESSICA

"Marry me, Jessica." Lucas' words reverberated in my ears.

I glanced back and forth from the sparkling diamond ring to Lucas' face, my heart pumping and palms sweating. My best friend—and probably the most desirable bachelor in our town—had just knelt before me and proposed with a remarkably heart-felt and romantic speech. Meanwhile, there I was panicking and blinking back tears.

Everything Lucas had said leading up to his proposal rang true. I believed him when he said he would do everything he could to make me happy. We could absolutely achieve something similar to the idyllic future he had just outlined for me if only I said yes.

A life with Lucas would mean I'd be safe, cherished, and free to pursue my dream career of teaching history. I could have chil-dren, raise them in the same small town where my grandma raised me after my parents died, and I could travel—or not—as often as I wanted.

I didn't have to consider my other option for long because, well, frankly I spent most of my time stressing about those possibilities already. My other option was a life of uncertainty, one where I might never have kids, might never even marry. That option definitely didn't involve me staying in my hometown or any one place for a long time, and it likely wouldn't permit me to hold down a stable teaching job.

But that second option involved Aiden. And Aiden was the love of my life, even if he did also happen to be an elf, slated to become king of his people right around the time I'd be graduating college.

"Jessica?" Lucas prompted, his emerald-green eyes pleading with me.

"I'm sorry Lucas. I...I...I have no idea what to say."

He licked his lips, patiently waiting, still kneeling before me.

"You caught me completely off guard. Five minutes ago I was packing and I didn't even expect to see you, let alone for you to tell me all this."

Lucas dropped his head and a short laugh escaped his lips. "I guess that's better than a flat out no and a slap across the face," he said, gazing back up at me with a weak smile.

"Will you stand up?" I asked, pulling on his wrists.

He shook his head. "No, I need to know..."

My heart was pounding a million beats a minute and I felt tears drying on my cheeks now. "I can't answer that, Lucas."

Lucas frowned.

"I..." I peered at the clock. "I'm supposed to leave for the airport in ten minutes. To meet Aiden. So I can't say yes," I inhaled deeply, realizing what I really wanted was to go back in time and keep him from ever asking me to be his wife. "But I can't lose you either. I do love you Lucas, and I need you in my life. I just can't...what happens if I say no?"

He closed his eyes for a moment and then he rose from his knees and sat beside me on the bed. "Nothing. I want you to say yes now, but I know that's not...realistic. I can't hate you, Jessica."

Lucas ran his fingers through his dark brown hair. "Lord knows I've tried."

"I'm sorry. I don't deserve you," I said, wiping my eyes.

He nodded. "That's the truth."

I shoved him playfully. I thought about everything he had said, and we were both quiet again for a moment, the atmosphere turning somber. "I'm not asking you to wait for me or anything," I said. "I want you to live your life, to be happy."

"I know."

"Can I call you this semester?"

"Of course, Jessica. I'll be pissed if you don't."

"So we're still friends?"

His head bobbed once, then he held the open ring box out towards me.

I gaped at the ring again. "It's gorgeous," I said.

"It's yours," he said. "You should keep it."

I shook my head. "It's only appropriate to keep the ring when accepting a proposal."

"I'm only taking the ring back if you say no." He snapped the box shut and dropped it on my lap.

I eyed the box but didn't touch it.

Lucas reached over and wrapped my fingers around it. "Just keep it till summer. Maybe it'll remind you of me, and that the offer still stands."

I reluctantly nodded.

We both stood and Lucas wrapped me in an awkward goodbye hug. "Safe travels," he said.

I forced a smile while fighting back tears. He started out the door, then paused.

"Just don't reject me by text, okay? Or by phone for that matter. If you get a better offer and you decide to say no, it's got to be in person. Deal?"

"Yes. Goodbye, Lucas," I said.

I watched him drive off, then returned to my packing, unable to process any of it just yet. When the car came to take me to the airport, I wasn't quite ready, so I asked them to wait while I finished.

Ten minutes later, my luggage was in the trunk and I was comfortably seated in the back seat, alone. I reached into my purse and pulled out the ring, studying it for several minutes. I closed my eyes and let myself dwell on the future fantasy life I could have with Lucas. It wasn't the first time I'd considered a life with him, and with the weight of the small diamond hot in my hand, I knew it wouldn't be the last time either. It was a pleasant daydream of a fulfilling life, but it didn't give me butterflies.

One year ago, I could have been perfectly satisfied with a promise of a lifetime with Lucas. But now that I knew that giddy, breathless feeling that overtook me when I was with Aiden, I couldn't settle for anything less. A life with Lucas meant a life without Aiden, and that would probably kill me.

AIDEN

I paced nervously around the airport unloading zone waiting for Jessica to arrive. It wasn't like her to be late, and my mind flitted to dark places. What if she had been hurt? What if there was an accident on the interstate? What if she had changed her mind? I pulled out my phone, ready to call her when I saw her step out of a black Lexus. The driver helped her out of the car then went to the trunk for her baggage. I tipped the guy then pulled Jessica to me.

She let me kiss her, but her heart wasn't in it. Unfortunately, I didn't have time to decipher her mood. Jessica was terrified by the prospect of a tiny private plane and had insisted we fly commercial. If we missed this flight, I'd surely be late for my meeting. We zipped through security and arrived at the gate with nary a moment to spare. It wasn't until we were comfortably seated in our first class reclining seats with matching flutes of champagne, that we could truly catch our breath.

"I missed you," I said.

She smiled and peered out the window.

"Shall I distract you while we take off?" I offered suggestively, knowing she was uneasy about flying. I squeezed her hand.

Jessica sipped her champagne, turned to me, then burst into tears.

Clearly, this was more than jitters about flying.

"Hey," I said, wrapping my arms around her as best I could without unbuckling either of us and inviting negative attention from the nearby flight attendant. "It's okay. What's wrong?"

She took a breath, shook her head, then started rummaging around in her purse. I retrieved a tissue from my jacket, assuming that was what she needed, and offered it to her. Jessica accepted it and dabbed at her eyes. She opened her mouth and started to say something, but began crying harder instead.

I rubbed her back as she slumped over her lap and dismissed the concerned-looking flight attendant. "I hate seeing you sad, Jessica. If you've changed your mind, it's not too late. We can fly to London, explore the touristy sites for a few days and then you can go back home."

She shook her head. "It's not that. I'm sorry. I just hate good-byes. I've never been away this long," she said.

"You don't have to apologize. You sure your grandma wouldn't want to fly over to visit sometime?"

"She doesn't fly," Jessica said.

"Okay," I said, continuing to rub her back as she turned towards the window. Being homesick was understandable since she was going to be in England a full semester. Jessica and her grandma were very close, especially since each one was all the family the other had since her parents' death over a decade before. I absentmindedly ran my fingers along the tips of her long, straight brown hair, trying to think of some way to perk her up.

I remembered the last text from Jessica before I'd left for the airport. She had just said goodbye to her grandma and was so excited to go. She seemed so giddy then. What had happened in the interim?

I didn't want to push the subject with Jessica, so I focused on distracting her instead. She calmed down by the time we reached cruising altitude and fell asleep an hour after that. I pulled out a stack of papers held together by an oversized binder clip and plopped them on the tray in front of me, ready to do some work. Then I patted my pocket expecting to find a pen, and came up empty. I had some in my briefcase for sure, but I didn't want to risk waking Jessica when I stood to reach into the overhead bin.

Her purse was on the floor beside her feet, so I picked it up and reached in, knowing she'd have plenty of pens. I found a pen right away, but at the same time, my hand brushed up against something unexpected. I peered into the purse and saw a black suede jewelry box. As I opened the box, it didn't even occur to me that its contents might be private or that my actions constituted snooping.

The moment I saw the sparkling diamond ring, I snapped the box shut and dropped the purse. Clearly, I was not intended to have seen that. My mind raced, poring over the possibilities. I swallowed the growing lump in my throat. There was only one explanation that made sense—Lucas. Jessica wasn't crying about leaving her grandmother; she was sad about being away from Lucas.

I had accepted Lucas' presence in her life, but I didn't particularly like him. He was a jock and a party-boy, and he bounced from one woman to another with a frequency that suggested he was incapable of deep, romantic feelings. I knew what Jessica saw in him—he was familiar and safe for her. She'd grown up with him, but they'd never actually dated. And of course I understood why he was interested in her, although since he could clearly have any girl on campus, it stumped me as to why he was so insistent on winning her affections.

Since Jessica and I had begun dating, we'd had our ups and downs, brought on mostly by my ties to the elf kingdom and my obligation to marry an elf woman and become king. When I hadn't been there for Jessica, Lucas was, and for that, I would be forever grateful. But I was with her now, and we were trying to make it work. That should have been enough for Lucas to back off.

I gazed over at Jessica, who was sleeping surprisingly peacefully, given that she was on an airplane. I assumed she wouldn't be on a cross-Atlantic flight with me if she had accepted Lucas' proposal, and the fact that she wasn't wearing the ring surely was a good sign.

But why was the ring in her purse if she'd turned him down? And how the hell could I ask her about it when she hadn't meant for me to see the ring to start with?

CHAPTER TWO

JESSICA

After my inopportune meltdown at takeoff, I fell into a hard, deep sleep. My roommate Claire hadn't been kidding when she suggested I start with just a half of the anxiety pill she'd offered me for the flight. Had I taken the whole pill instead, I would've been comatose the duration of the flight.

I felt better when I awoke. Aiden, who appeared to have been working the entire time I slept, eyed me warily, likely unsure if I was about to start sobbing again. I wished my feelings about my relationship with Aiden were more straightforward, but it was just so complicated no matter how I tried to spin it.

I'd started to fall for Aiden before learning he wasn't like me. Until he'd told me he was an elf, I, like most people, never even imagined such a thing existed outside of storybooks and movies. Aiden and other elves blended well with humans. The only truly noticeable physical feature shared amongst them all, aside from insanely good looks, was a slight point at the tip of the ears. But there were other differences between humans and elves which weren't apparent from the outside. Elves had extraordinary hearing, sight, strength, speed, and stamina. They didn't get sick, and they aged much slower than humans. Although many elves lived among humans, they were still a very close-knit, well organized group with their own political subdivisions and agendas. By virtue of his birth, Aiden was destined to become the leader of his clan and had been training for that role his entire life.

By any rational standards, Aiden and I had no business being together, but we were. Worse yet, we were in love. It was that kind of end-all, be-all love that was completely irrational and totally overwhelming and absolutely perfect.

I briefly considered confessing to Aiden about what had happened before the flight, but quickly dismissed the idea. Telling Aiden about Lucas' proposal felt like a betrayal to Lucas, but keeping it from Aiden, well, that didn't seem significant. I hadn't accepted the proposal, so it didn't really affect Aiden. Besides, he already knew Lucas had feelings for me. This changed nothing for me and Aiden. I only wished I could be so confident that it wouldn't change things for me and Lucas.

I pushed all thoughts of Lucas—and everyone else at home—out of my mind and snuggled up to Aiden. I had absolutely no reason to be sad. I was embarking on a journey I'd dreamed about for years with a man I loved. Life was good.

"Are you hungry?" Aiden asked.

I inhaled sharply and ascertained that I was actually starving. I nodded enthusiastically, so Aiden motioned for the flight attendant, who quickly brought us the meals they'd apparently tried to serve us while I was napping. I hadn't flown in over a decade, and this food was decidedly better than I remembered airplane food being back then. I wondered if it had actually improved with time or if this was just a benefit of first class.

Aiden and I made small talk for a few minutes, then I noticed him glancing at his notepad again.

"More work?" I groaned.

He chuckled. "You do realize the purpose of my trip is to work, don't you?"

"Yes, but now?"

Aiden shrugged. "What would you have me do now? Our options are fairly limited here." He paused. "Shall I recite Shakespearian sonnets to you while we fly over British waters?"

I nodded enthusiastically.

"I was kidding." Aiden's tone was dry but the sparkle in his bright blue eyes made me giggle more. He reached his hand across my lap pulling both of my hands inside his. I relaxed against him and smiled. It was hard to believe I was thousands of feet above the ground and felt this comfortable, but Aiden had that effect on me.

I managed to distract him from his work for the last leg of the flight and before long, we were disembarking. We made our way towards the baggage claim and quickly spotted the man—a decidedly elfish man—holding a sign reading "Eklund" in all caps. Aiden shook hands with the man, introduced us both, and asked him to take me to the car.

I shook my head. "I'd rather stay with you." After sitting for hours, it felt good to stretch my legs. Plus I was in a foreign country and had no interest in being separated from the only familiar face on the continent.

Thankfully, Aiden understood, sending the driver, Quinn, outside with our carry-on bags and gripping my hand firmly as we awaited the rest. Soon, we had all the luggage loaded and were on our way. Aiden glanced at his watch nervously as the car slowed with traffic.

"I won't have long to help you get settled before I need to leave for my meeting," he said apologetically. "I should be back in time for a late dinner though. If you're not too tired I can take you out to a true English pub."

I smiled. "Sounds perfect."

The car slowed again as it neared a gate. I had hoped Aiden's home would be more centrally located in town, but now that I saw the massive estate, I realized why it was on the outskirts. It wouldn't have fit anywhere closer to the city. We cruised down a long, treelined path, slowing to a stop along a circular gravel drive in front of an oversized brick house. No neighboring houses were visible.

The driver hopped out and held open the door before I'd even fully registered the sight.

"Come on, I'll give you the quick tour before I have to leave," Aiden said, exiting the car and offering me his hand. I timidly followed him in through the front entrance, smiling politely as we paused by the two maids holding open the solid wood door. They introduced themselves with such formality that I practically expected them to curtsey.

"Nice to see you. I'm going to give Jessica the tour before I leave," Aiden said, whisking me off to the side before I could really talk with them.

The foyer led to a wide hall, flanked by oversized rooms on both sides. "Parlor, dining room, living room," Aiden said as we walked past. "Library," he said next, slowing the pace as he knew that would peak my interest. "There are bathrooms at both ends of this hall," he continued, pointing down a separate hall at the back of the house, "and the kitchen is there, along with the laundry and other rooms you'll not need."

I wrinkled my nose. "Your maids are not doing my laundry."

"They are unless you're going to force the driver to schlep you to a laundromat in town each week," he said.

I relented, as we had reached a set of French doors leading to the back yard. Aiden swung the doors open and turned to me, gauging my expression and smiling as my eyes lit up.

"This is gorgeous," I said, taking in the huge grassy expanse, lined with a wide patch of wild flowers and then a densely grown forest. I spotted a barn in the distance, and remembered Aiden promising me several horseback rides.

"We have to keep moving," he whispered, dragging me back into the house. We made our way up a narrow stairway, which

Aiden reassured me led to the same second floor as the main stairway we'd passed in the foyer. There was a striking grand piano and then a hall shooting off in either direction.

"I promise we can explore more later, but this will be our room while we are here," he said, leading me down to the far end of the hallway to the right. Aiden opened the door and let me pass through the doorway first into the surprisingly large suite. There was a sitting area to one side, complete with a sofa and cozy looking chaise along with some chairs, a massive four poster bed facing a fireplace, two dressers and nightstands, a large mirror, and a gorgeous mahogany desk near a window. Although the flooring and most furnishings were a darker wood, the room felt cheery and bright due to the large windows. I approached the far window, near the sitting area, and was pleased to find that it opened onto a small balcony overlooking the gardens.

"Bathroom is this way," Aiden said, gesturing to another large room with sparkling cream-colored marble floors, dual vanities with mahogany-framed mirrors, an oversized claw foot tub, and a modern shower with multiple shower heads. There were several doors off of the bathroom, which I assumed were the main closet, linen closet, and probably a smaller room housing the toilet.

"Wow," I said. "This is great, Aiden."

He smiled.

And it was great, really. The house had all the charm of the older home it was, but all of the modern conveniences thanks to well done renovations. The property was idyllic and the room would be perfect for studying. It was just a little, well, cold and impersonal. And isolated. It also struck me as the sort of house that may have been haunted at some point in the past.

Aiden's smile turned downward. "You hate it," he said. "You can pick a different room if you don't like this one. I suspect most of them are empty now."

I bit my lip, wishing there were some way to control my heart rate so he couldn't decipher my every mood change.

I shook my head. "No, it really is gorgeous, and I'm sure this is the best room. I had only expected something closer to campus. That's all. Maybe a little more centrally located in London. This feels a bit—country."

Aiden sighed and turned towards our luggage, which I hadn't even noticed in the corner of the room. He hoisted his larger suitcase onto the bench at the foot of the bed and began rummaging around for something.

"I'm sorry, Jessica. I was sure you'd love it here. I thought the noise and bustle of the city center would ruin your idyllic image of London." He retrieved his toiletry bag from his suitcase and headed into the bathroom, shutting the door part way. "We could arrange for someplace closer to campus for you tomorrow if you like."

I sat on the end of the bed, regretting having admitted my disappointment. This place was perfect; it just wasn't what I had anticipated. That didn't mean I had to be so negative.

"I don't want to go somewhere else," I said, and it was true, especially if Aiden weren't there.

He emerged from the bathroom, now shirtless, and began changing into a dressy shirt from a hanging garment bag. I stood to help him with the buttons, not because he needed any assistance but because I loved standing that close to him. He kissed the top of my head as I finished the last button.

"It's fifteen minutes to campus," Aiden said. "Twenty to thirty at most to the touristy London attractions."

The knowledge that we only *felt* far away from everything perked me up.

"Are you going to rest while I'm gone?"

I hesitated. "I had planned to walk around the city," I said, knowing I was too far to do that.

Aiden nodded. "If you're ready in a few minutes, you can

drive out with me and Quinn can take you wherever you'd like to go. Then you can just text him when you want a ride back."

"I'm fine with public transportation," I reminded him.

"Let's save the double decker bus for this weekend," Aiden replied with a wink.

AIDEN

Dinner that first night in London was amazing. Well, the food was nothing to write home about, but witnessing Jessica's enthusiasm about England was priceless. Her voice was so animated as she recounted the details of her afternoon that she had to pause to catch her breath. She shared with me her observations about differences in the clothing, language, and vehicles before stopping abruptly.

"I'm so sorry. I didn't even ask about your afternoon. How was your meeting?"

I laughed. "It was fine. Nothing interesting to share. Tell me more about your adventures. And what do you have planned for tomorrow?"

Jessica whipped out a folded sheet of paper and placed it on the table. "Here's what I've come up with so far. If there's anything you'd like me to save for the weekend so we can do it together, just let me know. I wanted your opinion on everything anyway."

I bit my lip to suppress more laughter. I had never before seen her so excited about something. I glanced down at her overly ambitious list and noted she'd listed many of the popular tourist attractions but also some lesser known historic landmarks.

"First off, this is an excellent list, but there's no way you can see all of this in one day. Isn't the best part of having an entire semester here that you don't have to hurry through all the places you want to visit? Slow down and experience them all fully. Second of all," I paused, tempered by Jessica's pouty expression, "we won't be doing any sightseeing here this weekend."

"Why not? I thought you had the whole weekend free, and my classes don't start until Wednesday!"

I sipped my beer, enjoying the anticipation of her reaction to my surprise. "I'm sorry, but I am going out of town until Tuesday evening."

Jessica's expression fell and her shoulders slumped down. She looked too sad for me to continue the ruse.

"Oh, cheer up. You're coming with me," I said.

"I am?"

I nodded. "We are headed to Paris for a long weekend. I thought we should see all the holiday décor before they take it all down for the spring."

"Paris," she repeated calmly. "Paris, France?" She squealed loudly before repeating our destination a third time and then running around the table and flinging her arms around my neck.

I captured her mouth for a kiss, though both of us were grinning too widely for any real passion. Then I motioned for the bill, eager to be alone with her.

When we returned to the house, we made a beeline for our bedroom. The bed had been turned down and a fire was roaring in the fireplace.

"Talk about ambiance," Jessica said with a shy grin as she slipped off her boots, mittens and scarf.

I removed my own coat and then held the back of hers as she shrugged out of it.

"Are you tired?" I asked. I figured she must be after walking around the city for hours on the same day she flew across the Atlantic.

Jessica shook her head, the mischievous look in her eyes one I knew well and loved. I pulled her towards me and pressed my lips against hers. She moaned into my mouth, reminding me that, thanks to the holidays, which we'd each spent with our respective families, we hadn't been truly alone together for two weeks. Jessica apparently felt the same sense of urgency, as she quickly began fumbling with the same buttons she'd fastened earlier that day.

I kissed each part of her smooth, creamy flesh as she undressed, then I grabbed a blanket and pillow from the couch and created a makeshift bed on the floor by the fire. I was already a bit warm, but without the fire, Jessica would be freezing in this old house that lacked the benefit of modern insulation. Jessica happily joined me on the floor, lowering her body onto mine in a way that made my breath catch in my throat as her bare breasts tickled my chest. We kissed for a few more minutes before she pulled back.

"Do you have protection?" she whispered.

I crawled out from under her and retrieved a small foil packet from the nightstand.

Jessica eyed it warily.

"This is from my suitcase," I said, reassuring her it wasn't years old.

She leaned in to kiss me again and then froze. "Did the maids unpack that?"

I shook my head. "No. I did." Before she could come up with more reasons to delay, I reached for her hips, lifting her onto my lap. I leaned forward, nipping her bottom lip playfully before placing a trail of soft kisses along her jaw. Jessica giggled as my breath tickled her neck, but as my kisses moved lower, her laughter turned to soft moans and she arched her breasts closer to me.

"I think you're going to enjoy Europe," I whispered, gently toppling us both onto our sides and reaching my hands down her torso.

THE REST OF THE WEEK WAS IDYLLIC. I FELL INTO THE HABIT OF watching Jessica sleep each morning before getting up to run, shower, and dress for work. She demanded I wake her before I left, and I was equally insistent that she go back to sleep after I departed. I worked during the days, but had the pleasant frequent distractions of texts and pictures from Jessica, documenting her touristy explorations. We made love each night that week, and every night I fell asleep with Jessica in my arms. I couldn't imagine a more perfect future than one where I followed this routine with her.

It was a stark contrast to my travels the prior summer, when I was essentially shadowing my uncle Marius, my kingdom's current leader. It had been the final step in my own preparations to become king. Jessica and I had broken up right before I left the country, when she had learned of my betrothal to Gwyneth, an evil witch of a woman my parents had selected for me to marry when I was still a young child. Although Gwyneth had trained her entire life to be my queen and to support me in all my work, conversation with her was tedious and tenuous. She was pretty and polite, but I was never attracted to her and never even developed the slightest fondness for her.

I never had learned if Gwyneth was directly involved in her brothers' scheme to kill Jessica. Jessica and Lucas had, thankfully, foiled that plot without any help from me. Regardless, Gwyneth was out of my life now for good, and the experience was reprehensible enough that my family and the higher-ranking leaders in our kingdom all backed off of their efforts to find me a suitable elfish bride before I was set to take the throne. I knew the respite wouldn't last forever, but I was determined to enjoy it while I could.

JESSICA

Paris was heavenly. Paris had always been one of those places

I thought would be amazing to visit, but I had never even really dreamed of a trip to Paris because I assumed I'd never actually go. The reality was better than anything I could've imagined anyway. We stayed in a boutique hotel with a view of the Arc de Triumph, and the entire city glowed with the magic of the holiday lights.

We were only there a weekend, but we made the most of it. We slept late, enjoyed chocolate croissants and the best chocolat chaud I'd ever tasted, then set out on a flurry of tourist adventures, ambling through many museums, exploring the iconic monuments, and finishing our last evening with a chilly but romantic boat ride along the Seine. I found that baguettes consumed in Paris were decidedly better than baguettes from anywhere else, or any other type of bread in the world for that matter. I probably gained five pounds from the bread, fresh cheeses, wine and delicious steak.

"I don't want to leave," I pouted, watching the city lights fade to a distant twinkle as our jet took off to return us to London.

Aiden squeezed my hand. "I'll bring you back in the spring," he promised. "When it's warmer, there are several gorgeous gardens we can explore. Oh and you'll love the palace at Versailles. And the wineries in Bordeaux. We'll have to do a more extensive tour of all of France when your classes are over."

"I'll hold you to that," I said. Then I glanced around the plane once more. It was his family's private jet, and while I was nervous —okay—terrified, about flying on it initially, I had to admit it was nice. We had plenty of legroom and it was so luxurious I nearly forgot I was flying thousands of feet in the air.

"You could unbuckle your belt and get more comfortable," Aiden said with a grin that told me he knew exactly what my response would be.

"Not a chance." It was a short flight anyway. When we arrived back at the London house, Aiden carried our luggage upstairs. Then, a maid magically unpacked my suitcase while I showered and changed into my pajamas. I wanted to be well rested for my first day of classes.

"Thank you for a wonderful weekend," I said to Aiden before he flipped off the light. He kissed me again, softly, before heading downstairs to catch up on work from the weekend.

When I awoke the next morning, Aiden was already downstairs, chatting in the study with two elves I didn't recognize. He excused himself to kiss me goodbye as I left, wishing me a good first day, and insisting Quinn, the driver, chauffeur me to campus.

I was excited and nervous about my classes in a way I hadn't felt since the first day of college. I didn't know any of the other students, any of my professors, or how different the classes would be from my university classes back home. Luckily, my classes would all be in my native language, an obvious advantage over the study abroad programs in other countries.

My first class was 19th Century British Literature. I was also taking History of the United Kingdom, Anatomy of War, and Landscapes over Time, a geography-focused history class. My final class, Comparative Policies, was focused on the current governments and political arenas of Great Britain and the United States. The first three classes met Mondays and Wednesdays and the other two were on Tuesdays and Thursdays, granting me three-day weekends for travel excursions.

A nerd by nature, I was genuinely excited about all of my classes. Now that I was nearing the end of my college experience, I could finally take courses than interested me without worrying about any of the stupid prerequisites or other courses needed for my degree. When I returned to campus in the fall, I'd take one final history course and then the rest of the education classes I needed for my teaching certificate, leaving me free second semester to complete my student teaching experiences and graduate on time with a Bachelor's Degree in history and a license to teach.

I met with the university's study abroad counselor before class and he introduced me to the other students visiting for the semester. There were roughly twenty of us, but less than a dozen from the U.S. Luckily, I quite literally ran into a girl from Wisconsin on the way out the door. Her name was Julia, and she was in three of my history classes. We made plans to meet for lunch that day, and I was so relieved that I texted Aiden as I reached my first class and proudly told him I'd made a new friend.

The classes themselves seemed very similar to my classes in America, although the professors all had formal British accents which made them sound much more intelligent and sophisticated than my American professors. I suspected my main problem in class here would be that I'd get so caught up enjoying the melodic way their words sounded when they spoke that I'd forget to listen to what they were saying.

At lunch, I picked up a sandwich from the deli where Julia and I had planned to meet. Just as I was grabbing a napkin to take to a table, I felt a tap on my shoulder.

"Hi!' she greeted me. Her energy and perkiness reminded me of Claire, my best friend and roommate from college back home. The instant familiarity had a pleasant calming effect. We found a table nearby and made small talk while we ate, swapping basic background tidbits about ourselves.

"So where are you staying? Are you in the university apartments near campus?" Julia asked, folding the paper wrapper from her sandwich.

"No, I'm about twenty minutes away. I'm staying with my boyfriend," I said, feeling awkward about how that sounded.

Her eyes widened with intrigue. "You have a British boyfriend? How did you guys meet? Is that what brought you here?"

I shook my head shyly. "No, he's American," I said, realizing that wasn't exactly true. I'd always assumed he was Norwegian by birth, but come to think of it I didn't actually know where Aiden was born. "His family does a lot of business in England, so they have a house here and that's where we're staying." I sipped my tea, then continued, anticipating her next question. "He's not in classes here. He graduated last summer but he's here for work, so the timing was perfect."

"Cool," she said. Then she glanced at her phone and wrinkled her nose. "We should get back. Class starts in twenty minutes."

I agreed, and we headed back to campus together.

All in all, it was the perfect first day of classes. The entire week, actually, was seamless, and on Thursday night, I went out for dinner with Julia and some of our other classmates. I had wanted Aiden to come along, but I later decided it was for the best that he had to work since it forced me to come out of my shell and actually get to know other people.

CHAPTER THREE

Lucas

Winter break sucked. I hadn't spoken to Jessica since she left and knowing she still took off for England with *him* after I bared my soul to her, well, that really sucked. I scolded myself for ever considering it might turn out differently.

Jessica was not spontaneous and she certainly wasn't the type to get caught up in the moment. But for some reason, I had convinced myself that if I really poured out my heart to her and told her every goddamned thing I was thinking and feeling, then she would realize she was being an idiot. And I'd hoped that she would see that she felt the same way for me, that she had for all this time, and that she was only with *him* because she was too scared to risk ruining her friendship with me.

Whatever.

It could have been worse.

She could have thrown the ring at me, kicked me out of her house for even attempting that kind of stunt moments before she was set to leave the country with *him*. But she didn't. And she didn't exactly close the door on a possibility of a relationship with me sometime in the future. Until she had *his* ring on her finger, I was still in the game. And when I play, I play to win.

Thank God for sports. It was the busy season for hockey, and I was the left wing and lead scorer of my university's team. This was my last season playing at the collegiate level, since I'd just signed to join the Hawks for the next season. The contract gave them all the power of deciding when I'd actually start playing for them and whether I'd be on their junior league roster first or actually play for the Blackhawks. But, so far, their plan was to keep me out of it all until the season ended and then I'd start training with the team over the off-season. I guess that way they could watch how I did with the guys and make a final decision based on how I performed at training camp in August.

Either way, it was my last college season, and I wanted to leave with my kick-ass legacy in place. I also had to manage to avoid injury this season, which was harder than usual since my decision to go pro essentially put a target on my back for all of our opponents.

Whatever. I could take it.

On top of that, I was swamped with classes, since my mother was determined that I would someday graduate. She'd begged and cajoled and somehow gotten the school to agree to let me take correspondence courses this summer, then take a sabbatical the next year. I'd finish up my degree with correspondence courses the following summer. I didn't quite understand why she was so focused on the damn degree right away when I could just finish down the road when my hockey career puttered out. But, since the woman had spent thousands of dollars on my hockey training and dedicated hours each week to washing my hockey gear and driving me to various matches and practices, I figured I owed her.

The one plus to Jessica's absence was that I could flirt with other girls without fear of getting caught. Not that I wasn't allowed to hang with other girls before, or that Jessica would even make a big deal out of it if she were in town. Now that I'd laid it all on the line for her, I just didn't want her to question my sincerity if she saw me making out with Jenna or Chrissy after class.

Since Jessica was currently shacking up with *him*, though, I wasn't going to feel any guilt. If I needed a girl or two to keep my mind off of Jessica, I deserved it. When she came back, if she wasn't engaged to *him*, I would refocus my efforts. Until then, it was all fair game.

JESSICA

By the fourth week of classes, I'd settled into a comfortable routine. I had a decent grasp on all of the material and really enjoyed four of my classes. Julia was doing a fair job of filling the empty space in my heart left by the absence of Claire. And I was finally accustomed to the presence of others — the house staff—constantly surrounding Aiden and me in his house.

Aiden and I had made good use of the long weekends, spending one weekend exploring Norfolk and another eating our way through Yorkshire, leaving me excited for other adventures throughout England. Unfortunately, when I brought up the topic of our next weekend adventure, he told me his father was arriving that weekend and wanted to have dinner with us.

We really hadn't spent much time together in London, so I didn't initially see this as a problem. Then Aiden told me his father would be in town for several weeks, and that he would likely be too busy to travel with me for the duration of his father's visit. I couldn't blame him; he'd told me before we planned the trip that he would be busy with work. I was still bummed.

And even though I'd already met his father, albeit briefly, I was really nervous about dinner. I'd never before had a serious boyfriend, so I wasn't accustomed to the meeting-the-parents tradition. In general, though, parents loved me. I was soft-spoken, well-mannered, and had good grades. In high school, the parents of all of my friends trusted and liked me. Even Claire's father, a conservative Presbyterian minister who Claire claimed disliked everyone, quickly warmed to me. But somehow I knew things would be different with Aiden's dad.

"You look great," Aiden said, likely tiring of watching me fidget with my shirt. I was wearing my dressier jeans and a button-down white blouse with a pale pink cashmere sweater. Normally I found the sweater warm and comforting, but today it just felt itchy.

"You have nothing to be nervous about. Just be yourself," he said.

I let out an exaggerated sigh. One of Aiden's many special talents as an elf was heightened senses. His extraordinary hearing and sight made it impossible to hide my moods from him, as he could quickly gauge my breathing and heart rate for clues. Since this gift was shared by all elves, Aiden's dad would be able to sense my anxiety just as quickly as Aiden had. The only thing worse than being nervous about meeting someone was having that person know I was nervous about meeting them.

Aiden chuckled, coming up behind me and enveloping me with his arms. I was still in front of the mirror, and I couldn't help but smile at the sight of us snuggled together. We looked like an adorable greeting card. Aiden, with his thick blond hair and bold blue eyes, was always striking to look at, and with his body wrapped around mine, I looked pretty decent, too.

"Let's go," he said, dragging me by the hand downstairs.

When we reached the dining room, his dad was already in the room, standing by a window with his back to us.

"Father, I'm sure you remember Jessica, and Jessica, my father, Ivar," Aiden said politely, clearing his throat awkwardly.

As Ivar turned, I smiled warmly, despite the cold, false smile on Ivar's face. I glanced uncomfortably at Aiden, who nodded reassuringly and pulled out a chair for me.

"You have a lovely home here," I said, desperate for him to like me. "The entire property is gorgeous."

"Thank you. Although title to the manor actually belongs to Aiden."

"Oh," I bit my lip, certain Aiden hadn't mentioned that.

"Are you enjoying London so far?"

"Yes. It's always been a place I've wanted to visit, so this has really been a dream come true."

One of the maids came around with wine, filling both men's glasses with red then shying away as I shook my head dismissively at both. Aiden reached for my hand under the table and squeezed it softly. I knew the move was meant to comfort me, but it just made me even more self-conscious. If Aiden sensed my nervousness, his father surely could too, and I didn't even want to imagine what he thought, seeing Aiden touch me under the table.

"And your classes?"

"Great. I can't imagine a more appropriate setting to learn history and literature."

Ivar nodded before sipping his wine.

"Jessica is a history major," Aiden said. His father remained disinterested.

We continued the small talk as the salad course was served. I felt like Ivar was finally warming up to me, and I started to relax while he and Aiden began to discuss business matters. I tried to follow the discussion throughout the main course as Ivar and Aiden both debated multiple political issues, swapped opinions on different candidates for various elf government positions, and reminisced about family friends.

Then, Ivar abruptly changed topics.

"Aiden tells me you were raised by your grandmother," Ivar said, addressing me.

I noticed Aiden shoot a warning look at his father. "Yes," I replied calmly. "My parents were in an accident when I was younger."

"Tragic," he said, his tone not exactly matching the sentiment. "Was there an investigation, do you know?"

I turned to Aiden, bewildered. But he appeared just as confused as I felt.

"I mean to say, was there definitive proof it was an accident, and not a crime?"

"Father, I don't think this is relevant or appropriate dinner conversation."

Ivar looked dismayed as he turned to me. "Oh. My apologies. I don't spend as much time with humans as my son, so I'm not as familiar with the...particulars about what you consider acceptable topics of discussion. In our culture, we would want to know if a relative had been murdered."

Aiden started to speak but Ivar cut him off with another apology and a shake of his head.

"I'm sorry. I'm sure Aiden has told you my life has been dedicated to security measures for our leaders. I suppose that makes me more comfortable with such talk than I should be. We shall discuss something else."

I sipped my water.

"What were your parents' names?"

"Father!" Aiden scolded.

"It's fine," I said, still confused by his father's preoccupation with my parents, but not bothered by the innocent questions. "Kathleen and Joseph."

Ivar smiled. "Very nice names. Traditional. Did they go by nicknames?"

"Uh, my mom called my dad Joey, but I don't really remember whether everyone called him that or just her."

"What about your grandparents?"

"My grandma's name is Betty. My grandpa was Emmett, but he died before my parents did."

"Betty is your mother's mother, right? What about your paternal grandparents?"

"They both passed away a few years ago."

"What were their names?"

"Ethel and Fritz."

Ivar nodded as though this were fascinating. "Were you familiar with your great- grandparents? Fritz's parents?"

I shook my head, intrigued as to why Ivar had suddenly taken such an interest in my ancestry. "I never met them. I suppose they died before I was born."

"You suppose? But you aren't sure?"

It was such an odd line of questioning that I really wasn't sure how to respond. I chewed deliberately, hoping Aiden would intervene and point out the ridiculousness of it all, but he didn't. I swallowed the bite of chicken and wiped my mouth.

"I really have no idea," I said finally. "Not having parents meant I didn't exactly have the same familial relationships other kids my age did, but then again I'm not sure that many people know their great-grandparents well. If they were alive, they certainly didn't make any effort that I know of to be a part of my life, which seems a pretty rotten thing to do given the circumstances."

Ivar nodded, then feigned interest in his food as dessert was served. I again turned to Aiden for some support, but instead he simply smiled as though his father had said nothing strange.

We ate in silence for a few minutes before the discussion turned to Aiden's six siblings. They chatted amicably about all of them, taking turns sharing any updates they had, and then Ivar began interrogating Aiden about whether he knew why Cordelia and Elgin weren't having children yet. Aiden said he hadn't discussed it with Cordelia, and Ivar didn't seem to believe him.

Then, when Aiden dared to say he didn't think it was his business, his dad went nuts.

"Not your business? How do you figure? Whose business is it if not yours?" He shook his head in irritation. "She should have already had at least one."

Aiden held up a hand defensively. "Fine. I'll ask her about it." He used a tone clearly designed to appease his father, which may have worked, except I sort of giggled. I didn't mean to, and in retrospect it was a bit gutsy since, as an only child, I don't have firsthand knowledge of the type of personal details shared between siblings. But it seemed ridiculous to me that Aiden would have some say in when his sister had children.

Predictably, the giggling turned Ivar's attention back to me, only now he was clearly irritated.

"And where exactly do you see this relationship headed? The last I heard, Aiden was going to stop fooling around over six months ago, yet here he is in England with you, and the last I checked, you were still considered a human."

"I guess I'm just that likable," I said snarkily, disregarding the strange comment at the end. Then, remembering who I was talking to, I calmed myself. "I don't think either of us knows where this is going, but we are both happy with how things are now."

Ivar grimaced. "How much has my son told you about the expectations for his position?"

I glanced at Aiden, who was visibly annoyed at his father's question. "Well, I know he was supposed to marry Gwyneth and..."

"Father, what is your point?" Aiden interrupted, pushing his plate to the side, causing me to startle as it clanked loudly into his water glass.

Ivar glared at his son. "I am simply inquiring about her level of knowledge. I am curious exactly what you have told Jessica."

"She knows I am going to be king. She knows what the traditions say. She knows the type of work I'll be doing and the challenges I'll have."

Ivar chuckled. "I don't even think you truly understand the challenges you'll face, Son."

Aiden started to speak again but I patted his leg.

"Sir, I understand your concerns. I know you're disappointed and that you don't approve of Aiden's involvement with me, and honestly I don't blame you. But I also know he didn't set out to hurt you or to mess up everyone's plans. And I'm sure I seem naïve to you, but I have to believe that your people, as sophisticated a group as they clearly are, will understand that you can't always choose who you love."

Ivar was silent for a long moment. He slowly chewed another bite of his cheesecake and then nodded for the maid to remove the plate. "Jessica, as a history major, I assume you have some knowledge of the various monarchies in this country and surrounding ones."

I nodded, uncertain where he was going with this.

"Then you appreciate the importance of a legal heir in those regimes," he concluded. "Well, I'm sure you also are aware by this point that we don't even know if it would be possible for you and Aiden to conceive a child. And even if it were, that child would never be in line to rule our people."

"Royal monarchs almost always married someone outside their own nation," I countered. "And the offspring of those couples was the legal heir to the throne and had no trouble succeeding the throne." I was about to remind him that Aiden's son wouldn't be heir anyway, thanks to their people's unusual line of succession. Rather than pass the throne directly from father to son, it went from father to his oldest nephew. But before I could continue, Ivar chuckled sardonically.

"Jessica this isn't a matter of nationality. We can't just issue you a green card and make you one of us. There are significant genetic differences. Your child could never lead our people because nothing anyone does could make your child an elf. Your child will not have any of the gifts and abilities of our people. It would be akin to letting a cat rule a kingdom of dogs."

"Father!" Aiden chastised.

Ivar shrugged. "I'm not saying dogs are better or vice versa, just that they are indisputably different creatures altogether and that this would be nothing like an interracial marriage or even an international one."

I swallowed. I understood what he was saying, and as much as I hated it, I couldn't think of a counterargument. Indeed, I was fairly certain there was no counterargument.

"If you choose to marry Jessica," Ivar said, now addressing Aiden directly, "You should know that you would be affirmatively ending our family's line to the throne. You would be the last Eklund ever to serve your people. Are you ready to end that legacy?"

I felt my eyes brimming with tears and was about to excuse myself from the table when he continued.

"Jessica, if you were as understanding of Aiden's obligations as you purport to be, you would be more supportive of his other option—to marry an elf woman and procreate with her, while continuing his relationship with you."

Aiden stood abruptly. "Enough! I will not have you alienating Jessica in *my* house," he said, overemphasizing the ownership of the home. "And we both know what you're saying isn't even true. My children are never going to take the throne regardless of whom I marry. Cordelia's firstborn son would be in line to be our next king."

Ivar nodded calmly. "Yes, and then your grandson. Except he will be half human, and wholly incapable of meeting the physical demands of the job, let alone garnering support for his policy decisions." He stood and turned to me. "I apologize for ruining the tenor of our dinner here. It has been a pleasure to get to know you, Jessica. I have no doubt that you are an upstanding young lady. I simply question whether you both have thought through the full effects of your relationship. Goodnight."

I watched, flabbergasted, as Ivar sauntered peacefully out of the room.

Then I turned to Aiden, who heaved a heavy sigh before reaching for his wine goblet and draining the contents in one long sip. He turned towards the wall and suddenly, his fist shot out, punching a hole in the side.

"Aiden!" I shrieked.

He shook his head.

The maid scurried in, eying both of us warily. I wondered how much the staff knew of their masters' abilities and lives, or how much of the conversation they'd overheard. This maid, Kelly, seemed extremely uncomfortable around Aiden. She clattered the dishes together nervously as she gathered them, avoiding all eye contact with him.

Although, as I gazed back at him, I decided he did look more than a tad frightening at the moment. His unnaturally blue eyes had an icy gleam to them and his entire face had hardened as though he were focused on a single, malicious thought. And the effortless way he slammed through the wall was deeply disturbing.

Not knowing what to say to calm Aiden and certain I'd feel better if I kept busy, I stood and started helping clear the table. But, as Kelly returned looking visibly panicked at the sight and Aiden quickly trained his cold stare on me, I realized that was probably not the right thing to do. I placed the dishes I'd gathered back onto the table and stepped closer to Aiden. I rubbed my hand along his firm arm.

"Let's go upstairs," I suggested.

Aiden swallowed audibly and reached for his wine again, frowning when he saw that he had already finished it. He glanced around the room, spotted the bottle, and refilled his own glass, causing an even more horrified look to appear on Kelly's young face. Then he nodded to me, placed a hand on the small of my back, and silently guided me to the stairs.

When we reached the room, I saw that it had already been prepared for bed, as always. The bed was turned down, the fire was on, and a pitcher of ice water with two glasses sat on a small tray by the couch. As much as the thought of someone—basically a stranger—moving things around so thoroughly in my bedroom had initially creeped me out, I now realized that I could definitely get used to this luxury.

Aiden unbuttoned his shirt and tossed it over the couch, where I knew it would be retrieved, laundered, and ironed in the morning, only to magically reappear in the closet later.

I racked my brain for the right words to say to comfort Aiden, but came up empty. So instead I watched him pace the room angrily, pausing only for sips of his wine. It was a pity Aiden was so incensed at the moment because he looked incredibly sexy in his formal slacks and ribbed, sleeveless black shirt.

I stepped into his path and he stopped, enabling me to twine my arms around his waist. He kissed my forehead before setting his goblet on the nearby table and placing both hands on my hips. He guided me backwards to the point where we could make eye contact.

"I'm sorry about my father. I shouldn't have subjected you to that."

"It's not your fault," I said, knowing he needed comforting even though I did feel he'd done a lackluster job at best in defending me. "You couldn't have known he'd say all that."

"I did, though," Aiden said, releasing his grip on me and resuming his pacing before plopping down on the couch. "He's never been pleased with me and he's told me all of these things many a time."

I considered that for a moment, unsure whether Aiden had told me this before and I just didn't fully understand or if, as I suspected, he hadn't detailed the extent of his dad's issues with me. "So you knew he was okay with you continuing to see me if you married someone else?" I asked finally, starting with the aspect that plagued me the most.

"I did," he said without hesitation. "It's not that uncommon of a scenario, really, in your world or mine."

I frowned, realizing what he said was the truth but desperately needing him to add something—anything, really—to emphasize how repugnant he personally found the idea. But Aiden was silent. "What have you said to your dad about that idea?"

Aiden breathed a laugh. "Of course I told him I didn't want that."

I closed my eyes and exhaled with relief. "But he keeps bringing it up?"

"My father likes to remind me that I have duties in life. He treats me like an impetuous child and tells me it isn't about what I want."

"But…" I began.

"Jessica, I can't talk about this now. I'm sorry," he interrupted, raising his fingers to his brows and rubbing.

I sat beside him on the couch. I hated seeing him this stressed, but I'd be lying if I said I wasn't disappointed that he wouldn't talk about any of it with me.

"Do you want to watch TV?"

He shook his head.

I scooted closer to him and he wrapped his arm around my shoulders, pulling my head to rest against his chest.

"I'm sorry," he repeated. "I hate that no matter what I do, I hurt someone. Any choice I make, someone is disappointed." He sighed, then continued, in a completely different tone. "You don't need to clear the table, Jessica. Or make the bed or wipe off the mirrors. It's not like when you're a guest at someone's house and it's polite to help out the host. The staff is here to do these tasks, and they're compensated well for it."

I was taken aback by the sudden change in topic, but started to explain myself when he interrupted again.

"You don't have to worry about them liking you."

His tone annoyed me more than his words, but given his mood, I knew it was best to let it go. Instead I asked the other question on my mind.

"Do they know? About what you are?"

"No," he answered quickly. "We've never told them. I'm sure they've made some observations, but like I said, they are well paid, and bound by confidentiality agreements." Then he frowned. "Actually, I think they're frightened by me. The maids, anyway. And they look at you like some gullible innocent that they worry I'll eat for dinner tomorrow."

Now that he mentioned it, I had noticed a difference in the way the staff, especially the maids, looked at me compared to how they viewed everyone else in the house. And Kelly specifically always looked surprised when I returned home after class, like she couldn't imagine escaping this place only to come right back.

"Why not use elves then, so you don't have to worry about that stuff?" I asked.

Aiden chuckled, as though the notion of his own kind working as a maid was preposterous. "My people are better suited for other tasks," he said. "And besides, there would still be confidentiality concerns given the nature of my family's work."

I interpreted his response to mean that he felt that housekeeping and similar chores were beneath elves, which of course meant he shared his dad's clear opinion that elves were superior to humans. Every fiber in my body ached to start an argument over this with Aiden, but I knew now was not the time. So instead, I stood.

"I'm going to take a bath," I said, heading to collect the book on my nightstand. I almost offered to let him join me, but didn't, out of concern he might actually take me up on the offer.

"I think I'll head down to the library for a bit," Aiden said after I started the water. "Clear my head and do some work, I guess. You don't need to wait up."

I nodded, well aware that given our different sleep needs, it was rarely wise for me to wait up for Aiden. I tossed a handful of grapefruit-scented bath salts into the water flowing out of the faucet and placed a fuzzy white robe and towel next to the tub. Suddenly, I remembered another question I had for Aiden.

"Aiden?" I popped my head out of the bathroom, uncertain if he'd already left. He turned to me. "Why was your dad asking so many questions about my family?"

He frowned thoughtfully and shook his head. "I don't know."

"Didn't it seem odd to you?"

Aiden shrugged, then left.

I softly closed the door to the bathroom and tested the water temperature. I mentally calculated what time it was back home right now and wondered what my grandma was doing at that moment, or Claire, or Lucas. Grandma had probably just finished eating. Claire was likely flirting with a guy instead of studying. And Lucas...well, he was harder to predict. Since he'd decided to go pro with his hockey, he was essentially rushing to finish as much of his studies as he could while amping up his practice schedule as well. The last I'd heard, the plan was for him to start training with the team over the summer and begin playing in the fall. I wasn't sure when—if ever—he planned to finish his course load and graduate.

I worried about Lucas, in that respect. He assured me that even as a rookie, he'd make enough playing hockey to support himself and save plenty for years to come. He said even a handful of years playing professionally would yield enough to support him for life if he lived modestly. I suspected he hadn't calculated the effect of taxes on that hefty salary, or the fact that, as a well-known, professionally hockey player, he wouldn't live modestly.

But summers were light for hockey players, with it mostly

being a recovery season, so really he could probably take a few college courses each summer and still finish his business degree within a couple years. Lucas never had considered himself much of an academic, and I was always reminding him that hockey was not his only talent. He wasn't the dumb jock, no matter how much he tried to wedge himself into that stereotype.

I shut off the water and chastised myself for dwelling on Lucas for so long. He had a mother to lecture him about his life choices and didn't need me, thousands of miles away, stressing about his future. Especially while his ring sat cold and alone at the bottom of my nightstand drawer.

AIDEN

The house was quiet when I went downstairs, the dinner mess apparently having already been cleaned by the staff. The light in the library was still on, but the room was empty. I sat in the tall, antique armchair by the far wall, remembering how I'd preferred that chair even as a child. When I was small, I could curl up in the chair and be completely encapsulated by its firm upholstered sides, free to experience a comfort I suspected was shared by cats who assumed a similar position in most chairs. I scrolled through emails on my phone and had just shut my eyes when I heard footsteps.

"That always was your favorite chair," my father said, sitting across from me.

I didn't bother opening my eyes.

"I expected you'd be upstairs with your precious Jessica now," he said.

"No, you didn't," I replied, unwilling to pretend we didn't both know that his intent had been to drive a wedge between Jessica and me, or that he hadn't clearly succeeded in his mission.

He tilted his head to the side, acknowledging my point. "If she truly loved you, she'd support what you need to do."

"Jessica does love me. She just doesn't understand why the things you say I need to do are so important. And she certainly doesn't love elves in general. We've given her no reason to." Between the comments, ranging from snarky to downright vicious, the literal attacks on her person, and the general treatment as though she were a second class citizen, it was unlikely elves could ever redeem themselves to Jessica.

Father didn't respond right away, which I hoped meant he was truly considering my words. "It's the only solution," he finally said. "You're smart enough to know that."

"It's not an option," I replied firmly.

"Why not? Because you have the final say?"

I inhaled slowly through my nose, willing the fresh air to calm my already seething nerves. "What queen would even agree to that scenario, to just be a pawn to create a new generation?"

My father chuckled. "Any queen. She would go into the engagement fully informed about your relationship with Jessica and fully consenting to it continuing. If you're so concerned about her happiness, you could even authorize her to have a similar arrangement on the side. Or not. Either way I am certain many, many women would be more than willing to marry you and ensure that our people continue our great legacy."

His answer caught me off guard. I'd always been so dismissive of this so-called solution that I'd never even considered the possibility of my future wife in the scenario knowing about Jessica from the start. I'd always assumed it would be a secret I'd keep, much like it had been with Gwyneth, until her brothers discovered the truth. Unfortunately, there was still a significant, insurmountable problem with my father's plan.

"I love Jessica," I said. "The thought of being intimate with another woman physically nauseates me."

My father raised an eyebrow. "You've done it before," he said lightly.

I didn't let myself dwell on whether he was simply guessing or actually knew when or with whom I'd been intimate. "I wouldn't do it. I couldn't."

"Well, you wouldn't have to, actually. Science these days has made it so that your queen can bare your offspring without you ever touching her."

I swallowed uncomfortably, hating that my father had, yet again, solved another aspect of the problem with this idea. Yet I was still deeply bothered by the notion of a woman who wasn't Jessica carrying my child. What if it changed my feelings for the woman, seeing her belly swell with my baby? And if the pregnancy didn't change my sentiments, would I still love the child, even if I resented its mother?

"No," I said.

"It's pretty common, you know, what you're feeling now," my father said. "You're about to undertake a huge new role and you panic, act out, buck the system, so to speak. We should have seen this coming sooner, I suppose." He stood and walked to the corner of the room where a fully stocked bar was apparently beckoning to him. He dropped two ice cubes into a highball glass with a loud clink then poured an amber-colored liquid from the largest decanter. He held up the glass, and I nodded, so he prepared another drink, carrying them both over to where we sat.

"Why were you asking about Jessica's great-grandparents?" I asked.

My father's face lit up. "Ah yes. I was hoping she would know more about her ancestry. Do you have any knowledge of her relations? I was particularly interested in her grandfather Fritz."

"I don't," I said, taking a swig of the whiskey and relishing the slight burn as it slid down my throat.

"He was born in Germany, I gathered, and it seems his father never came to the United States."

I shrugged. My father's knowledge on the topic exceeded my

own, and he was clearly not ready to tell me what piqued his interest to start with.

We sipped our drinks quietly for a moment before my father spoke again.

"Marius would like to meet Jessica," he said.

"No."

"You must realize they'll meet eventually if you continue to pursue this relationship."

I frowned. I had actually intended to insulate Jessica from as many people in my family as possible for as long as possible. Marius was at the top of the list of people I wasn't eager to have her to meet. As calculating and cold as my father was, Marius was ten times worse. I often wondered if he'd always been that way or if it was simply a side effect of the job. And if it was the latter, what did that say about my fate?

Father sighed. "Regardless, it wasn't a request. He's still your king and while he can't compel her, you have no choice in the matter. I can hold him off until summer, I'm sure. But if she's still in your life then…"

"Fine," I said.

My father remained in the study for several minutes more, but neither of us spoke. Finally, he bid me goodnight and left. I exhaled the tension out of my torso.

CHAPTER FOUR

JESSICA

The days after our dinner with Ivar would have been awkward, except that I barely saw Aiden or his dad. Aiden kissed me as he left in the morning, apologizing again for his father the prior night, and then returned long after I'd gone to bed, two days in a row. The third day didn't start out much better. I had waited up late for Aiden the night before, but eventually fell asleep on the couch. He must have returned home at some point because when I awoke, I was in the bed. How he managed to move me without waking me was a mystery.

I patted the bed beside me and sighed, finding it empty. But then I heard a rustling across the still dark room.

"Aiden?"

"Yes, Jessica, it's me. I'm headed out shortly. Go back to sleep."

I rubbed my eyes wearily and glanced at the clock. "Will you be long?"

He leaned in and kissed my forehead without answering.

"Aiden, wait," I pleaded as he started towards the door. "You can't come home early today?"

"I'm sorry, no."

"I haven't seen you in two days. You leave before I wake up and come home after I'm in bed."

"It's my fault that you sleep a lot?" His abrasive tone caught me off guard.

"It's six o'clock in the morning, Aiden. I waited up until midnight last night and you still weren't here."

"I'm sorry," he said, not sounding the slightest bit apologetic. "You knew I'd be busy this semester when you agreed to come.

"I'm bored all day. And lonely. I don't have anyone to talk to. I'm the only human other than your staff within walking distance!"

"You could read a book, watch a movie, listen to music. Enjoy yourself. Some people wish they had more free time."

I sighed. He wasn't going to even attempt to understand, and this early in the morning, I couldn't even formulate a coherent argument. "You don't even bring me tea before you leave anymore."

"You can ring Arielle at any time and she'll bring some up for you," Aiden said.

"That's not the point." I buried my face in the pillow, hoping to go back to sleep before I said something I'd regret.

I felt the bed shift as Aiden sat beside me. "I have to go," he said.

"Then go."

"I'll try to get home early."

I didn't answer, and I didn't lift my head off the pillow until I heard the door click shut. I was just starting to accept that I couldn't fall back asleep when I heard a knock at the door.

I smiled, relieved Aiden didn't actually leave me on that note. "Come in," I called.

The door swung open and Arielle appeared, a floral pot of tea on a tray beside a mug, saucer, and small vase of flowers.

My face must have revealed my disappointment, as she quickly offered to leave and bring a fresh pot later if I preferred.

"No. This is fine, thank you."

"What would you like for breakfast this morning?"

"I'm not really hungry," I replied, hoping she'd leave me alone soon.

Arielle's nose twitched. "Mr. Eklund said to make sure you ate something."

"Toast then," I said. "Or fruit. Whatever will be fine."

I snuggled back under the covers for a moment until she returned, then made my way to the balcony with my drink. It was another foggy day, the mist rising eerily off the hills in the distance and stretching up towards the low-slung clouds. The air felt thick and sticky already, even though the temperature was still cool.

My first class was at nine, so I did some homework and left a bit early, hoping to catch Julia to chat before class. That afternoon, in between classes, I walked around campus and the center of town for awhile then decided to call Lucas.

"Well, hello, Ms. World Traveler," he greeted.

"Hi," I said, surprised that he actually answered and trying to calculate the time in Chicago. "Are you headed to practice now?"

"Yep. Mr. Responsible."

There was a lengthy silence. I started regretting calling him.

"Jess?"

"Yeah?"

Lucas laughed. "Just seeing if you were still there."

"Sorry. I'm not sure why I called. I didn't have anything to say really, just missed hearing your voice."

"Yeah, you haven't called me back since…you left."

I sensed from his hesitation that he was about to say since he proposed. "Sorry, I just wasn't sure what to say."

"How has your trip been? Do you like London?"

"Great. Really nice. Classes are good, the people are friendly and have these lovely accents..."

"Jessica," he interrupted. "Are you okay? You sound..."

"Lonely?" I supplied.

"I was going to say tired, but yeah."

"Honestly, it hasn't been what I expected so far. Aiden is busy all the time and I don't know anyone here. I've met a couple people in my classes, but it isn't the same, and when I'm at the house it's just weird because I'm all alone aside from the servants trying to wait on me."

"There are servants?"

"Yes. I mean, not tons. A cook, a daytime cleaning lady and a nighttime cleaning lady, a butler, some guards."

"So you got what you always wanted," he said.

"I never wanted all that," I snapped.

"Whoa, calm down, girl. I was joking."

"Oh. Right." I sighed, having forgotten that Lucas knew me better than anyone. "I'm sorry."

"Stop apologizing."

"I can't help it. I called you so I wouldn't feel so lonely but it's my own fault I'm here and it isn't right for me to complain about it to you when I chose this. Besides, I'm just in a mood now. It really hasn't been all bad. The first two weeks were amazing. But the last week..." I didn't even know where to begin.

"You could just come home. You're allowed to change your mind," he added. I suspected he wasn't just referring to the summer trip.

I ignored the comment. "I hate how awkward this feels, you and I, now."

"It doesn't have to be awkward. Until you make up your mind, I'm just the same old pal Lucas."

"Lucas, I did make up my mind. I told you before I left."

I couldn't stand the thought of making him wait for me all

semester, even if his offer was more tempting now than ever. If I were with Lucas, I'd be home. And even come summer once he left for Chicago, I'd be close to home even if I went with him. Or maybe even at home. I could see us making a long distance relationship work. He could visit me at home one weekend and I'd drive up to Chicago the next. I could work and save some money for an apartment after graduation and I could keep an eye on my grandma.

"Jess?"

I'd zoned out while he was still talking.

"Sorry. I'm so sleepy I can't think straight."

"Go take a nap then."

"Later. So how are your classes?"

"Good. I'm not taking anything too intense, since I've got to keep up my GPA for the scholarship, but they're all going well so far."

I smiled as Lucas delved into further detail about his course load. Lucas sounded really happy when he talked about his classes. Happy in a way he usually reserved only for hockey talk. I let him chatter on about the ins and outs of his business classes for a few more minutes before asking about his plans for summer.

"I haven't heard too many details yet," Lucas said. "I know I'll be moving to Chicago and training with the full team at Johnny's and United, but they pretty much hold all the cards about what and when."

"Kinda like being in a fraternity," I said.

Lucas laughed. It was a familiar, comfortable laugh that helped me relax and realize our friendship may not be permanently strained.

"How's everything going with the frat brothers anyway? You like any of the new guys?"

"Yeah. But I'm still just hanging with Jack a lot. When we aren't at the rink, we play video games and hit up some of the bars near the apartment to pick up..." his voice trailed off awkwardly.

"It's okay, Lucas. I told you not to wait for me. I'm spending the semester with Aiden, and you should be dating other people, too."

He sighed. "Don't worry about it, Jess. I'm not sitting at home pining over you."

"You couldn't pine if you tried."

"Hey, I just got to the rink so I should probably go. You gonna be okay?"

"Yes. I've got a busy afternoon planned. A walk, maybe a nap, perhaps I'll hang out by the stables for a bit if the sun comes out and warms it up some."

"Sounds titillating." Lucas said. "Oh, I almost forgot. I checked up on your grandma last weekend."

"You did?"

"Yeah, I went back home for Chris' birthday and I had some free time so I went over to see how she was doing."

"And?"

"She seemed good. I trimmed some bushes for her, cleaned the gutters, changed the smoke detector batteries and picked up some groceries."

"Oh geez, Lucas, I'm sorry you had to do all that."

"It's fine. She gave me fifty bucks."

I laughed. My grandma was always assigning random tasks to Lucas that she could just hire someone to do for her—at a higher cost, of course. "Thank you for checking up on her. You know you don't have to do everything she asks you, though."

"I don't mind."

"Thanks, Lucas. Alright, stop stalling and get to work." As I hung up, I realized I felt better, but I was also acutely aware of how much we hadn't said. Lucas had mentioned his brother's birthday and I hadn't even asked how Chris was, or his other brother Jacob, for that matter. I didn't know how many points he'd scored at his last match.

I didn't even know what he looked like. I mean, I knew the basics, but during the season, it wasn't uncommon for Lucas to change daily as various bruises and cuts took up residence on his body. Not knowing whether or where he'd suffered minor injuries as of late was a weird feeling for me. After being so close to Lucas for so long, there was now so much distance, and I didn't think it was all caused by the Atlantic.

AIDEN

My week had been a nightmare. After the disastrous dinner with my father, we launched into the real reason for his visit—days of back to back meetings with Marius and the leaders of other elf clans in the area. While I'd met all of the other leaders before, this was the first time I truly needed to impress them with my qualifications to lead our clan, so for the first time in ages, I felt nervous.

On top of the actual work anxiety, I was still annoyed with my father for instigating a disagreement with Jessica and unhappy about how I'd left things with her. She was not pleased with me, or quite possibly any aspect of life, this week. I couldn't blame her. I just couldn't deal with the whole issue of marriage and the line of succession right after the confrontation with my father, and I simply did not have the time or energy this week to explain to her why I was so distant this week.

To make matters worse, when I returned home, Jessica was already asleep. Her phone was on the nightstand beside her and it lit up with a new text message just as I bent over to kiss her. It was from Lucas, and he was thanking her for calling earlier, saying he enjoyed talking to her, and expressing hope that the rest of the day was better.

I didn't make a habit of reading Jessica's text messages, and I regretted having seen this one. It bothered me, to put it mildly. I wondered how often Jessica called Lucas. Did they talk regularly still? Or was this a one-time thing so she could whine about me? I didn't consider myself an insecure man normally, but given that Jessica had an engagement ring from Lucas hidden in her nightstand—not that I was snooping—I couldn't help but feel uneasy about this text. I had an urge to wake her to discuss it but thought better of it. She was allowed to call friends back home and anything I said tonight was just going to start another argument.

I undressed and climbed into bed beside her. She stirred slightly, sighed, then settled back against her pillow without fully rousing. I scooted up behind her and draped my arm around her, letting the familiar fruity scent of her hair soothe me to sleep.

The next morning, I skipped my run, even though I desperately needed it for my stress level and mental clarity. Instead, I brought breakfast up to eat with Jessica and ordered flowers and chocolate to be delivered to her later. When everything was set up, I woke her.

She rubbed her eyes as she sat up. Jessica was adorable first thing in the morning. I handed her a cup of tea then slipped under the covers beside her.

"What time is it?" she asked, bringing the steaming mug to her lips without fully opening her eyes.

"It's 5:30. Sorry to wake you but I wanted to spend time with you before I left."

"No, it's okay. I'm glad you did," she said, smiling as she noticed I was still in the thin sweatpants and tee shirt I'd slept in.

We talked for a few minutes about her classes and then I attempted to explain why I'd been so busy this week. I kept hoping she'd bring up her call with Lucas, but she didn't. I didn't pry. I assumed, at least, that if she planned to marry him, she'd let me know.

"I should shower soon," I said when I noticed it was already 6.

Jessica, who had been picking at her oatmeal, abruptly dropped her spoon and pouted.

"I'm sorry. I'm all yours Sunday." I promised.

She groaned. "It's a long time till Sunday."

I agreed.

Jessica nudged the breakfast tray to the foot of the bed and quickly pulled her shirt over her head. I felt my eyes widen at the sight of her smooth, creamy skin and perky breasts. Jessica wasn't normally this brazen, and I loved that she could still surprise me.

I was still appreciating the view when she rose to her knees and dipped her fingers beneath my shirt, lifting it up. I took the hint and helped, then cupped her chin in my hands and pulled her in for a kiss. We didn't have long, and I needed to make this memorable if I was still competing with a guy four thousand miles away. Her lips parted willingly, and she leaned against me, tripling my aching need for her as her nipples pressed against my chest.

I loved kissing Jessica, and it was one thing I would never tire of, but the second she moaned into my mouth, I couldn't wait any longer. I pulled away from her mouth, kissing, licking, and sucking my way down the rest of her body, teasing her as she arched against me. I slipped my hand beneath the band of her pajama pants and dipped my finger ever so slightly into her, eliciting from her the most delicious moan yet. I teased her another moment before withdrawing my hand, tipping her back onto the bed, and removing our remaining articles of clothing.

By 6:15, I was in the shower, with Jessica joining me a moment later. She was smiling, satisfied, and—dare I say it— happy. I suspected she'd need a nap later, but for now, she looked full of energy. And I may have skipped my run, but I felt like my alternate workout was infinitely better for my mental status.

"I'm not going to be able to concentrate today," I told her after our shower, as I tightened the loop on my tie.

"Good," she replied, lounging on the chaise in her bath robe. "Maybe I should text you some naughty pictures throughout the day just to be sure of that."

I knew she was kidding, that she would never be the type of woman to do that, but the threat alone was a pleasant distraction from the parade of meetings awaiting me. "I love you," I said, leaning in to kiss her again.

She smiled, and I left.

JESSICA

Aiden continued his punishing work schedule the next month, but we somehow managed to reconnect in meaningful ways in the little time we did have together. He surprised me with cards, flowers, and random gifts throughout the day that reminded me he was thinking of me. We also made a habit of waking ridiculously early at least once a week so that we were together in a more private way, more often than just the weekends.

It didn't hurt that I'd also finally gotten the swing of things in my classes, learned my way around London, and made some real friends in town. I was grateful that I was finally feeling comfortable and settled in my routine, since Aiden's sister Cordelia was now staying at the house too. His father had come and gone a couple times, and both Genevieve and Oliver had visited. But this was the first time I'd seen Cordelia since late fall, and her presence had the potential to make me very nervous.

Cordelia and I had never been particularly close, what with our first encounter involving her intentionally causing me to drive into an icy lake. But she had saved me a few times since then and she did seem to be a competent doctor, so I was attempting to give her the benefit of the doubt. Since her arrival in London a week ago, she'd been randomly drawing samples of my blood, without ever fully explaining why.

On that particular night, Aiden was actually home for once and I was stuck studying for mid-terms. I forced my way through one last page, then noticed Cordelia hovering in the corner of the room, hiding something behind her back. Startled, I simply stared at her, awaiting her explanation.

"I need a blood sample," she said calmly.

"You already took one a couple days ago."

She hesitated. "I know. I need another."

I was so eager for a distraction from my studies that I almost consented, but Cordelia was behaving so strangely I knew there had to be more to the story.

"The first time you gave me some of Aiden's blood, you took one sample of my blood later. The second time, two, and now this time, let me guess…you'll need three?"

She nodded. "Probably."

"Why?"

Cordelia sighed as though I'd asked the dumbest question ever. "Each time you're injected with Aiden's blood, it seems to take longer to leave your system."

This made sense to me, but I didn't know why it mattered to Cordelia. "So?"

"So I want to know exactly what is going on."

"Basically I'm your lab rat?"

Clearly interpreting this as consent, Cordelia approached me with the needle. I yanked my arm back.

"Really? I've saved your life three times now, and you can't be bothered for a tiny blood draw?"

"Seriously? You tried to kill me, Cordelia! You can hardly count what happened after that as saving my life."

"Po-tay-toe, po-tah-toe," she replied. "You of all people should be interested in supporting my research."

"Oh, really? Why is that?"

"Well, for starters, you seem to get hurt a lot when you're with

Aiden. Don't you want to know what the long term effects of all those blood transfusions are?"

I did my best to remain expressionless.

"And now that Gwyneth is out of the picture, Aiden is going to have to marry someone. Someone who can carry his babies, obviously."

I chewed on the inside of my cheek, still desperate to appear nonchalant.

"There are very limited studies on the effects of elf blood on a human, over time. There have been other cases where a human has received a one-time transfusion, and it eventually leaves their system. But each time you get some of Aiden's blood, more of it remains in your system, and for longer. I'm working on a hypothesis about a long-term, daily maintenance dose, possibly to see if that could help a human carry an elf's child, maybe even deliver a full-elf child."

"How would that be possible?"

Cordelia shrugged. "Why should I tell you more?"

I sighed, thrusting my arm to her, veiny side up. She tied the rubber tubing just above my elbow. Used to the process by now, I made a fist then looked away as the needle pierced my skin.

"Obviously, you're not my favorite person in the world, and I think Aiden is making a huge mistake by continuing his involvement with you," she said, removing the needle, capping the vial of blood, and dabbing my arm with a cotton ball. "But he is my brother, and soon to be king, so I feel some obligation to help him out."

"So you think it's possible…" I tried to formulate my words in my head, "for Aiden and I to have children?"

"Maybe. Maybe not. You're not the same, you and Aiden, obviously. And that might kill the baby in utero. Or you. If you can even conceive." She paused. "I don't know what the baby would be either, probably some half-breed of sorts…" her voice trailed off, the tone of it so casual I almost forgot she was talking about life and death—specifically, mine.

"Are you distracting her, Cordelia?" Aiden asked.

I startled, not having realized he was even in the room.

He bent over and kissed my forehead before sitting beside me. I saw an oversized book in his hand, indicating he was planning to read while I studied.

Cordelia flashed him a quirky smile and hopped up. "Thanks," she said, holding the blood vial in her hand.

I nodded, then turned to Aiden. "Did you hear what she was saying?"

He glanced down. "I heard enough."

"So do you think…"

"No," he interrupted. "You're not going to be a guinea pig. It's not safe. There has to be another way."

"Surely it's been done before, somewhere," I said.

"No," he repeated, this time with finality.

I sighed and tried returned to my studies, but of course I couldn't focus. If what Cordelia was saying was true—if there were some way for me to carry Aiden's child and for that child to actually be a true elf, all of our problems were solved. Well, most of them anyway. It seemed odd to be so preoccupied with my hypothetical offspring with Aiden when he'd never even asked me to marry him, but I suppose I accepted that figuring out the issue of our progeny was somewhat of a prerequisite to the marriage part if Aiden weren't going to completely abandon his post.

I didn't really have another chance to discuss it all with Aiden. He left the next morning for Germany and was gone for a week. I was slightly hurt that he didn't even invite me along, even though I would've turned down the invitation because of my class schedule. I told myself he knew he'd be too busy with work to spend time with me there. The house was eerily quiet in his absence, and I found myself chatting up the two cleaning ladies frequently and spending most of my evenings in London's West End with Julia and my classmates.

On the day Aiden was set to return, he was hours later than expected, and he didn't even bother to call. He left early the next morning for meetings and returned back to the house well after I had eaten dinner and finished all of my homework. He purported to have eaten earlier and went straight to the desk, where he hunched over his laptop, furiously scribbling notes on a crisp, yellow legal pad beside him.

Aiden furrowed his brow, sighed, and rubbed his forehead. He was the picture of stress. I hated it, and I hated feeling like he was blocking me out.

I tentatively approached and placed my hands on his shoulders, hoping he wouldn't rebuke the much-needed massage because it hampered his handwriting. Thankfully, he didn't. He continued working for a moment and then let his pen drop to the paper. A soft moan escaped his lips as his head relaxed back into my hands. I smiled as I felt the tension in his neck start to loosen.

After another minute, Aiden reached for my hand and pulled it to his lips, kissing it briefly. "Thank you," he said.

He spoke with a finality that I suspected was intended to stop the massage so he could resume working, but he needed more than a five minute pause. I leaned forward slightly, letting my breasts press into his shoulders as I moved my hands down slightly to massage the front of his shoulders and chest. Aiden smiled, then effortlessly tugged my hand, pulling me around and onto his lap in a fluid motion.

Aiden eyed me quizzically as if he didn't quite know what to do with me.

"I'm sorry I've been so distant lately. I've been under a lot of pressure."

"I know," I replied sympathetically.

He shook his head. "You don't know," he said, his tone leaving me uncertain as to what he meant by the response.

I paused before responding, determined not to let this turn into a fight simply because he was sleep-deprived and stressed out. "Then tell me."

Aiden stared out the window whimsically. It was pitch black outside, and surely even his expert vision couldn't see anything past the double-paned glass.

"Are we telling each other everything now?" he finally asked.

I frowned. "What do you mean?"

"You have your secrets, why should I not have mine?"

"I don't have secrets," I replied without thinking.

"Oh?" He broke his gaze from the window and faced me. "Why were you crying on our flight over?"

A lump formed in the pit of my stomach. Did that mean he knew about the proposal? God, why hadn't I told him? Was that what was causing his stress?

My thoughts raced. All this time, I'd blamed Aiden's work for the fact that we were growing apart, but all along, it was me. Everything was my fault.

"Jessica?" Aiden's voice snapped me out of my thoughts.

"I'm sorry," I said. "I didn't tell you because I didn't want to worry you. How long have you known?"

He sighed. "I found the ring in your purse during our flight. You were asleep and I was looking for a pen. That's all I know."

"Oh, Aiden, I really am sorry."

"Perhaps you could fill in the gaps so I don't speculate further."

I nodded. "Lucas came over the day we left. I thought he was just coming to say goodbye, but he asked me to stay and he, well he sort of proposed."

"Lucas asked you to marry him," Aiden said matter-of-factly.

"Yes."

"And you said...."

"Aiden, I'm here with you now. What do you think I said?"

"The ring is in your nightstand drawer, Jessica. I suppose I'm not positive what you said."

I couldn't believe he had found it there. I wondered if he stumbled across it randomly or was actually looking for it, but I probably wasn't in a position to inquire. "I said no, that I loved you. But he told me to keep the ring to remember him by or something. So I did. And I would've told you all this sooner but I know you don't like Lucas and you're already so stressed out that I didn't want to make it worse."

Aiden didn't respond. I couldn't quite decipher his expression, but it certainly didn't seem angry. I waited another minute and then I spoke.

"Is that what has been bothering you lately?"

His expression softened. "No."

"Then what is it? I know you've been working so hard, but you seem distant even when you aren't working."

Aiden traced his thumb absentmindedly across my bare thigh as he thought. The sensation quickened my pulse despite the seriousness of our discussion. "It's my father," he finally said. "He's very concerned about my relationship with you and the perception it will give my people."

"Our relationship is none of their business," I insisted, knowing even as I said it how ridiculously untrue it was.

He continued as though he hadn't heard me. "It makes me look weak. And if my people believe I'm putting you—a human—before them, it makes my loyalty questionable." Aiden paused. "It's a lot of political mumbo-jumbo, really, but the essence of it is that I can't maintain my family's power if I don't come across as a strong leader."

"They'll just have to accept you," I said, realizing how stupid my words sounded.

"They don't, Jessica. Not everyone is loyal to my family. There are other leaders in our world and they could usurp our power altogether if I don't do exactly what I'm supposed to do."

"What other leaders? What do you mean?"

"There isn't just one nation of elves. My people are part of the northern clan. That's what I am set to rule. But there is also the southern clan and the eastern clan. If my people aren't satisfied with my leadership, they can protest it and come up with a new leader. And if the other clans perceive us as weak or even as a threat to the elfish way of life because of my connection to you, they can try to overtake our clan altogether and make it part of theirs."

As a history major, I understood exactly what Aiden was explaining. It was the essential problem faced by every single monarch from the middle ages to the present. One must rule strongly or risk losing the nation's sovereignty.

And yet all I could focus on was the fact that his people had other options. It didn't have to be him. That's what he was saying when he claimed there were all of these threats to his power.

"Wait, so you could just leave all of this behind and come home and lead a normal life without being king of anything? You chose this?" I wasn't sure what to say to any of it. I'd always assumed Aiden was just a pawn of his father, that if he couldn't lead, no one else could either. But this...this all made it seem so voluntary. "I feel like I don't know you at all!"

Aiden gripped my leg roughly and pulled it across his lap so I was now straddling him, my groin pressed firmly against his waist. His smoldering stare burned into my eyes and caught me completely off guard. "You do know me, Jessica. You know me," he repeated, his gaze so intense I felt myself sweating.

"I...I..." I stammered, totally flummoxed. I knew that look in his eyes and couldn't focus on anything but the increased yearning deep in my core when Aiden looked at me that way. "You're just trying to distract me, Aiden. We need to talk."

Aiden stood abruptly, knocking the chair to the floor as he did. He carried me across the room, my legs still wrapped tightly around his waist, and leaned over the bed, not increasing the space between our bodies even for a moment.

"What I am doing is proving my point, showing you that you do know me. And that I know you. We can talk all night if you want, but it won't change the fact that you and I are on the same team here. We both want the same thing, and you know that."

His face was so close to mine that I felt the breath escape with his words at the same time as I processed their meaning. I was still confused, unsettled, and slightly annoyed, but my mind went blank the second Aiden pressed his lips to mine.

CHAPTER FIVE

AIDEN

As our bodies stilled, we remained entwined with each other. Jessica's arm was draped across my chest, her delicate leg thrust between my own legs. I listened to her breathing, observed her heartbeat, and I sensed the moment she fell asleep. I didn't dare move just yet, but I was wracked with guilt, and it was only worsened by my close proximity to her. I couldn't think straight with her intoxicating scent flooding my nostrils and her hair tickling my bare chest.

I slowly slid my hand down her chest and pulled it out from under her thin nightgown, blushing that we hadn't even bothered completely undressing in our haste to have each other. That—the urgent and overwhelming need for her that drowned out all logical thoughts and made it impossible for me to make wise decisions around her...that was my problem.

There was no question about it—Jessica and I were no good for each other. We were from completely different worlds and she was just as certain to be my undoing as I was to be hers.

The more time I spent with my father, the more I respected and understood him. He was no longer the distant and authoritarian man incapable of showing warmth even in the privacy of his own home. Now, I could see the rationale behind his actions. He was principled, not cold. He was determined, not stubborn. Most importantly, I could now see how badly he wanted me to succeed. His every move was driven by his resolve to help me reach my potential.

Jessica whimpered in her sleep, tensing her hand briefly into a fist then relaxing her fingers onto my chest again. God, she was perfect.

I was screwed. There was nothing logical about my feelings for her, nor could I deny the intensity of them. I could be fully entrenched in some tactical political scheme, and with one touch from Jessica, all I would be able to think about was being with her. Even just the sound of her voice made me wild. The passion I felt for her consumed me, and, at this rate, it was bound to drive me insane.

We were drifting apart and I hated it. I couldn't deny that it was entirely my fault. I had dragged her along on this trip, promising it would bring us closer together, and then the moment we arrived, I began pulling back. I couldn't help it, though. The deeper I delved into the true happenings in my own community, the more dedicated I became to the cause—and the more I realized Jessica would be the kiss of death to my family's reign, not to mention to my own political career.

But worse than that, I was learning more and more about the dangers Jessica could face because of her relationship with me. And that was what caused the crushing guilt that made it impossible for me to sleep next to her delicate and innocent perfection.

I scooted my legs out from under Jessica's then stilled for a moment before lifting her hand off my chest and sliding away altogether. I watched her sleep for another moment, envying the peacefulness that enabled her to sleep so soundly, certain I would never feel that serene until the day I died. Then I grabbed jeans and a shirt before exiting the room.

As I suspected, my father was still awake. He was holed up in his makeshift office in the library, speaking in hushed tones with a man I didn't recognize while sipping a glass of what I assumed to be bourbon. When he saw me, he smiled, his eyes having only briefly flickered with disapproval as he observed my mussed hair and clothing.

"Aiden, please join us," he said jovially. He reached for a large decanter, plopped some ice into an etched crystal glass, and poured me a drink.

"I'm not interrupting?"

My father shook his head. His companion stood. "I must be on my way, actually," the man said. He bowed respectfully to me and left.

I watched him go then sat across from my father.

"You're right," I said without waiting for him to speak. "We need to find a way to fix this."

His expression revealed he hadn't expected that from me. It took him a moment to respond.

"Well, you know your best chance is if you're able to marry someone with elf blood."

I knew he would say that. He'd been consistent in that, at least. "It's not someone," I replied. "It's Jessica. There will be no one else. Instead of wasting your time thinking of other solutions, you need to assume this is how it will be and figure out how to make that work."

I braced myself for my father's typical response, that I didn't know what the future held and I shouldn't be so resolute. But it didn't come.

Instead, he simply said, "I can't guarantee that it would be enough, even if she were to become like us."

For once, we were actually on the same page, it seemed. I hid my shock at this and pressed on. "So why don't we bring the analysts in now, figure out a likely scenario and get a fair grasp on public opinion before we mess with any testing?"

"We can't waste time and resources analyzing hypothetical what-ifs before we even know if it is possible. We don't even know that she'd agree."

I broke eye contact. I knew that was a deliberate jab as my father was aware I had virtually no control over Jessica's actions or decisions. Obviously, such a scenario was unheard of in our culture, especially given my position.

"Let me worry about her," I said.

My father tossed his head back and laughed. "Son, we have an entire army worrying about her, thanks to your recent conduct."

I sipped my drink, unwilling to get into that discussion again.

"So you're telling me that if our researchers can figure out how to make it happen and the analysts tell us it will help your position, then we can count on her to cooperate?" he asked.

I swallowed the lump rising in my throat. "Yes." I tried to convince myself that it was the truth. After all, she had seemed excited when Cordelia told her each injection of my blood took longer to leave her system. She had willingly let Cordelia test her blood after. Of course, I knew the difference here. My father wasn't suggesting we continue to test Jessica's blood but that we subject other humans to a battery of tests to see if a human could become an elf, simply by transfusing enough elf blood into the human.

He nodded. "You realize there won't be definitive answers on long term effects in the near future, right?"

"Yes." I paused. "This won't hurt anyone, will it?"

My father hesitated. "No. We know the effects of our blood on injured people. What we need to study is the effects of it on healthy humans."

"They'll be willing participants?"

He shrugged. "I suspect there will not be full, informed consent, but they certainly won't use unwilling people." Then he sighed. "If you agree to this, you're not going to have oversight over each detail. You'll have to let others do their jobs."

I sipped my drink again. Delegation wasn't my strong suit, especially when it came to Jessica. It didn't help that I was doing all of this behind her back, moments after deflecting my negative mood onto her and forcing her into a defensive position about the engagement ring.

"We can't do the testing without your authorization," my father said, snapping me out of my thoughts.

I nodded.

"I need you to actually say it, Aiden."

"I'm authorizing you to do the testing," I said, finishing the rest of my drink and setting the glass on the desk with a loud clink.

"Very well then," he replied, retrieving a paper from his desk drawer and sliding it across the surface to me. "Sign here, and I'll see you in the morning."

I did as I was told and went straight upstairs where I found Jessica, still sleeping soundly.

Jessica

The next month flew by. During the week, I kept busy with classes and my newfound friends while Aiden worked nonstop. On some weekends, we traveled together. We went to the Cotswolds one weekend and Bath another. At other times, I invited him out for dinners or drinks when meeting up with my classmates, but he always purported to be too busy. Julia was starting to tease me about having made up my illusive boyfriend. She invited me to Devon one weekend and I quickly said no, then reconsidered and agreed. Aiden had already said he'd be busy then, so why shouldn't I go have fun with Julia?

Not surprisingly, Aiden was less than enthusiastic about me going. I reminded him that I was quite independent before he came along, and that I could certainly handle two nights without him. After many threats of sending a guard with me, he finally acquiesced.

Julia and I spent our first day exploring Dartmore National Park, capturing glimpses of wild ponies and admiring the rugged, breathtaking scenery. We spent the night in Salcombe, planning to explore the shops and marina Saturday before returning to London Sunday.

We stayed in a cute bed and breakfast in a shared room with two small beds. We ate dinner late, then changed into our pj's and drank wine on the floor between our beds. It reminded me of slumber parties I'd attended as a child, with that same cozy vibe that made everyone prone to oversharing. We started by talking about our mutual classmates and professors, what we missed about the U.S. and what we loved about London. I asked Julia about her family and friends back home, which of course led to some discussion about the long-term boyfriend who'd broken up with her right before our semester abroad. So, I wasn't surprised when she asked about Aiden.

"What's the deal with this mysterious boyfriend of yours? Will I ever actually meet him?"

"Probably not," I mumbled, topping off both of our drinks. "He's turned into a total workaholic since arriving in London."

"What does he do?"

I was accustomed to answering this question by now. "His family owns a large international business and he's taking over in January. That's why he's so busy now, plus he's under a lot of pressure to really prove himself to the rest of the family and other people involved in the business."

Julia raised an eyebrow and helped herself to some licorice. We'd learned the hard way that American favorites like red licorice cost triple in England compared to back home, but it was so worth it for the familiar treat. "But won't he be even busier once he's officially in charge?" she asked.

"Yes," I agreed reluctantly.

"Do you think you'll get married someday?"

"I don't know." I struggled to explain the complications facing my relationship with Aiden without revealing too much. "His family doesn't really approve of me and if he married me, he might have to give up the job."

She wrinkled her nose. "That sucks. Is his family like crazy rich?"

I nodded.

"Rich people are so weird."

I agreed with her assessment and bit off another bite of licorice. I steered the conversation back to happier topics, but still went to bed confused about where things stood with Aiden. When I was with him, and we were alone and he wasn't preoccupied by work, it was perfect. He made me happy. He made me laugh. He made me feel loved. I could deal with all the other complications if that was all it was, but lately it was more. I couldn't shake the feeling that he was intentionally pulling away from me. I had assumed living together in London would bring us closer, but instead I felt more distance between us than ever.

AIDEN

My sister Genevieve arrived in England the day Jessica was set to return from her weekend away with her friend. Eager to reunite with my sister without my father breathing down our necks, I took her out to a pub, returning home when I thought Jessica would be arriving. Instead, I found she had beaten us home by a half hour and was currently walking by the stables chatting on her phone with none other than Lucas.

I had missed her over the weekend and had wanted a happy reunion, but between her annoyance with me for not being home when she returned and my resentment that she called Lucas to pass the time, I knew our reunion was doomed from the start. So, instead of waiting around for her to hang up the phone, I went inside and pulled up some contracts Marius wanted me to review.

When Jessica came inside to find me, I was still worried I'd snap at her for talking to Lucas. I knew I had no right to be jealous, that I needed to calm down. I read a few more sentences and then turned away from the computer.

Seeing her gorgeous face for the first time in two days instantly changed my mood. It was impossible not to by happy looking at her. I reached for her, desperate for a kiss, but she held me at bay.

"Why am I here if you don't have any time for me?" Her tone was accusatory, but her eyes were soft. I knew she felt hurt, not angry, and it was entirely my fault.

"You're here because I want you here. I need you here." I paused. "I know this trip hasn't been what you expected and that it seems like I'm always working. But even on the days I don't get to talk to you, I'm glad you're here. The time I spend watching you sleep is the best part of my day."

Jessica eyed me warily for a moment before her expression softened. This time, she let me pull her into my arms.

"I missed you," I said. "And I'm sorry I wasn't here when you returned. My father is working on my last nerve and I was desperate for a few minutes out of the house with Gen. And then when I came back…"

"I was talking to Lucas," she finished. "I'm sorry, Aiden. I had to call him because his last final was this week and my cell phone didn't work in Devon. He's moving to Chicago tomorrow to start training, and…" she paused. "And you don't care about any of these details." She laughed at herself.

"I had fun with Julia, but it would've been a romantic trip with you, too."

I smiled. "We don't need craggy hills and seascapes for romance. We could make our own romance right here."

Jessica giggled and hopped onto the bed, welcoming me with both arms.

We had a perfect evening reconnecting, and we had dinner brought up to the room so I didn't have to share a moment of my attention with my father or anyone else. Jessica's final exams were fast approaching, so she would be the busy one now, even though she'd done so much work this semester that she probably could've aced her tests without studying.

One week later, my father summoned me to his office in downtown London. I knew he must have something important to discuss, since he rarely called me to him while we were at work. I went to him immediately, closing the door behind me when I arrived. I had the feeling the nature of our discussion was more clandestine than normal, in part because it affected Jessica and in part because I suspected, although hadn't confirmed, that Marius was unaware of what we were doing. Certainly he would support the testing if it resulted in a solution, but at this point he was firmly resolved in his position that I marry someone other than Jessica.

I turned hopefully to my father, then hesitated, realizing I hadn't spent much time in his office here. Generally when we met, he came to my office. His was significantly smaller, but similarly furnished to my own, except that along the far wall in my office there were file cabinets and his wall was lined with vaults I assumed housed weapons. My mind briefly flashed to the times in my childhood when my father had taken Oliver and me for target practice. Oliver was always a much better shot than I, although now we both would likely qualify as sharpshooters by human standards.

"Sit, please," my father said.

I did as he asked.

"I'll get right to it. The results did not show what we had hoped. Within a matter of days of receiving elf blood, healthy humans have no trace of elf blood in their system."

I frowned. "That's not possible."

"We've confirmed the results, Aiden. Cordelia has looked over it all as well."

I shook my head. Obviously, someone had made an error somewhere. "Cordelia found traces of elf blood in Jessica's system weeks after she was injected with my blood."

"I know that."

I considered the possible explanations for a moment before figuring it out. "It's the cumulative effect. Each time they have elf blood, it lasts longer. We just need to keep going."

"No, Aiden they've done that. They have given the subjects more blood more times than Jessica has ever…"

"That doesn't make sense," I interrupted. I stood and paced the room. I made my way over to the window and looked out. Dozens of floors below us, at ground level, I spotted an elf guard. It wasn't Elgin, since he had a hard time looking inconspicuous and tended to stay closer to me these days. From this height, I couldn't tell who exactly it was even with my impeccable eyesight. But the fact that a guard was there—for me—reminded me that I was different.

"It's me," I said. "It has to be my blood. Or someone in our lineage. That's why it isn't working."

My father paused, seemingly not ready to disappoint me given my enthusiasm. "Aiden, sit down," he finally said. "You make people nervous when you pace like that."

I rolled my eyes while my back was still to him, grateful at least that he didn't add his usual bit about how pacing wasn't suited to my position, then I complied.

"We got these results a few days ago and that was Cordelia's initial thought as well. So we gave the subjects large doses of her blood and the results are the same. There was no trace of elf blood in the subjects' systems when we retested them last night."

I sighed. It made no sense. I supposed I could insist they continue the study, using my blood, but I knew enough about genetics to realize there was nothing special about my blood that wasn't present in Cordelia's.

Father remained silent for several minutes, I suppose to give my disappointment time to set in.

"If it's not our blood, then what is it? How do you explain Jessica?"

He hesitated, making me wonder what he was debating keeping from me.

"When is the last time she had any elf blood, before Cordelia's test last week?" he finally asked.

"It's been months," I said. "Before we came to London."

He nodded as though I'd confirmed his assumption. "And there's no chance any other genetic matter…or bodily fluid is in her system?"

His clear discomfort at that sentence confused me, until I realized what he was asking.

"No. We've always used protection," I said, feeling myself blush. I wondered if it was even possible to transfer the elf genetics to her that way. I supposed it would be more pleasant for her if I could heal her via sexual intercourse rather than a needle piercing her skin, but it didn't seem plausible.

"We don't have reason to believe that would do anything," my father added as though reading my mind. "I just wanted to be certain we weren't drawing conclusions without addressing every other possibility."

I frowned, having no clue what he was getting at.

"Cordelia tested Jessica's blood when she first arrived here, and it showed the exact same levels of elf blood as the sample she took after you first gave her blood to heal her. At first, we thought the effects of your blood simply lasted longer each time you gave her a dose, but now it seems like she has some elf blood in her system all the time."

"That's not possible," I said, too perplexed by it all to protest that my father and sister had taken it upon themselves to test Jessica without asking me first.

My father slid a paper across the desk to me. I glanced down, recognizing it to be blood test results, but I knew I wouldn't be any more convinced by the numbers since the error clearly had to have been made in the testing itself. The samples had to have been switched, or mislabeled, or something.

"The reason her tests are different, Aiden, isn't because of your blood, but because of hers."

I took a moment to process his words, to let their full meaning sink in. I inhaled slowly and stared him in the eye, afraid to allow myself to consider all the possibilities this revelation might open up.

"You're saying Jessica has elf blood—that Jessica is..." I paused, not believing what I was about to say. "Part elf?"

He nodded solemnly then raised a hand. "We'd have to do further testing to confirm this, but it's the only explanation that fits, and I'd already suspected that..."

"You suspected this?" I cut him off, my mood instantly flipping from hopeful to irate. "And you didn't tell me?"

"Calm down, Son." My father's expression suggested he was embarrassed by my reaction, despite the absence of any witnesses.

"I will not calm down. You should not have kept something like this from me..."

"I didn't know anything for certain," he interrupted. "And we still don't. What I was going to say before you got all worked up was that I suspected her grandfather Fritz had some involvement with our people. There are records of a German-born elf named Fritz marrying a human, abandoning his ancestry, and moving to the United States."

I frowned, struggling to process all of this new information. "That's why you were so interested in Jessica's relatives," I concluded.

My father nodded. "I was hoping she could confirm some of the details for me so I could be certain, but she knows even less than our genealogical records show."

"When were you going to tell me? And when did you first suspect all of this?"

"I planned to tell you when I had reliable information, which is why I'm telling you now. And frankly, I've suspected this from the start, when I first met her. There was something off about her."

"Off?" I repeated doubtfully. "If what you're saying is true, and Jessica's grandfather was an elf, that makes her what—one-fourth elf? You can't possibly expect me to believe you can sniff out someone with that diluted of elf ancestry."

"I've spent my entire life focusing on the most minute details. My success at my job depends on my ability to recognize things others would miss." He paused. "And frankly, I suspect you sensed it, too. How else do you explain your extreme attraction to her when you'd never before found any human the slightest bit interesting?"

He paused for me to consider his words before continuing. "She hasn't ever gotten sick as long as you've known her, has she? Didn't that seem odd to you? Humans are constantly falling ill. The average is, what, four colds a year, plus maybe a bout of influenza or some stomach virus every year or two? And how does she maintain her physique? Does she spend a lot of time in the gym? Because I've never heard of her exercising the entire time I've known of her and she appears to me to be exceptionally fit. Even her features—they're just too symmetrical, too perfect to be human."

I frowned, annoyed at his persistence and at myself for being so blind. How hadn't I noticed it before? Or had I, and I just dismissed it as my own bias? Certainly I'd always *considered* her to be perfect, but it didn't occur to me that she actually *was* a bit too perfect. "Enough," I said. "This could be a good thing, right?"

He nodded. "Your offspring would be five-eighths elf, but in several generations the distinction would be insignificant enough that perhaps your descendants could eventually retake the throne."

I didn't really care about my lineage. I acknowledged it as a concern, but not a pressing one. I wanted answers about the immediate future.

"What's the next step?" I asked eagerly.

"We'd need to run some more tests on Jessica."

I didn't like the sound of that, and presumably my expression reflected as much because my father continued with his explanation.

"If we are going to approach Marius with the position that you plan to marry Jessica, we need to know for certain whether she can bear children and what exactly we could expect from those offspring."

"If Jessica is part elf, that alone is proof that an elf and a human can have children."

"No one will take our word for that. We need to be able to prove it. The other clans are going to be watching closely what you do. If we don't tread lightly, we're still inviting anarchy or even war."

My father was being overly dramatic, of course. I'd learned that, when he was a child, the elf purists were still a powerful faction, but the reality was that it hadn't been a big issue in modern times. Still, I personally would've felt better knowing for certain that Jessica could safely carry our child to term before accidentally or intentionally impregnating her.

"The more elfish we can portray her to be, the better this will be for everyone."

"What do you mean?"

"Aiden, right now no one outside of our immediate family is aware that we suspect Jessica to be one-fourth elf. If we can pump her up with elf blood and somehow establish that she's actually more like fifty percent elf, that would benefit us greatly."

"How would we do that?" His idea intrigued me. Obviously, I knew how we could get additional elf blood into her, but devising some sort of test to show her elf makeup during the time the extra blood was still coursing through her veins seemed tricky. And convincing our potential enemies to believe the results of the test seemed even less likely.

"We leak the information, timing it well. And we make them think it's their idea to test her then."

I considered this, happily feeling optimistic about the future for the first time in ages.

My father apparently didn't like that I was dawdling. "Well? I assume you agree?"

I flung my hands up. "I need to think about it."

"No, you need to conduct yourself like a leader and be decisive. Take action for once."

"I am not approving any plans without talking to Jessica first. She should be involved in these decisions since it's her life we're discussing. And besides, I think she deserves to know what you've learned about her grandfather." Also, I was desperate for a moment alone with someone who would share my enthusiasm.

My father frowned. "Really? I would have thought you'd want to protect her. How do you think she's going to react if you've tell her she's part elf and everything will work out magically and then we learn that she can't even carry an elf child or that she could never pass as more than one quarter elf? You're risking getting her hopes up for nothing."

I hesitated. I did want to protect Jessica. I certainly didn't want to disappoint her. But keeping this news from her any longer than I had to was wrong, even if the reason to delay made sense. Although, we hadn't actually been seeing eye to eye lately.

Another disappointing blow might be the last straw and then this would all be for nothing.

"I don't want to lose her," I said.

"Then you need to act quickly to ensure this plan goes off without a hitch."

"I'm not authorizing someone to start injecting her with a lot of elf blood without her consent," I said finally. "And she's not to be given anything but my blood, so get Cordelia over here now to start drawing it."

My father nodded. "So I can get the ball rolling on everything and you'll talk with her tonight?"

I agreed then scurried out of his office, eager to surprise Jessica with all of my news.

CHAPTER SIX

JESSICA

My phone rang less than a half hour before my exam. I glanced at the caller ID, frowning when I saw it was Aiden. I supposed that he was calling to wish me good luck, but honestly I didn't think I could handle the distraction of even an innocent call from him, and the way things were going lately, I worried what started as an innocuous conversation would turn into another argument. Then, I really wouldn't be able to focus on my test. So, I switched my phone off without even listening to the voice mail.

The test turned out to be surprisingly easy, although I may have over-studied in an attempt to avoid Aiden's family. Writing the essay portions was downright pleasant, I decided. And it didn't hurt that this was my last exam- really my last task of any level of difficulty here in London. I was basically home-free till fall.

I had originally planned to stay in Europe several weeks after classes ended to travel more, assuming I might not have another all-expenses paid trip to England. But I was homesick. I had never gone this long without seeing my grandma. I missed the sunny Midwest weather, American foods, and non-accented voices. I was nervous about seeing Lucas, but eager nonetheless. And Claire—oh how I missed Claire. While I'd made new friends, it wasn't the same. They were friends I'd keep in touch with, sure, but not the kind of friends I could cuddle with in bed on a rainy day, eating popcorn in our pj's and watching early nineties action movies.

I hadn't told anyone back home that I might return earlier than anticipated so the thought of surprising them all excited me, too.

When I'd mentioned to Aiden that I was considering heading home shortly after exams, he hadn't tried to convince me to stay. In fact he'd basically said the opposite, that I'd have plenty of future opportunities to visit Europe again with him and that I should head home to spend time with my grandma before school started up again if that was what I wanted. He, of course, wasn't coming back to the States for a few more weeks regardless.

I sighed, wishing I could pinpoint what was going on between Aiden and me, or better yet, actually fix it. It was obvious he was tense and that he felt guilty about leaving me alone so often, but I hated the feeling that he was trying to distance himself from me. Most of all, I was terrified that spending this semester together had made him realize he didn't actually want me by his side the rest of his life.

"Hey, can you believe we are done?"

I startled at the loud voice coming from behind me. I turned to see Julia, and she was practically jumping with excitement.

"Why don't you look happy? You should be thrilled! We did it!" Then she paused. "Uh oh- do you not think you did well?"

I shook my head, trying to dispel the bad mood with the movement. "No, I'm pretty sure I aced it. How about you?"

She nodded enthusiastically. "So listen, a bunch of us are going to a pub for a celebratory drink or five. Want to share a taxi?"

I considered the offer briefly before nodding. "Sure. Just let me text my boyfriend where we're going."

Julia laughed. "Is he going to come along? Will I finally meet Mr. Mysterious?"

"I doubt it," I said.

"You know, I'm starting to think you made him up just to stop Dustin from hitting on you," she teased. "Not that it worked."

I giggled. Our classmate Dustin was a hopeless flirt. Even if Aiden weren't in the picture, Dustin wouldn't be my type, but he sure was fun to hang out with.

Once we were in the car, I texted Aiden. "Test went well. Off 2 celebrate w/Julia," I said. I noticed I now had two missed calls from Aiden, but I was determined to be a carefree, normal college girl for the night.

My phone buzzed with his reply. "Congrats. Really need to talk to you. Please call."

I rolled my eyes thinking of the times I'd really needed to talk to him when he'd blown me off because of a meeting. I deserved a night out. I wasn't going to feel guilty.

I clicked my phone off again and chatted amicably with Julia the rest of the ride to the pub. After we arrived and ordered the first round, I thought about Aiden again. What if something had happened? What if my grandma was sick or had fallen?

I had nearly made up my mind to call him when Julia pulled me aside.

"Okay, what is going on?"

"Aiden keeps texting me to call him."

"Why?"

I shrugged. "I don't know. At first I thought he was just being needy but now it occurred to me he could be calling because something happened."

"If something bad actually happened, don't you think he'd say so in his text?" Julia shook her head. "Sounds like he just doesn't want you out having fun without him. Why don't you tell him he can come have fun with us or talk to you later?"

"Good idea," I said, impressed with the simplicity and logic of it all.

"Not in mood for serious talk right now," I texted. "You can come join us while we celebrate or we can just talk later."

We were on the second round of drinks before he replied. I assumed that meant he was considering my offer. His text was curt. It said, "Fine. Have fun. Text me when you want Quinn to pick you up."

I frowned at the fact that he wasn't even going to pick me up. It really did stink that my friends here would never meet him. Oh well. His loss. I was determined to enjoy the night regardless.

Four hours and a few too many beers later, I texted Aiden that I was ready for a ride home. Then I headed to the bathroom with Julia. We got distracted by a game of darts on our way out, though, and by the time we stumbled out to the front of the bar, I saw Quinn's town car. I was about to offer Julia a ride home so she wouldn't have to pay for a cab when the back door of the car opened and I saw a figure start to exit.

"Aiden!" I shrieked excitedly, pulling Julia by the hand. "I guess you'll get to meet him after all," I told her.

We reached the car right as the passenger climbed out. It wasn't Aiden at all, but Oliver.

"You must be the mystery boyfriend," Julia said, offering her hand to Oliver. "We were starting to think you were imaginary."

Oliver seemed both bewildered and amused, so I clarified before he had a chance to make any inappropriate or opportunistic comments.

"No, sorry, Julia. This is Aiden's brother Oliver. I don't know why he's here." I glared at Oliver.

"He's cute," she said, louder than I suspected she intended.

I gave her a huge hug. "Call me once you're back in the States," I said. "We will have to do a reunion someday."

She nodded. "I'm going to miss you!"

We hugged once more, and then I crawled into the car, Oliver following closely behind.

"So what are you doing here?" I asked, searching the car for bottled water. "When did you even get to London?"

"Today," he said, answering my latter question first. "And Aiden wanted me to personally assure that you arrived home safely. He has been going crazy all evening wanting to talk to you about something."

"Then why didn't he come?"

"He and our father are in some top secret closed door meeting with Marius."

I rolled my eyes, nearly falling over from the ensuing dizziness.

Oliver laughed. "Wow, you are drunk! I can literally smell the alcohol on your skin."

"We were celebrating exams," I said.

"I wasn't judging you."

"It sounded like judgment."

He reached into the front, retrieved a bottle of water, loosened the cap and then handed it to me. "Shit," he mumbled. "Aiden told me to give you a bunch of his blood. I don't even know if I should still do that with you...like this."

"Why would he tell you that?" I asked, dribbling a bit of the water down my chin.

Oliver shrugged. "No clue. Also no idea why they suddenly flew me in last minute. But I guarantee you it is something big and important and I am not going to be the one to screw up this time."

He pulled out his phone and typed an inhumanly fast message to someone while I wracked my already-fuzzy brain to try to think of a reason Aiden would want me to have blood.

"I'm not hurt," I said. "This must be some misunderstanding."

Oliver's phone chimed. "Nope," he said. "Aiden says to go ahead with it."

Before I could question him further, he grabbed my arm and stabbed me with something.

"Ouch!"

"Hold still, Jessica, jeez."

"What are you doing?"

"I told you. Aiden said to give you some of his blood. Two vials now, then an IV overnight."

"What? That's ridiculous. I'm going to call him so he can explain."

I reached for my phone, but Oliver swept it away.

"He's in a meeting," he repeated.

I rolled my eyes, but the gesture again made me nauseous. Ugh. I really had overdone it with the alcohol. "Wait, is this because I'm drunk? Is he trying to sober me up?"

"No. Although I'm sure he wouldn't approve of you getting trashed with some random kids in a pub. Geez, you *are* high maintenance," Oliver said as though he were agreeing with someone. I was too tipsy to read too much into the statement.

I huffed but leaned back against the seat. I let my eyes drift shut, then decided that doubled the dizziness. "Can you roll down the window?"

Oliver complied quickly. "Do we need to pull over?" He was eying me like I held a grenade.

"No," I said, praying that remained true. "But some music would be nice."

Quinn's gaze met Oliver's in the rearview mirror and Oliver nodded. Quirky late-nineties pop music blared through the speakers. Not exactly what I'd meant, but it would do.

I shimmied side to side, feeling much better when I moved. Actually, my whole body was pulsing with energy now. I wrinkled my nose, realizing that was the effect of Aiden's blood. The weasel had totally been trying to sober me up. Well, too bad for him, I was going to enjoy my buzz as long as I could.

"Do you dance?" I asked Oliver.

"In cars? No."

I smiled. "In public. Like at bars or clubs."

He nodded with a grin.

"Aiden doesn't. He can dance, really well actually, but I can only think of a handful of times when he actually danced with me."

"I suppose he just doesn't want to end up on the next edition of Elf Kings Gone Wild," Oliver mused.

I looked to him with alarm before realizing he was obviously kidding.

"There is dancing at most of the official gatherings we have," Oliver said. "Ballroom dancing, mostly."

I was okay with that. I didn't actually know how to waltz or foxtrot or whatever, but I was confident Aiden could teach me and he'd lead anyway. It really wasn't about the type of dancing or even the music. Mostly I just enjoyed feeling his body move against mine. And I wanted to know that he wasn't embarrassed by me. I had never been big on PDA, but I was acutely aware that Aiden had no issues with public make out sessions back on campus, but now, whenever his family or anyone connected to his elf world was around, he would at most hold my hand chastely.

"He probably wouldn't ever invite me to something like that," I finally said, dashing my own hopes of a Cinderella-style royal ball with my own elfish prince. I gazed out the window watching the last of the London cityscape blur past the window; we were nearing the estate.

"Everyone wanted him to break up with you last year, you know," Oliver said suddenly. "He's fought for you time and time again. Aiden has risked our entire family legacy, maybe even the safety of our people, for you."

"What is your point?" I demanded, annoyed by his tone.

Oliver looked away. "I don't know. I guess just that he really likes you. Sometimes I can't tell if you realize that, if you even appreciate the sacrifices he's made."

I turned back to the window. I wondered how often Aiden had spoken with Oliver over the semester. As far as I knew, they hadn't seen each other much since we left, although I supposed Oliver could have been in one of the other countries Aiden visited for some meeting and he just didn't mention it.

Oliver had always been Aiden's best friend. While their relationship had definitely taken a hit last summer when Oliver basically betrayed Aiden and me, Aiden had assured me that things had been strained between them for some time before that because of their different life paths. Still, I knew my existence was one of the biggest wedges between them, and I hated being responsible for pulling Aiden away from his brother, especially when he didn't exactly have any real friends who weren't relatives, as far as I could tell.

"You're a good brother," I said.

"Yeah, I am," Oliver replied in his normal cocky tone. He rolled the window up as I heard the gravel of the private drive crunching beneath our tires.

Oliver glanced down at his phone. "Aiden's still not home yet, but he said to call him after you get home."

He helped me out of the car and steadied me as I wobbled with my first step. Then I swatted his hand away, insistent that I could walk fine on my own. He followed me up the stairs and to my bedroom, and just as I was about to ask when he was going to leave me alone, he dropped my purse on the floor by the door. Oops. Guess I'd left that in the car.

I kicked off my shoes, determined to ignore Oliver's judgy stare.

"I'm going to have someone bring up some crackers for you. And maybe a ginger ale?"

I shrugged nonchalantly, but actually that sounded perfect.

I opted to call Aiden before my shower, but the call went to voice mail. Figures, I thought. I made my way to the bathroom, taking my pj's with me, and had just turned on the shower when my phone buzzed with a text from Aiden. He apologized for not answering, said his meeting was almost over and that he'd rush home, and that I should let Oliver start me on an IV with blood overnight.

"Why?" I texted back.

"Please just trust me. I'll explain when I'm home. I have news," he replied.

I sighed, then stepped into the shower.

I lingered in the steamy glass enclosure until my skin started to prune. Then I shut off the water and slowly got ready for bed. Just as I pulled my tank top over my head, I heard a knock at the door. I peeked my head out, assuming it was the maid with my snack, but I saw that the crackers and drink were already on a tray near the bed. I dried my hair with the towel one last time before hanging it up and plodding over to the door.

It was Oliver, his hands full of medical equipment. I groaned.

His eyes wandered down my body then back up again, and I was thankful that I was wearing shorts and a tank top to sleep and not a skimpy nightgown or sexy camisole.

"Aiden wants this started now," he said. "Why don't you get comfortable in bed and I'll set it up. Then you can go to sleep whenever."

I huffed out a breath of air and turned to get a cracker. "No," I said. "Unless you can tell me what all this is for, we'll just wait until he gets home."

Oliver's expression remained unchanged. He grabbed the glass of soda and set it on the nightstand next to a bottle of water. He stuck the plate of crackers next to it and placed the TV remote there, too.

"It's not up for discussion," he said finally. "You may be in a position to disregard what Aiden tells you to do, but I'm not. I actually have to do what he says. And you and I both know I can make you cooperate if you won't do so willingly. Please don't make this harder than it has to be."

I cocked my head at him, trying to determine if he was actually willing to force me into the bed if I refused.

His eyes narrowed, suggesting both that he shared his brother's uncanny mind-reading ability and that yes, he would do whatever it took to get me hooked up to the damn IV.

I sighed, not wanting to even envision the awkwardness of that scenario. I shoved another cracker into my mouth then went to the bathroom to brush my teeth. I shot him an annoyed glare as I returned, climbed into bed, and situated the covers around me.

Oliver rolled his eyes, shoved a pillow under my arm, then began wiping my hand with a disinfectant. I felt a slight pinch as the needle pierced the skin on my hand, and then a coolness traveling up my arm. He fiddled with the bag, then stepped back, inspecting his work.

"Good. Aiden can take it out for you when he gets home."

"Which will be.….?"

"Soon. Not sure exactly. But if you need me before then, text. My room's just down the hall."

"I don't have your number," I said.

"Really?" He picked up my phone and fiddled with it, I supposed entering his number.

I glanced down at my hand, feeling like an invalid. "So this is Aiden's blood?"

Oliver nodded. "He was insistent that we only used his. He thought you'd be more comfortable with that."

I was. "It's so much though. Have you been stockpiling it?"

"No. Cordelia took a bunch this morning, then more this evening before he left. I think she'll draw more later because he wants you to have more in the morning."

I frowned. Something was fishy with all of this. "And you really don't know why all of this is necessary?"

Oliver opened his mouth to say something and then shut it, shaking his head. "I'm just as out of the loop as you are. I have my suspicions, but I can't say anything."

He left before I could press him for more.

I clicked on the TV, determined to wait up for Aiden, but late night British TV was a bore. My buzz had worn off, leaving me drained. I drifted off sometime after 1 a.m.

CHAPTER SEVEN

AIDEN

My entire body buzzed with excitement as I left the meeting with Marius. I was annoyed that it had lasted so long, but apparently our current king wanted to run every last detail by his entire team to ensure our strategy didn't have any holes. Interestingly enough, when he presented the issue to his advisors, he led them to believe that Jessica was legitimately at least half pureblood elf. This prompted me to speculate as to how loyal his "trusted" advisors actually were in his mind, but it also reassured me. The fewer people who knew the truth about Jessica, the safer she would be.

The final plan was simple. A "secret" email suggesting I intended to marry Jessica rather than a full-blood elf would be leaked. The southern and far-eastern clans were already acutely focused on our clan because of the upcoming transition in power, so we knew they'd home in on that information and immediately want to flaunt it as a potential weakness. We weren't sure how soon they'd want to act, but we knew the second they questioned it, we'd have to present her immediately for confirmation or they'd suspect our ruse. So we planned to keep pumping Jessica full of blood until either—or both—clans had run their own independent tests.

Cordelia assured me that they had given significantly larger doses of elf blood to the humans in their recent trials over a period over two weeks with no negative effects, and Marius was certain the other clans would push for confirmation within a matter of days. So, I felt confident in Jessica's safety, if not slight discomfort, in the meantime.

I couldn't wait to get home to tell her the news. I wasn't sure how readily she'd accept the fact that she was already part-elf, but she would be thrilled to see the potential for a real future between the two of us. We couldn't trust Oliver with all of the information, and I hadn't wanted to tell her over the phone, but clearly she would have suspected something huge in light of the blood we were forcing on her.

I pictured her eagerly awaiting my arrival and big announcement, but when I burst through the front door, Elgin hot on my tail, the house was silent. Too silent, really. Elgin stopped me, then called for another guard to come inside with us to search the house before we went any further. The guard hadn't even finished his search of the first floor when Oliver stumbled down the stairs.

"Brother!" He greeted me warmly, pulling me close for a hug. He smiled at Elgin and shook his hand before turning back to me. "What is going on?"

"Where's Jessica?" I asked.

"In bed. In her pajamas."

I raised an eyebrow.

Oliver laughed. "I personally tucked her in."

Anyone else I would not allow to tease me about her this way, and possibly not even Oliver could get away with it on a different night, but tonight, I was in a good mood. "Did you give her all the blood?" I asked instead.

He nodded. "What is going on, though?"

Before I could answer, Cordelia swept in through the library door. She scowled at her husband and whispered an accusation about him being out too late. It struck me as cranky and odd, even for Cordelia, but whatever. I couldn't focus on anything but Jessica tonight.

I motioned for both of my siblings to follow me into the library, promising to update them both at the same time. As I spoke, Cordelia withdrew another liter of blood. Since she was more involved in the recent happenings than Oliver, he had more questions. But both of them seemed excited at the unexpected turn of events.

"So how are they reacting to the email so far?" Oliver asked.

I shrugged. "We don't even know if they've seen it yet. Or if they ever will," I admitted. "We won't know anything until they ask us directly about her."

Cordelia removed the needle from my arm. "Well, we will be ready when they do," she said. She handed the bag of freshly collected blood to Oliver. "Refrigerate this and give Jessica the entire contents of the bag already in there first thing in the morning."

He frowned. "Where are you going?"

"Bed. I'm exhausted," she said.

We both watched, confused, as she trudged back up the stairs. I didn't think I'd ever seen Cordelia exhausted before. I turned to Elgin for explanation, but he was watching his wife with a concerned expression as well.

"We're fine here, Elgin. Go with her," I said.

He hesitated, then made his way up the stairs.

"I'm going to talk with Jessica now," I said.

Oliver nodded. "Her IV should be done by now, but since she's going to get a new one in the morning, I'll just disconnect it so we don't have to stick her again tomorrow."

I considered insisting on doing this myself, since I didn't really want my brother around my sleeping Jessica, but I wasn't sure I could do it correctly and didn't want to risk hurting her. "Be quick," I told him, eager to talk to her alone.

The room was dark aside from the blue glow of the TV, but Oliver and I both could see fine. He disconnected the IV and twisted something near her hand then nodded at me, signaling he was done. I whispered my gratitude, impressed that he was successful that fast and without even waking her.

Once alone with my beloved, I slipped out of my shoes and unbuttoned my shirt, loosening my tie enough to pull it off over my head. I tossed it on the couch along with my shirt, socks, belt and pants. Then I knelt beside the bed and slowly smoothed her hair, determined to wake her as gently as possible. She groaned and shifted slightly, her arm folding closer to her chest. Dang. She was really in a deep sleep. I watched her for a few minutes and then thought better of waking her. She would be too groggy to process all of this information now anyway, so I should just wait until morning.

I got myself ready for bed and climbed in beside her, wrapping my arm around her and pulling her close. I knew this new discovery wouldn't make our future together an easy one by any means, but it was more than enough reassurance for me that we were doing the right thing by fighting for each other.

I must have drifted off at some point, and when I opened my eyes, Elgin was at my side. I startled, then quickly slid out of bed.

"King Stefen has requested an urgent meeting with you, Ivar and Marius," he said, his voice too soft to disturb Jessica. "Marius wants you on the plane in twenty minutes."

I started to protest, but there was no point. Elgin was only the messenger. Besides, this was good news. If the King of the Eastern Clan wanted to meet with me this morning, then he must have received our message about Jessica. Our plan was working. I quickly dressed. I glanced at Jessica, so peaceful in her sleep that she looked like a princess, but didn't wake her. Hopefully she'd sleep in and I'd be back by her side before she awoke. Either way, I didn't have time to explain everything now.

JESSICA

I awoke abruptly to the sensation of someone holding my hand. I groaned without fully rousing, about to remind Aiden that I had greater sleep requirements than he did. But instead, a voice decidedly not Aiden's apologized.

I opened my eyes to see Oliver. He fastened another tube to the IV in my hand. Now I groaned louder. God I was tired. What time was it anyway?

"Sorry. Go back to sleep," he said, starting to slink away.

"Wait. Where's Aiden?" I could've sworn I felt him at some point in the night, but I was alone in the bed now. Glancing across the room, I saw his discarded clothes but no other sign of him.

"He had to fly to Russia. Last minute thing. He'll be home as soon as he can. He told me to let you sleep till he returned."

I rolled my eyes. As if someone could sleep through having an IV swapped out. "Well what's going on? Did you talk to him last night?"

Oliver froze like a deer in headlights. That man had zero poker face.

"Tell me what he told you then," I said.

He shook his head.

"Oliver!"

He stepped closer. "He wants to tell you himself. All I can say is that Cordelia's been doing some research and they've got really good news for you and Aiden."

"That tells me nothing. Why are they pumping me full of Aiden's blood?"

Oliver hesitated. "They're going to trick the other clans into thinking you're one of us. So you need to have tons of elf blood in your system and then Aiden will let the other clans test a sample of your blood."

That sounded too simple to be true. If that was possible, why hadn't they done this sooner?

I asked Oliver. He got all squirmy and insisted he couldn't tell me more.

"Wait, so who exactly will test my blood? You or Cordelia?"

"No, I think they'll want to use one of their own people to guarantee the results."

I cocked an eyebrow. That made sense, but I wasn't exactly comfortable with the notion of strangers poking and prodding me. "Aiden agreed to all this? Without asking me?"

"It was his idea. And he said he tried calling you like a million times yesterday." Oliver scurried out of the room before I could interrogate him more.

I tried to go back to sleep, but I was too eager to talk to Aiden now. I texted him asking when he'd be back but he didn't reply right away. The maid came up with some breakfast, and I assumed even she knew more than I did as she didn't even bat an eye at my IV bag of blood. My phone buzzed as I finished eating and I quickly grabbed it, eager to see what Aiden had to say.

But it wasn't Aiden. It was Julia. "I have your backpack you left at the bar last night," she wrote. "Need a proper goodbye anyway, so meet me at Susie's in an hour for brunch and I'll return your bag."

I gazed around the room and realized I must have been very drunk not to even notice the absence of my backpack last night. I started to text back that I couldn't make it, then stopped. Aiden hadn't returned yet—he wasn't even answering his text. And I did need my backpack before I left the country. Plus, one last brunch at our favorite local eatery would certainly help the time pass quicker until Aiden returned. I texted back a thumbs up sign and then sent Oliver a text asking him to come up.

He was there in a flash.

"I need to get up now. Can you unhook this contraption?"

He frowned. "You're not going anywhere."

"I am going to the bathroom, thank you very much." I glanced up at the bag, which had literally just dripped its last drop. "Besides, it's empty."

He sighed and knelt beside me. He pulled out the needle and carefully peeled the tape that had held it in place off my hand. I rubbed my hand and twisted it gently. He looked at my hand and frowned. "Hold on a sec," he instructed.

I did as he asked, although he was gone more than a minute.

He returned with a medicine dropper and I watched curiously as he squeezed two small drops onto my hand. They stayed on the surface, but within a few seconds, the bruise from the IV needle started to heal. Oliver gazed up higher on my arm, lifting it to hold it level, and dripped more blood onto my bicep where he'd injected me with blood the night before.

"Alright," he said.

I smiled appreciatively and waited for him to leave before making my way to the bathroom. When the maid came up to make the bed and collect the laundry, I asked her if Quinn could drive me to town. She informed me he wasn't there, but that she'd call me a taxi. I agreed, and I headed downstairs ten minutes later.

Signs of life were everywhere in the house, but I didn't actually see any of the many residents I knew had been there the night before. I assumed many of them were with Aiden, and as I passed the library, I realized there was some closed door meeting going on inside. I smiled at the guard at the door, then went outside. I spotted a taxi turning towards the private drive and jogged down to the guard at the gate.

"It's for me," I said, meaning for him to open the gate.

He frowned. "I wasn't informed that you were heading out."

I shrugged my shoulders and walked outside the gate. "Well, I am. Be back soon." I stepped into the taxi and gave directions on where to go.

Julia was already at our usual booth when I arrived. She waved at me but didn't stand. I leaned in to hug her. "Wow, you look like you had a rough night," I said sympathetically.

She nodded. "Yes, this is the worst hangover of my life." She shoved my backpack towards me then gave me a quick once over. "But you were much more wasted than me and you look fabulous and well rested. What the hell? What's your secret?"

I couldn't very well tell her I was so pumped full of elf blood at the moment that I could practically pass for a non-human species, so I just shrugged. "Just lucky I guess."

We made small talk for a few minutes, ordered, and then my phone buzzed. It was Aiden texting me to call him. Finally!

"Sorry," I mumbled to Julia. "I have to take this. Be right back," I said. I started to call him as I stepped out the side entrance of the restaurant into the quiet alley.

Right as I heard the phone start to ring, I felt a sharp prick in the side of my neck. I raised my hand to swat at the errant bee or whatever that had stung me, but then the world went black.

CHAPTER EIGHT

AIDEN

I smiled as I answered Jessica's call, but she didn't speak. Instead, all I heard were muffled male voices. I hung up, deciding she probably had her phone in her pocket and inadvertently called me when I had texted. I waited a moment and called her again, but it went straight to voice mail. I dialed Oliver, assuming his was one of the voices I heard in the background. Thankfully, he answered immediately.

"Can I talk to Jessica?" I asked.

"I guess so. You can't try her phone?"

"I did. Isn't she with you?"

"No, Jessica's still upstairs," he said.

I started to question who was with her, whose voices I had heard, when I realized Oliver was speaking to someone in the background now.

"Actually Aiden," Oliver said, his tone less certain now. "The guard just told me she left over an hour ago."

"What do you mean she left? Where did she go? Who is with her?" A slur of curse words flew through my brain. That was not good at all. I'd just promised the King of the Eastern Clan that he could send a representative back to the house now, with me, to test Jessica's blood. If we couldn't find Jessica right away, the whole plan would be ruined. They'd assume we were intentionally keeping her away.

"We don't know where she went. She left alone," Oliver said. "In a cab."

I charged him with finding her and making sure she was home before I returned with the king's ambassador. We were scheduled to land in roughly three hours, and I was sure I couldn't wait that long to find out what had happened.

"I'm sorry," I said to the ambassador, speaking his native Russian with relative ease. "Ms. Grove was at home asleep still when I left, but now it seems she's gone out on her own and my staff isn't sure where to find her."

He expressed some shock at the fact that someone so close to the soon-to-be king was allowed to wander off into the city alone, a sentiment which truly, I shared. "I apologize," I reiterated. "We had no idea why King Stefen was calling me. Had I known he was curious about Jessica, I would have brought her with me or at least asked that she remain at home."

He nodded, skeptically. I shot Elgin a nervous glance, wishing he were on the ground helping Oliver, Cordelia, and my father figure out where Jessica had wondered off to.

By the time we landed, I was a nervous wreck, but was doing my best to hide that from the ambassador. If Jessica's stubborn need for independence—her insistence on always showing me she would do what she wanted whatever the risk—actually caused this plan to fail, I wasn't sure I could be alone with her without wanting to strangle her. It was so typical of Jessica.

I dialed Oliver before I even stepped off the plane.

"Update me," I said.

"We got the number of the taxi she took off the security

footage. We called the company and tracked down the driver so we just found out where she went. I'm on my way now with Quinn and Saron."

I sighed, hoping the driver, guard, and my brother were enough to wrangle my wayward girlfriend back home.

We drove home quickly, arriving before receiving any further word of Jessica. My father and Marius offered to entertain the ambassador in the main parlor while I paced nervously in the library and awaited updates. After what felt like an eternity, I heard footsteps approaching. I turned just as Cordelia and Elgin entered. Elgin, as always, was impossible to read, but one glance at Cordelia's face and I felt like my chest was being crushed.

I shook my head, willing her to say something to contradict her expression.

"Aiden they found her phone in an alley. It looks…"

Elgin grabbed his wife's hand and stopped her mid-sentence. "Oliver will be back shortly with the human girl who saw Jessica last. No one needs to speculate in the meantime. Stay in here."

He closed the door, leaving my sister and I alone. She rushed forward and enveloped me in a hug. Cordelia was not a touchy-feely person, and an embrace from her was an unfamiliar, and, frankly, unsettling sensation. I pushed her back and turned to the window, saying a silent prayer while willing my brain not to jump to the darker possibilities.

Moments later there was a ruckus in the hall and Oliver burst into the library. He nudged forward a terrified-looking girl I assumed to be Jessica's friend, Julia.

I stepped forward and offered my hand, trying to ignore the way she jumped back from me. "I'm Aiden. You must be Julia?"

She nodded timidly.

"Jessica has told me a lot about you. I'm sorry we didn't get to meet sooner." I gestured to a chair. "Take a seat."

The girl didn't look like she wanted to sit, but she did.

"I already told the police everything I know," she said.

I glanced at Oliver warily.

"The police were still on the scene when we arrived," he explained.

"Did you talk to them?" I asked.

He shook his head. "No, but we have three guards there now."

"Send more," I said.

Oliver started to protest, then turned to Elgin, who quickly nodded and stepped out.

I really felt for Julia now. Her heart was racing and she probably thought we were about to kidnap or kill her. I needed her to relax if she was going to tell me what had occurred. "I won't take up much of your time. I just wanted to hear from you what happened. After that, my driver can take you home, or if you prefer, you can call someone now to pick you up."

She hesitated. "Um, yeah, actually, I, um, let me text my friend and he'll just swing by." She started typing on her phone. "What's the address here?"

I told her, then grew horribly impatient at her slow typing.

"Why did you ask Jessica to meet you?" I asked.

"She left her backpack at the bar last night. Plus we were both a little tipsy so I don't know that we really said goodbye."

"Goodbye," I repeated.

"Since Jessica is leaving town early," she explained.

I swallowed, not having realized she had definitively chosen to return home so soon. Clearly, we had spoken even less as of late than I thought.

"She got a text from you and said she had to call you or something, so she went out the side door so she could hear you better. Susie's has a loud brunch crowd."

I tried to picture the layout at Susie's but couldn't. I didn't even know if I'd ever been there. Apparently, it was Jessica's favorite restaurant, though.

"It's off of Towne Street. Safe, quiet neighborhood in the northeast side of downtown. Mostly shops and restaurants," Oliver said, as though he'd read my mind. "The side door opens into an alley. The side door of the art gallery next door is the only other door on the street. The art gallery was closed when Jessica called you."

"Go on," I said to Julia.

She shrugged. "That's really all I know. Jessica had already ordered her food, and she left her backpack at the table with me, so she meant to come back." Julia swallowed loudly. "I got the impression you two had been in some sort of fight or something lately, so I didn't think it was too strange when she was gone for a while. But after our food came, I went to tell her and she was gone. I initially figured she had come back inside without me noticing and was in the bathroom or something, but then I saw her phone. It was on the pavement, in the middle of the alley."

"Did you see anyone suspicious?"

"No."

"Did you hear anything unusual when she was outside?"

Julia shook her head. "It's really loud inside."

I turned to Elgin. "The phone?"

"Cops took it for evidence, but Saron swiped it," he said.

"Thank God," I mumbled. "Any prints?"

"So far just hers."

I turned to face the window, feeling the pressure in my chest building to the point of explosion.

"We'll find her," Oliver said gently, and I realized he was talking to Julia, not me.

She asked to be updated when we did, someone agreed, and then she left. I knew from the breathing in the room that several others remained.

I took a deep breath, struggling with every fiber of my being to retain my composure. This was all my fault. Again, I had placed Jessica in harm's way. I shook my head, knowing I couldn't let myself get emotional. I needed to stay clearheaded and focused. That was what would bring Jessica home.

Unless it was already too late.

A hand reached for my arm and I swung violently, knocking the arm off me along with a tall vase of flowers nearby. It crashed to the floor and splattered water everywhere. I glared at the person who had touched me. It was Cordelia. "Get out," I told her. I didn't need comforting now; I needed action.

I turned to Elgin, just as he shut the door behind Cordelia. "What's the plan?" I asked.

He stared blankly, a glum expression on his face. "We're reviewing security footage from all the nearby places of business. Once we know who took her, we'll find where they went."

I knew what he was thinking—that there were too many possible suspects to figure it out otherwise. It could've been people from within our own clan who didn't want me marrying a half-breed. Or it could've been the eastern clan, suspecting we were trying to trick them. Or the southern clan, or…

There was a knock at the door and my father burst in. "Wait outside," he said to the others, watching everyone aside from Elgin and myself exit before he spoke again.

"Aiden, there was no reason for Marius or me to be on that trip this morning. Nor did it have to be that early in the morning."

My father paused and I struggled against the urge to scream at him. The love of my life was missing and he dared complain about an unnecessary business trip?

"They set us up," he continued abruptly. They wanted as many of us gone as possible and wanted to throw us off our game so they could take her."

"How did they know she'd leave the property?" Elgin asked.

"They didn't. I'm sure they were prepared to take her from here. I suspect our meeting would have run longer if they hadn't been able to get her so quickly."

"So she's in Russia?" I asked, ready to go to her.

"I don't know. We can't assume that. And the ambassador hasn't said anything. He's starting to suspect something is going on, but I can't even tell if he's aware of the plot. He may be just another pawn."

"I'll kill him," I said with complete seriousness.

"Aiden!" my father scolded. "This is a good thing. If the eastern clan has her, it's because they want to test her, not harm her. They have nothing at all to gain by hurting her, and, quite frankly, given the debacle your relationship has caused us, it would greatly behoove them to keep her alive."

I registered what my father said, but I wasn't reassured. I brushed past him and was in the parlor in an instant.

"What have you done to her?" I shouted, lunging at the ambassador with a speed that knocked his chair backwards and enabled me to land on top of him, my hands at his throat.

"Jesus Christ," my uncle muttered. "Aiden! Aiden! I command you to stop immediately!"

I heard his words, but I didn't move. Even when I felt multiple pairs of strong hands pulling at me, I resisted. Elgin finally pried me off the bastard and pinned me to the wall. I struggled for a moment, then stopped. My uncle and three guards were now in front of the ambassador, protecting him from me and apologizing profusely. Elgin dragged me out of the room and pushed me through the front door. My father followed close behind.

"Aiden that is not how we handle things. We do not treat ambassadors that way. Do you know how much harder you just made your uncle's job? Why would he tell us anything now, after you attacked him?"

I kicked the gravel with my shoe. "He wasn't going to tell us anything anyway. You just said he was likely a pawn."

"So what good is it to kill a pawn?"

"It sends a message," I said. "And it would've made me feel better."

"You have to learn to control yourself to be a true leader."

I swiveled around to face my father and stepped closer so our chests were nearly touching. "This entire plan was your idea. You had better fucking find Jessica and she had better be unharmed."

I stormed off, with Elgin on my heels, before my father could reply.

CHAPTER NINE

When I opened my eyes, everything was pitch black. My head was throbbing, my mouth was dry, and I literally couldn't see anything. There was an odd buzzing sound, and I felt the floor beneath me vibrating. My eyes widened and I let out a sharp scream. I was chained to the ground of a cargo hold in an airplane.

I screamed until I didn't have any breath left. I tugged on my chains until I felt the cold metal slice through the skin at my wrists and ankles. I quieted only to catch my breath, and then I made out distant voices. I strained to listen, realizing the abundance of elf blood was making my normally average hearing superhuman.

"She's bleeding," the one speaker said. I didn't recognize the voice, but the accent was definitely British. "Mark it down and watch when it heals."

"It won't heal," the other voice said. "She's obviously human."

There was a snicker. "It's already healed, you moron."

I strained to see my wrists, but couldn't. Apparently my night vision hadn't excelled like my hearing. Or maybe I was still adjusting to the darkness. I did notice the stinging where the chains met my skin had all but disappeared.

"Did you get the first three samples?" one of the voices asked.

"Five. We are supposed to take one per hour, remember?"

Did that mean I'd been unconscious for five hours?

"Where are you taking me?" I asked quietly, my voice sounding fragile as it met the cool darkness around.

There was a silence, before one of the voices replied "a lab."

"Why? What do you want with me?"

"We just need to do some simple tests on you. If you don't fight us, this will be much easier and we'll have you back home in no time."

"What are you testing?"

"You, my dear." The voice was disturbingly calm. "We need to know if you were born an elf, or somehow converted to one."

"But I..." I fumbled for the right words, so many blurred thoughts racing through my head. "How would you even test that?"

"Blood samples. And of course we can tell by watching how your body heals from various injuries."

I felt my heart race in panic at the thought of future injuries at the hands of these faceless creatures. "Who are you working for? Who authorized all of this?"

The first voice laughed, then grew eerily close. "Why it looks here like your own King-to-Be, Mr. Aiden Eklund, authorized this little endeavor," he said. A paper was thrust in front of my face and a tiny light, presumably from a flashlight, shone on it. I could barely lift my head to see, but Aiden's signature was clear enough, as was my name, and several references to "blood samples" and "tests." My stomach sank. Why would Aiden do this? And how? How could he do this to me?

Then I remembered what they'd said earlier, the part about injuries.

"Wait, I'm not an elf," I said, pulling at my chains again. "You can't hurt me the way you can hurt an elf. I won't heal. I'm not an elf!" I screamed.

I heard the voice sigh. "I told you not to struggle," it said.

Before I could respond, there was another pinching sensation at my neck and again, I was out.

WHEN I NEXT OPENED MY EYES, THE FIRST THING I REGISTERED WAS searing pain down my back. The second was deafening screams. I didn't realize the screams were my own until the pain dulled, taking the noise down a notch as well. I tried to move, but I couldn't. I was seated on a hard floor. My arms were extended in either direction, thick black cuffs securing my wrists to some sort of chain attached to the wall. My legs were stretched out in front of me, similarly secured to chains. My shirt was gone, but I was still dressed in my bra and jeans. I shifted sideways, trying to free my arms, but they didn't even budge. I braced my feet into the ground and tried to lift myself or turn, but all I ended up doing was lifting my butt up a few inches, causing the cuffs to cut into my wrists and ankles.

I screamed again until my throat ran dry and my voice went hoarse.Then I willed myself to calm down. I had to start thinking rationally if I was ever going to get out of there. I squeezed my eyes shut, determined to focus on my other senses. I felt no sensation of motion and heard absolutely no sounds aside from my own quick, uneven breathing so I assumed I was no longer on the airplane.

I opened my eyes and looked around me, able to see several feet in each direction except directly behind me. As far as I could tell, the room was dark and empty with stone walls and no windows. The realization that I was locked in a dungeon hit me like a ton of bricks.

I tried to focus, to figure out what my captors could possibly want with me. They said they wanted to test my blood. But why? And why like this? Whoever they were, it was a fair guess that they personally had nothing against me and were doing this at someone else's bidding for payment. And if it was just a matter of money, well, surely Aiden had more. Aiden could pay any ransom to bail me out.

"Aiden." I whispered his name and felt tears dribbling down my cheeks. Why hadn't I taken his calls? Why had I been so unsympathetic to his duties lately? I pictured his sweet smiling face. I could feel the softness of his hair, the smoothness of his lips, and the roughness of his chin before he shaved in the morning. I smelled his woodsy aftershave, tasted the Arabica coffee on his tongue… I could practically hear his voice. And yet, he wasn't here. I was alone.

I told myself he'd come soon, that my rescue was imminent.

But then I remembered what my captors had said—that all of this was Aiden's idea. I'd seen his name on that paper—his signature, for sure. But why? He loved me, I was certain of that. If he needed me out of his life so that he could marry an elf and take the throne, he would just tell me. Aiden would not subject me to torture. There was no way to reconcile the Aiden I knew with the man who'd signed off on this.

But then, I thought about what Oliver had said. Even he had mentioned testing my blood, wanting to show people I was part elf. Was this really what they had meant?

I heard a clicking noise behind me and strained to see who— or what—approached.

"Help!" I shouted. "Who are you? What are you doing to me? I can get you money. Lots of it. More than whatever you're being paid to do this. Just let me have a cell phone."

"Shhhhhhhhhhh!" The voice responding to me came out as a hiss. It barely seemed human to me.

I was ready to disregard it, to ask more questions, but in a flash my shoulder was on fire. I screamed at the burning pain and then just as quickly as it had started, it stopped. I knew the monster was still behind me, but however I strained, I couldn't turn far enough to see. I gulped down a deep breath, desperate to slow my breathing so that I wouldn't hyperventilate and pass out, but then my lower back was searing. The pain was so intense that I saw flashes of light. I screamed again just as the burning moved to my rib cage.

"Stop it!" I begged, choking on my tears. "Please! Just stop it!"

But they didn't.

AIDEN

Fourteen hours and twelve minutes had passed since Jessica had been kidnapped. Every minute of that time felt like an hour. I couldn't eat, I couldn't drink, and I couldn't sit. I could barely breathe.

When Elgin finally came with the news that they thought they knew where she was, I didn't even let myself feel a moment of hope. I couldn't. There was still no guarantee.

"I'm coming," I said, following him out the door.

I vaguely registered my father protesting, but a moment later, we were both in a car, racing off to the airport.

I was briefed on the location once we were in the air—headed for Tennessee, of all places. Someone explained what they think had happened and why, but I couldn't focus. All I could think of was Jessica's peaceful slumbering face as I'd snuck out of bed that morning. Was it really that day? Or the day before? It was dark now, somewhere over the Atlantic. I didn't know where I was, or what time it was, and I didn't care. I just needed to get to her, and fast.

CHAPTER TEN

JESSICA

When they grew tired of burning me, they started cutting. My entire back throbbed, already raw and sore. I couldn't even venture a guess as to what they were using or where exactly. Every touch felt like a million glass shards embedding into my flesh. My eyes were on fire, and I ran out of tears. My voice was completely hoarse, my screams now coming out like strangled sobs. Even my lungs were struggling, with every breath feeling like I was trapped under water.

I'd abandoned my plan to stay calm and think rationally. I wasn't going to make it out alive, let alone escape. I tried to focus on my happy memories instead of dwelling on the fact that my last moments on earth would be spent in this musty dungeon.

I thought about my grandma, and how she'd insisted on making my birthday cake from scratch every single year. When I was fifteen, all of my friends served store-bought cakes at their parties, and I was so embarrassed that my grandma insisted on making my birthday cake that I decided not to have a party. So she threw me a surprise party, complete with a gorgeous home-made cake that was so perfect everyone assumed was from the bakery.

Why had she done that? It must have taken hours, so why not just buy the cake? Now I'd never know. Why hadn't I thought to ask her before?

I thought about Lucas, how he was living his dream. He was probably settled into his apartment in Chicago by now. I never sent him the housewarming card I'd picked out, and now I never would. I wondered if someone would find it amongst my things and know it was meant for him. I thought about how he'd probably have a horrible time with my death. But in the long run, it might actually be easier for Lucas to deal with my death than constantly waiting for me to realize I should've been with him.

I should have been with him. That was clear now. If I'd never met Aiden, I wouldn't be in a dungeon, dying. If I'd accepted Lucas' proposal, I would be home now with him and Grandma.

Home.

The word conjured so many feelings. I felt my eyes drift shut and I didn't even care anymore. I only wished I could lay down, either stretch out somehow or curl up completely. The stupid restraints were causing me to sit awkwardly upright. My leg muscles were cramping and my abs were burning.

I tried to think happy thoughts, and a vision of my mom popped into my head. She was gorgeous, perhaps more so because she never had a chance to age. In my mind she was always at her peak. She had thick, dark brown hair like mine, and huge brown eyes that always made me feel warm and loved. And my father, God how I missed him. He turned everything into a joke, and if I wasn't laughing at something he said, I was giggling from his tickle attacks. I missed his jokes. I missed my mom's bedtime stories. But mostly, I was sick of missing them for so long. I was ready to see them both again.

At least I could be with them again soon.

· · ·

AIDEN

An eternity passed before they tracked down Jessica. And then, once we arrived, they wouldn't even let me in first. They said it was for my own safety, but I knew what it was.

They were scared I'd walk in there and find Jessica's dead body and that I'd never recover. And they were right. I couldn't see that. I could barely handle breathing while the sheer possibility of it loomed in my mind.

So, I waited in the hall. It was some sort of warehouse that had a ton of lab equipment on one side and a giant white clock like you see in public school classrooms off to the other side. I watched the second hand tick all the way around the clock once and just as it was starting the second rotation, Elgin was in my face.

"They've got her. She's okay."

I felt like the wind got knocked out of me. I hunched over, certain I was going to be sick, and then I pulled it together just as quickly as it had hit me. I shoved past him, saw where my guards were hunched over Jessica trying to unlock the chains tying her to the wall.

My stomach tightened again. Chains. The bastards had used chains.

Jessica wasn't moving, her head was angled backwards and suddenly I realized Elgin might have been wrong. Maybe she wasn't okay. I flew across the room, diving to her level and gripping her body in my hands. She stirred, whimpered my name, then shut her eyes.

"Get her out of here!" I roared.

The guards were still fumbling with the key.

I tugged at the chains, expecting them to snap under my strength, but they didn't. These restraints were designed for an elf.

"Unlock the fucking chains!" I shouted.

I felt a hand on my shoulder and I swatted it away.

"Aiden. You're slowing them down!" Elgin scolded me, tugging me backwards.

I let him guide me to the back of the room, but only because Jessica seemed oblivious to my presence anyway. The lights flickered on and I got a better look at her. There were bloodstains on her jeans, her shirt was gone and her bra was soaked with blood and something else. Her eye makeup was smeared and there were pools of blood surrounding her.

My stomach lurched again, and then another guard threw a blanket over her.

"She's okay Aiden," Elgin repeated.

The final clasp unlocked with a snap and the guards lifted Jessica into the air. Relief washed over me and I turned, eager to make way for them to get her out of this wretched hellhole. As I turned, I saw two men and one woman, all elves, standing along the back wall. They were handcuffed and each was guarded closely by my men. I glanced down again and saw faint trails of blood leading from where Jessica had been chained to the opposite side of the room.

I snapped.

I lunged at the monsters, gripping the first one's head in my hands and twisting with all my might until I heard a sickening snap. My guards stepped back, astonished, and I moved on to the second man, torn between my desire to make him suffer and my need to have him ended fast. My second urge won out. As I moved towards the evil woman, Elgin grabbed me.

"Aiden!" he shouted, motioning for another guard to help restrain me. "She's awake!"

I didn't understand at first, thinking he was commenting on the psychopathic monster that had just tortured my sweet innocent Jessica. But no, he meant *her*. Jessica.

Jessica's soft brown eyes were wide open and staring at me, her face filled with horror.

I dropped the woman back into the hands of my guards and rushed to Jessica. I reached to take her from the guards, needing to comfort her in a way only I could, but she flinched, covered her head, and released a series of high pitch shrieks that caused me to stumble backwards.

"Get her outside," Elgin instructed the guards. He placed a hand on my chest and held me in place until they were through the door, then he nudged me along.

My father directed us to a cottage just north of Nashville. Cordelia was on her way, since I knew Jessica would prefer a familiar face helping her heal. Every time I moved near Jessica, she screamed. I didn't understand. I needed to hold her, to touch her, to see for myself that she was actually okay.

But she wasn't okay. Even I could tell that.

We injected her with two large doses of my blood in the car ride to the cottage. She had to be restrained for them to inject her because she fought too hard. When we finally got her to the house, she was unconscious. I remembered shaking the doctor we had with us, insisting something had to be medically wrong, causing her to sleep, and he insisted she was fine. I was so sure they'd given her something, some sleeping pill or hallucinogenic drug, but he said it was shock, and that it would wear off with time.

They tested her blood for anything suspicious, and they hooked her up to various monitors, but it didn't help. She drifted in and out of consciousness for hours, screaming inconsolably every time she awakened.

When Cordelia finally arrived, it was the middle of the night. She looked over Jessica, confirmed everything the other doctor had said, then took me aside.

"She needs rest," Cordelia said. "I want to give her something to help her relax."

"She's non-responsive already!" I protested, just as Jessica's eyes flitted open again and she began thrashing wildly.

Cordelia rushed in, held Jessica's arms in place and whispered something until Jessica stilled again. Her eyes remained open and I could see her shaking even from where I stood, but she was quiet.

I tentatively approached. With each step I took, Jessica's eyes widened, but she remained calm.

"Jessica," I whispered. "I'm here. You're okay. You are safe now. I promise."

She didn't move or respond.

"Leave us," I snapped at Cordelia.

Cordelia turned to leave when Jessica spoke. Her voice was soft and uncertain, but her word was clear.

"No," she said.

Cordelia hesitated. I swallowed hard, wiped a tear out of the corner of my eye, and backed away from Jessica.

"You're safe now," I repeated. "I love you." I backed into the hall and watched from a distance as Cordelia adjusted Jessica's IV. Then, Jessica's eyes eventually fluttered shut again.

Cordelia joined me in the hall. "I need to undress her, clean her up, and make sure all of her injuries have healed."

I nodded, not knowing what to do or say. Then I realized Cordelia was gesturing to the remaining guards I'd left in the area. I shooed them all away and watched from the door as Cordelia gently cleaned Jessica and then coated her with more blankets.

The next few hours stretched on painfully, with Jessica responding with the same terror each time she awoke. Finally, Cordelia came up with the idea to move Jessica outside once the sun was up so Jessica would instantly recognize that she was no longer in the dungeon. She gave her another dose of my blood before unhooking the IV. I helped her dress Jessica in one of the sundresses from her luggage which someone, I wasn't sure who, had brought along on the second flight along with Cordelia.

I had so many questions, and there were so many blanks to fill in. But I just didn't care. I needed my Jessica back to me—my real Jessica. Then I could worry about the details.

I kept my distance even after Jessica was moved outside, not wanting to risk scaring her further. But this time, when she awoke, she was calm and seemed like herself. I approached slowly, and she didn't panic, even when Cordelia backed away, giving us our first moment of privacy.

I reached for her hand slowly, barely touching her delicate skin with my fingertips. She watched my hand then turned her gaze back to my face, staring at me as though she didn't know me.

"You're safe now, Jessica. I love you," I said. I felt myself starting to cry again. "I am so sorry for…" I didn't even know how to finish that sentence.

I sat with her for several minutes, and would've stayed forever, but my father approached.

"Aiden you need to rest. She's in good hands with Cordelia, and I can stay with her a moment too if you want."

"I'm not leaving her."

"Elgin wants to brief you on what happened. If you won't sit down and close your eyes for a few minutes, at least listen to what he has to say. You're not doing any good out here now anyway."

"She's still acting like she's afraid of you, Aiden," Cordelia said. "Give her some time without you and she might make more progress."

I considered that, then hesitantly went inside. I knew I couldn't rest, but I did want to know what Elgin had learned.

He gave me the short story of what had happened. The eastern clan intercepted the message we'd meant for them to intercept but instead of falling for our trap, they'd set their own. They assumed we'd try to give her blood to artificially boost her elf-likeliness if they did the testing on our terms, so they'd taken her. The rest made no sense to me. That didn't explain why they'd hurt her—why there was dried blood coating her back and dripping down her arms. Nor did it explain why they'd taken her back to the United States.

I wasn't going to make sense of it all that day. I needed to get back outside, to Jessica. When I came outside, I saw her eyes were open and she appeared to be talking to Cordelia. I rushed towards her, but my father stepped in my path.

"Aiden," he said softly. "Wait."

"No, I want…"

"Stop," he interrupted. "She doesn't want you. She's talking now. She needed space from you."

"But I…" I shook my head, not even knowing what I meant to say.

"I wanted to talk to her, to find out if she saw anyone other than the three that were in that room with her. We need to be certain who ordered this before we strike back." He paused. "But it's you she's scared of. I don't know why, but she said you did this. She said you ordered all of this."

"That doesn't make any sense."

"It doesn't," he agreed. "And we told her that. But she's truly terrified, Aiden. You have to give her some space."

I rubbed my forehead, wishing this awful nightmare would end.

"Aiden," my father continued, pausing until I glanced up and saw he was dreading what he had to say next. "She said that she should have never left with you. I'm sure it's just the shock talking, but…"

My mouth fell open in disbelief. My father spoke the words as though quoting her directly, clearly surprised himself at what she had said. I didn't believe it. He had to be wrong. I needed to speak to her myself.

I started towards Jessica in a rush, but as soon as she noticed me coming, her eyes widened. She raised her arms to her face, cowering back against the lounge chair we'd placed her in. I froze. I didn't know why, but it was true. Jessica was scared of me.

I turned to Cordelia, who shook her head sadly. She patted Jessica's hand comfortingly and then came to me.

"Father said Jessica blames me, that she thinks this was my fault. He said she's scared of me."

Cordelia furrowed her brows. "Aiden, she's been through a terrible ordeal. The mind reacts in really unpredictable and inexplicable ways to trauma. It's just going to take her some time."

"Time," I repeated.

Cordelia nodded.

"But you don't think she's frightened of me?"

My sister hesitated, then swallowed audibly. "I don't know why, but she is. Her breathing and heart rate double when you approach her. Just give her some space and when she's out of shock, she'll come around."

"Space." I said. "Time and space." I shook my head in disbelief. "Fine, I'll go inside."

Cordelia shook her head. "Aiden, no. She's going to want a shower and a real nap in a bed. You need to go somewhere else for a while. I can't lie to her and tell her you're gone if you're just watching from a window."

"I'm not leaving her."

"She doesn't want you here, Son," my father chimed in, coming up behind Cordelia.

"Elgin will take you to a hotel for the night. We'll keep the rest of the guards here and I'll stay with her."

I started to shake my head, but my father gripped my arm.

"Aiden, she's not your prisoner. She's asking us to get rid of you and she's not going to feel safe if we aren't doing what she says. Just go, and we'll call you the moment she asks for you."

I cast one last glance at Jessica, still eying us warily, and swallowed hard.

"Fine. But I want hourly updates on her condition."

Cordelia nodded, and I walked away slowly, feeling like my chest was caving in.

CHAPTER ELEVEN

JESSICA

I felt the sunlight before I even opened my eyes. It was comforting, in a way, an instant reminder that I wasn't in that dungeon of a basement anymore. But it was also hot, oppressively so. The air was heavy and thick, and my throat so dry that I struggled to swallow.

I peeled my eyes open slowly and immediately saw Cordelia, calmly staring at me. I shut my eyes quickly, pained by the sudden brightness. "Water," I croaked.

I felt a hand behind my head and a straw pushed up to my lips. I sipped tentatively, certain I'd choke. The liquid was cool and refreshing and it slid down my throat with more ease than I'd expected. I drank greedily until the straw was abruptly pulled away.

"Pace yourself," Cordelia snapped.

I frowned and raised my hand to shield my eyes before opening them again, this time slowly. My location was unrecognizable, with blue, cloudless sky and green grass as far as I could see. "Where am I?"

"A friend's summer cottage, just north of Nashville. I wanted someplace private for you to heal. You kept panicking whenever you awoke and were inside.

"How long have I been sleeping?" I asked, glancing down at my body for clues. I was fully clothed, in a clean sundress that I recognized as my own but hadn't worn for years. I was positioned on an upholstered patio chair, the back propped partway up and my legs stretched out in front of me over the colorful material. There was an IV needle taped to my hand but it didn't appear to be hooked up to anything.

"You've been drifting in and out of consciousness for two days."

Cordelia reached over me and began to fumble with the hand I'd just noticed. "I'd like to give you more fluids intravenously along with some medicine. Is that all right?"

I nodded, surprised that she even asked, and that she was being so nice to me at all. "Where's Aiden?"

She frowned. "What's the last thing you remember?"

I sat abruptly, suffocating from the thickness of the air surrounding me. Cordelia handed me the water again and I forced a few sips down before trying to speak again. "What happened to Aiden?"

"Aiden is fine," she said, as though the question were absurd. She raised the back of the chair slightly. "Lean back."

I did as instructed. "Then where is he?"

"He left."

"He left," I repeated, letting the words sink in. "Aiden left me."

"He spoke with you first. I assumed you knew he was leaving. It's for the best." Cordelia shrugged calmly.

I bit the inside of my cheek to fight back tears, but my efforts were unwarranted. I was too dehydrated for my eyes to water and too fatigued to cry. I felt physically and emotionally exhausted, and possibly more hopeless than even before my rescue.

Cordelia left me alone for a while, and I drifted back into a restless sleep at some point, only to wake even thirstier than before. She refused to let me go inside, to escape from the thick, oppressive heat and unrelenting sun, claiming I panicked earlier whenever I awoke indoors because I didn't immediately remember where I was.

I didn't dare tell her that I didn't remember anything anyway. I didn't recall where I was, or why I was here, what exactly had happened, or why Aiden left me. But I was sure nothing would be better until he returned. Being outdoors on a day that humid was punishing, and only Aiden would be comforting. I traced my finger along the cushion of the chair, imaging it was his piqué shirt I was touching, then I inhaled slowly, as though I were breathing in his familiar scent, and squeezed my eyes shut, picturing his relaxed grin. I spoke his name over and over in my head, and could almost hear him say my name in response.

This ritual itself, the process of conjuring every aspect of Aiden as clearly as I could, felt oddly familiar. I had done it before, I now knew, recently, and often. I had been alone—he had left me previously, that is. And as I opened my eyes again, I realized I had been scared.

What had happened to me? Why didn't I remember it?

I raised my left arm, the weight of the clear IV tubing uncannily heavy, and rubbed my hand along my right arm and the right side of my body. I repeated this with my right arm on the left side, then checked my legs. I felt no pain, no signs of bruising or injury. But then again, I knew I wouldn't. That's why Cordelia was here.

She brought me a fresh cup of iced water and watched me drink. Why was I still thirsty? Couldn't she magically fix that the same way she'd erased the signs of whatever other trauma there had been?

Cordelia leaned closer, shining a light in my eyes. "Are you sure you're feeling alright?"

I nodded, trying to sound chipper and not suspicious. "Good as new. Just a bit thirsty maybe."

"You're not tired anymore?" she sounded skeptical.

Truthfully, I felt almost too spent to even answer her, but I sensed it wasn't wise to admit as much. "Nothing unusual." I handed the empty glass back to her. "Although something you said earlier made me wonder- did you overhear Aiden and I talking earlier, before he left?"

She cocked her head to the side. "Why do you ask?"

"Because I know you have impeccable hearing," I lied.

She flitted her eyes upward, as though my question didn't even merit a full eye-roll. "I have better things to do with my time than eavesdrop on my little brother. You still don't seem quite right to me, so I'm giving you one more vial of blood."

I was too tired to protest, so instead I closed my eyes again, hoping to piece together more of my recent past. I fell asleep again, or at least into that unsettling space in between wakefulness and sleep, where the sensation of falling suddenly jolts one awake. But I didn't fully rouse at the feeling this time. Instead, I remembered.

The memories came to me in flashes, fragmented pictures, and broken echoes of unfamiliar voices. I felt cold, hunger, and pain, but mostly fear. It was a smothering kind of terror, not localized to any one thing but rather amplified by the sheer unpredictability of whatever horror awaited me next. I tasted blood in my mouth, the metallic flavor filling my dry throat like a smoke. Then, I saw Aiden, with a look in his eyes that I'd never before seen in him or any human, for that matter. I watched the recognition wash over the first man's face moments before Aiden's hands reached his neck. The light flashed out again as I heard the sickening crack and a scream, then another thud, another crack, then silence.

My mind went blank again for a moment and then Aiden

turned to me, his wild eyes still gleaming fiercely. A bloodcurdling scream jolted me out of sleep.

Cordelia was at my side instantly. "Shhhhh. What is it? What's wrong?"

I gazed up at her and recognized the same look in her eyes as Aidens'. But when I opened my mouth to scream, I realized I already was.

I focused on the sun until my vision was obscured by dark floaters and I was able to calm down.

"What happened?" Cordelia asked.

I blinked several times. "I think a bee stung me or something," I said weakly, rubbing at my hip. I kept my hand in place, preventing her from confirming my story, and continued to fabricate. "I suppose I'll be healed in a moment with all this blood you're giving me. I'm all sweaty and this heat is giving me a headache, though. Can I shower now?"

She considered this request, but agreed. "Your bags are in the guest suite on the second floor. There's a shower in the private bath there. I'll show you the way. Just don't lock the door in case you pass out or something. I'm still not sure you're back to normal."

I followed Cordelia through the house, certain I'd never been inside before. When we reached the guest room, I immediately spotted my luggage. I went to my largest suitcase and unzipped it, taking a quick visual inventory before doing the same with my smaller bags. Cordelia, apparently satisfied I was not going to collapse, left, shutting the door behind her.

I sunk to the bed between my bags. All of my stuff was here. All of it. Someone had packed up my belongings from throughout the London manor and brought them all here. I glanced to the armchair beside the bed and realized even my backpack, the one I'd left with Julia, was here. My stuff was here, but none of Aiden's.

Had this been Aiden's plan all along? To pack me up and ship me off without so much as a warning? He couldn't have orchestrated the rest. He wouldn't have. I knew that.

There was a sharp knock on the door. "I'm fine, Cordelia," I snapped. I'd hardly been alone a minute.

"It's Ivar." The voice outside the door answered. "May I speak with you for a moment?"

I knew enough about Ivar to understand that he was never really asking permission, more like giving notice before he did whatever he wanted regardless of others' wishes. So I didn't bother saying no or insisting on time alone.

"Come in," I said instead.

He stepped into the room and pulled the door shut behind him. My muscles tensed at the notion of being alone with him, but he didn't come any closer.

"Jessica, I hope that you are feeling a bit better and that you find this room adequate." He paused. "I owe you an apology on behalf of my son. He should have never brought you into our lives and subjected you to all of this. I'm certain this is not how he planned for things to end, but as a ruler, one has to make impossible calls on short notice and sometimes it is unavoidable that someone gets hurt."

I didn't understand what he was telling me or why, but every time I opened my mouth to ask a question, no words came out. I was too bewildered by it all to even collect my thoughts, let alone verbalize them. So I let Ivar continue.

"I don't believe Aiden understood the magnitude of what he was subjecting you to when he authorized the testing. I am sure he did have feelings for you at some point and didn't want you to get hurt, but..." Ivar sighed. "Well, you know what they say about good intentions."

"Where is Aiden?" I asked.

Ivar glanced at his wristwatch, a massive gold band with an

ornately decorated face. "I suspect he's at the airport now. Probably not yet on the plane if you want to catch him on the phone."

"Airport," I repeated. "He's going…"

"To London," Ivar completed, frowning. "He's got a few more weeks of work there and then I suppose he'll probably settle down somewhere in New England for a bit. Didn't he tell you?"

I shook my head. "I'm still a bit fuzzy, I guess," I said.

"I'm sorry, Jessica. I thought he said goodbye when you two spoke. He did mention that you were still a tad frightened of him, which I suppose is completely understandable given the circumstances."

"What circumstances?" I was so confused.

Ivar gazed around his quizzically. "Jessica, you've been through a terrible ordeal. Aiden should have ended this long ago. He certainly shouldn't have let it come to this. I hope someday you can forgive him. I truly don't think he meant for you to suffer as much as you clearly did. He's a new ruler, and he made a mistake."

"So Aiden…this was his…" I heard my breathing increase as the realization of what he was saying washed over me.

"Fault?" Ivar guessed at the rest of my sentence. "It doesn't really help to lay blame. Was it his plan? Well, I suppose it went quite a bit awry from what he planned." He sighed. "The point is, I'm sorry. I won't pretend I am unhappy that things have ended between my son and you, but do truly regret the way things ended. You deserved better."

I didn't even know what to say. I wanted to scream, to cry, to sleep. I wished Aiden were there so I could ask him what happened, where I went wrong. How had I so horribly misread his feelings for me?

I realized Ivar was still watching me warily.

"You are, of course, welcome to stay here as long as you like. I know your last few days have been…tumultuous, to say the least."

He wrinkled his nose as he spoke as though the words were distasteful. "When you're ready to head home, one of my men can arrange for your transportation. We'll pay for you to fly wherever."

"I'm not flying anywhere," I said, suddenly nauseated from the rocking motion of the cargo hold mid-air.

Ivar nodded. "Of course. Well, someone could drive you…"

"I'll take a bus," I said, surprising myself a bit as the idea came to me. If Aiden was no longer protecting me, I wasn't safe relying on elves. The only reason I'd felt safe with any of them in the past was because I trusted their respect for him would keep me safe. "And I'll leave right after I shower and change."

Ivar hesitated before speaking. "Certainly. I can arrange for someone to drive you to the bus station."

"I'd prefer a cab," I said, convinced I'd feel safer in the car with a complete stranger over anyone from the elf community.

Ivar nodded again calmly. "I'll call one for you. Is an hour enough time for you?"

"Yes. Thank you," I said, turning to my suitcase. I just needed to hold it together for an hour until I got out of here. Then I could figure out my next steps. Once I was safe, I could begin the process of piecing together where everything had gone so horribly wrong.

"Jessica, I hate to bring this up now, but I must remind you of the Confidentiality Agreement you signed some time ago. The penalties are strict and will be enforced should you ever decide to…share your knowledge of our kind."

I clenched my jaw shut so hard the shock of my teeth clanging together reverberated into my eye sockets. What was wrong with these people? I inhaled and exhaled slowly. "I wasn't planning to tell anyone anything," I finally said, through gritted teeth.

"Very well. Thank you." Ivar reached into his pocket and retrieved his wallet. He began pulling out bills and then dropped a sizable stack of hundreds on the nightstand beside the bed. "For your travel expenses," he explained.

I started to refuse, to insist I didn't need his money, but I stopped myself. I hadn't gone through my purse, so I had no idea whether I still had my credit cards or whether I had any American money after being in the UK for so long. Ivar started to leave, then paused again, reaching into his other pocket.

This time, it was my cell phone. "The screen was cracked when you were abducted, but we had it replaced for you. It seems to be functioning now," he said.

He held it out to me, but I couldn't move. He waited a moment and then tossed it gently onto the bed before leaving me alone in the room.

I reached for the phone once I was alone and stared at it. I had no missed calls, no voice mails, and no text messages. I was truly completely alone. And no one cared.

I showered, dressed, and dragged all of my bags downstairs on my own, managing to avoid contact with anyone from Aiden's family. I asked the cab driver to take me to the bus station and used the drive to figure out where I'd go next. I couldn't take a bus directly home, although Ivar had given me more than enough cash to pay for it. But I wasn't sure I could face my grandma yet. How would I explain what happened with Aiden? Why I was home so soon?

Returning to campus with Claire was the next best option, but I'd face the same issues with her. I was barely holding it together, and I felt certain the next few days would be a nightmare.

I needed to go somewhere I'd feel safe, somewhere I knew I was loved and where I could talk about how horribly things had ended with Aiden without fear of breaking whatever ridiculous contract I'd apparently signed agreeing to stay quiet.

I booked a ticket on the bus for Chicago that was leaving in an hour. I sent a text to Julia, letting her know I was okay and that

I'd call her later and explain, but that left me with a full hour until my bus would depart.

I decided to use my time while I waited to figure things out. I just couldn't wrap my mind around it all. Ivar, possibly the coldest man I'd ever met, seemed embarrassed by his own son's cruel treatment of me, so I clearly wasn't over-dramatizing how awful Aiden had been. But I just hadn't seen it coming. Sure, things had been strained between Aiden and me. And sure, he was under a lot of stress, and we weren't communicating or connecting like we used to, but I hadn't expected that.

Had that been his plan all along? To let me finish finals then ship me off as a prisoner? I remembered how he had told me about Gwyneth the year before with the obvious goal of getting me to break up with him. Was this a repeat of that all over again? Did he want to end things with me but still lacked the courage to do it the right way, so instead he wanted to show me what a monster he could be, knowing I'd end it all then? If so, he'd succeeded. Whatever I thought I'd had with Aiden, I was obviously wrong. That chapter of my life was over, and I wouldn't look back.

The bus ride was long, and even though I was exhausted, I was scared to sleep. Every time I closed my eyes, awful visions popped into my head. I didn't want to face that yet. I thought about calling Lucas, but I had no idea what to say to him. Instead, I decided to call my grandma, since I knew she'd be expecting to hear from me. I kept the call brief, telling her my finals were over and went well, and that I was on a bus now, traveling. Of course I didn't mention that the bus was in the Midwest, but thankfully she didn't pose too many questions. Ever aware of expenses, my grandma was great at keeping our international phone calls short.

When I hung up, I still needed to hear a familiar voice, so I dialed Claire. She answered on the third ring, right as I was about to give up.

"Hey," I replied softly, not wanting to annoy the few other passengers on the bus.

"Jessica? Oh my gosh! How are you? How's London? Have you dumped Aiden for an even sexier Brit? Do they all have the dreamiest accents ever?"

Claire overwhelmed me with so many questions I wasn't sure what to say. When she finally quieted, I laughed.

"It's good to hear your voice," I said. "I missed you!"

"Oh, sweetie," Claire said. "I missed you, too. I was a little hurt that you didn't call more. I just assumed your trip was so fabulous that you'd never get homesick."

"Well, I'm homesick now."

"Sorry. You sound a bit...off. Or maybe that's the international connection?"

I was tempted to lie to her as I did my grandma, but I knew she'd understand and not take it personally if I was back and didn't visit right away. "Actually," I began hesitantly. "I came back early." I paused while she shrieked excitedly. "I just got back to the U.S. though, and I'm not coming home yet. I...my grandma thinks I'm still in England."

"What? Why did you leave early? Is everything okay?"

"The trip was mostly great, but my classes are over and Aiden and I..." I wasn't sure how to finish that sentence. We didn't exactly break up, and I certainly couldn't tell her that Aiden authorized strangers to kidnap and torture me for his own publicity. Or that he had the gall to think it was for my own good-or at least the good of our relationship.

"Oh, honey," Claire gushed. "Okay, you don't need to tell me about it. That's fine. Where are you now? Want to meet up?"

I gazed out the window, searching for a sign. As best I could tell, I was pretty close to home. "I guess I'm about an hour south of Chicago," I said. "I'm headed to see Lucas."

Claire was silent. I actually smiled a little picturing her shocked face.

"He, um, well, he actually asked me to marry him before I left for London and…"

"Wait- who asked you to marry him? Aiden?" Claire interrupted.

"No, Lucas. Aiden never proposed."

"Lucas asked you to marry him. Then you went to London with Aiden. Now you've broken up with Aiden and are headed to Lucas' apartment?"

I was about to confirm that she was more or less right, when she continued.

"Sweetie, no. You can't go straight to Lucas. You need some time after a break up. You're not thinking straight." She paused. "And remind me to lecture you later about keeping this tidbit about Lucas from me all semester!"

"I know," I said. I appreciated her point, but I wasn't sure how to explain it. Claire was great—she was an amazing friend. But Lucas was Lucas. He was the only one who could make me feel safe now. And he was the one I needed to be with, not Aiden. If I waited any longer, I'd talk myself out of it, whereas the sooner I was with Lucas, the more I would realize that a future with him was what I actually wanted.

I didn't trust myself not to make excuses for Aiden or rewrite history to make him less of a villain if I returned to campus or even home. "I've got to talk to him, though. In person."

"Well, okay," she said finally. "If you're sure."

"I am."

"My temporary roommate will be here until August, but you're welcome to crash in my room anytime."

"Thanks," I said, knowing her offer was sincere.

"So can you tell me about London?"

"Actually, I'd rather hear about your semester."

Claire yammered away for the next forty minutes, giving me just enough time to panic about my decision after we hung up.

It was already dark when I arrived at the bus station. I had briefly considered heading straight to a hotel and trying to catch Lucas the next morning, but I knew I'd just stew the whole night. Besides, I really couldn't stand the thought of a night alone. I had his address in my phone for the card I'd planned to send, so I gave the cabbie the address and prayed Lucas was still awake when I arrived.

CHAPTER TWELVE

LUCAS

It was almost ten when I got a text from Jessica. "U busy 2nite?" it read.

I replied in the negative, but there was no response. I figured it was already the middle of the night in London anyway. I returned my focus to the video game. I was creaming Jeff, my new roommate and fellow Blackhawk.

An hour later, I was bored, so I headed back to bed. I had just stripped down to some boxers and a sleeveless undershirt when I heard a noise near the front of the apartment. Whatever. It was none of my business what Jeff was up to.

But a moment later, he was knocking on my door. I opened it quickly.

"There's a girl at the door," he said. "Long brown hair, skinny, big boobs," he said, adding, "hot."

I shrugged.

"Well, I don't know her," he said, so I followed him to the door, wondering why he didn't just let her in if she was as hot as he claimed.

"Jessica!" I said, the second I saw her. I opened the door and stared at her for a moment, trying to convince myself she was really there.

She looked back at me, expressionless, then flung herself into my arms.

Jeff shook his head, then trudged back to his bedroom.

"Are you okay?" I asked. "It's after eleven. Are you alone?"

She gazed up at me now, her giant brown eyes glistening with tears. "Am I too late?"

"What?"

"You were right. I chose wrong, and I should have never left." she said, her voice shaking. "Will you still have me?"

I looked around her and realized she had a large suitcase, a smaller rolling suitcase, and an oversized duffel bag with her. I didn't dare ask myself exactly what she meant, but I knew what my answer was.

I pushed the door shut behind her and pulled her into my arms for a proper hug. "Yes. Of course, Jessica. Always," I said, kissing her hair. She clung to me for several minutes, shaking.

"Are you okay?" I asked, suddenly realizing she couldn't be this distraught over me. I considered the possibilities and felt my entire body tense with fury. "Did he hurt you? Jesus, did he…?"

"No, no, Lucas. Nothing like that."

She wasn't convincing, though I could tell she was trying to be.

"What happened?"

She shook her head. "I don't want to talk about it now. I'm just tired."

I nodded hesitantly, grabbed her bags, and led her back to my room. I set her stuff in the corner and found myself staring back at her again, uncertainly. She seemed thinner than I remembered her, and she did look tired. But mostly she looked terrified. Of what, I didn't know.

I pulled her close again, desperate to stop her trembling. "Are you cold?" I asked.

"No, she mumbled, her breath hot on my ear. "I'm tired."

We pulled apart again and I wiped the tears off her cheeks. She leaned in and kissed me, suddenly, and I nearly stopped breathing. It was a short and totally unexpected kiss, but a welcome one. I glanced over her body, and realized she could never sleep in the cut-off jean shorts she was wearing. I flipped off the light, then gestured to her shorts.

"You planning to sleep in that?"

She shook her head so I started to lift her tee shirt up over her head, leaving the black tank top on beneath.

Her body tensed, so I backed off and sat on the bed casually. "Can I get you anything?"

She shook her head, and tentatively slipped out of her shorts, revealing hot pink and black lacy underpants. My breath caught in my throat and I was thankful it was dark in the room.

"You're so beautiful," I murmured.

I lifted the covers on the bed for her to climb under. She moved slowly, but within a moment, we were side by side in the double bed. I sensed uncertainty still on her part, so I kissed her cheek tenderly and rolled her onto her side facing away from me. I wrapped my arm around her side and pulled her close to me.

"We can talk in the morning if you want," I whispered.

She didn't answer, but within a few minutes, her breathing evened out and her body relaxed into mine. I tried to forget the image of Jessica in her lacy panties, but between the touch of her silky tank under my fingertips and the smell of strawberries in her hair, I was going insane with desire.

And beyond the pure physical need pulsing through my body, I had several unanswered questions weighing on my mind. I forced myself to think of something asinine until finally, I fell asleep.

When I awoke, the arm I'd been laying on was numb and I had to piss like a racehorse. I felt like I'd slept for ages, but according to the clock, it was only three a.m. I delicately scooted away from

Jessica, removing my arm from her body last, then crept out of the room silently.

I splashed some cold water on my face after washing my hands, remembering the perfect body I'd left curled up half naked in my bed, then paused before re-entering my room, eager to get my desire under control before climbing beside her again. I heard a strange noise and opened the door.

The room was nearly pitch black, but I could make out Jessica's figure. She was sitting straight up in bed, breathing hard. I hurried over and crouched beside her, wrapping my arms around her from the back. She jumped when I touched her, then quickly leaned against me. She was shaking again.

"I woke up and you were gone," she explained, her voice weak.

"I'm sorry, Jessica. I just went to the bathroom. I'm back now."

Her long hair covered her face and I carefully brushed it behind her shoulders so I better could see the outline of her face. "Are you cold?"

"No," she said.

A sour feeling filled the pit of my stomach. "You're safe now."

"Yeah."

I didn't know what else to say. Obviously something had happened. Something was very wrong. But I didn't want to force her to tell me before she was ready.

"Do you want to talk now?" I asked finally.

"No," came her rapid reply. Her breathing grew quieter, though. She sniffled, and I pulled off my undershirt, mostly because I was dying to feel her body against my bare skin.

"Here, wipe your eyes on this," I said, handing it to her.

She laughed softly. "I'm so sorry. I should have never left, Lucas," she said after a lengthy silence.

"It's okay, you're back now," I said, hoping it was the truth.

"Is it too late?" she asked.

I considered her question, even though I knew the answer already. "No."

"Do you still..." Jessica hesitated. "All those things you said before..."

Now I laughed. It was just absurd that someone so amazingly sexy and beautiful and delicate could ever feel insecure. "I want you now more than ever, Jessica. I haven't stopped thinking about you since you left."

She squeezed my hand, then tentatively raised it to her lips. I responded by kissing the back of her head again, inhaling the fruity scent of her wavy hair.

Suddenly, she pulled away, crept out of bed, and grabbed her purse. She carried it back to the bed, first retrieving her cell phone, which she quickly placed face down on the nightstand, disregarding the slew of messages visible on the screen, and kept digging. Finally, she found what she was looking for and tossed her purse back towards her suitcase. She pressed a small box into my hands.

"Now that I'm back, it seems like you should have this," she said.

I quickly realized it was the ring I'd bought her. I frowned, not equipped to deal with so many mixed messages in the middle of the night. "Jess, I bought it for you. I told you, just keep it until you've decided."

"But I have decided," she said.

I took a deep breath, willing myself not to snap at her for rejecting me moments after seeking reassurance that I still liked her. "I don't want it," I said finally.

Jessica was quiet for a minute as though I'd confused her, and then she turned. "No, Lucas, I don't think you understand. I'm saying yes. I'm saying what I should have said three months ago. I just thought you should put it on me," she said.

I replayed her words in my head again before speaking. "You want to marry me?"

"Yes."

It was hard for me not to jump on the bed with excitement, or to tackle her and make love until the sun came up, but the rational part of me knew to take it slow. She was still shivering from something. She'd shown up at my doorstep late at night after some obvious trauma. After waiting for her to come around for years, I wasn't about to rush her into something she didn't actually want.

"You don't have to say that to stay here, Jessica," I finally said. "I'll keep you safe from whatever regardless. We don't have to be engaged. We can wait until…"

"We've waited long enough, Lucas."

My heart beat faster. She placed her left hand in mine and wiggled her fingers.

"Kiss me," I said, needing one last bit of assurance.

She turned her body more towards me and leaned in, planting her mouth on mine. Her kiss was sincere and needy, if not the kind of kiss you'd expect to lead to anything more. I kissed her back eagerly, wondering if I'd really get to kiss these lips the rest of my life.

When the kiss ended, I slid the ring on her finger. I saw her squint down at it in the dark.

"Are you happy now?" I asked teasingly.

"I will be," she said, settling back against me.

I scooted to the middle of the bed, pulling her along with me, then stretched out on my back. She curled beside me, her head on my chest, her hand on my abdomen. I pulled the covers over us and placed my hand on her lower back, against the small strip of bare skin between her shirt and panties. She didn't flinch, and before long, I could tell she was back to sleep.

I lay there focusing on the wide array of amazing new sensations—her breath, pouring onto my chest in even, warm spurts, her hair, tickling my sides as she shifted in her sleep, and the weight of her perfect breasts resting against my stomach.

I heard a buzz, and saw her phone vibrate with yet another message. I glanced at Jessica, confirming she was asleep before reaching onto the night stand for her phone. The texts were all from Aiden, of course. I tried not to read them all, but quickly skimming them revealed that she had left without telling him. He was worried about her.

I clicked on the most recent one, which read "I need to know if you're okay," and pressed reply.

I typed, "Jess is fine. She's with me. –Lucas," and clicked send before I changed my mind. I didn't want to piss her off by messing with her phone, and as much as I hated the guy, I felt for him. Worrying about Jessica was the worst feeling in the world. And until I knew exactly what he had done to her, I was going to treat him the same way I did the players on the losing team after each of my hockey matches—with dignity and respect.

But I sure was curious what had happened.

Despite lying awake for what felt like an eternity, I woke before Jessica. I tried to remain as still as possible, relishing in the closeness of our bodies. She shifted suddenly, and thrust her hand downward. I inhaled sharply and tensed my stomach muscles as her fingers grazed my groin. Then she sighed, turning again, and I realized she wasn't fully awake yet.

Remembering her panic the night before, I decided to rouse her myself instead of risking a panic attack while she tried to figure out where she was. I ran my fingers through her hair softly and kissed her forehead.

"Morning," I said.

She moaned softly and it took all of my willpower not to rip off her remaining clothes and take advantage of her half-asleep state.

"Are you awake, Jessica?"

She raised her hand to her face, rubbed her eyes, then turned to me, her hand still on my chest. "Sort of," she said. "What time is it?"

I glanced at the clock. "Nine." I instantly wished I'd let her sleep longer.

"Do you have practice this morning?"

"No. It's Saturday. You can go back to sleep if you want."

I caught her glancing down at her finger with a hint of surprise, as though she'd forgotten the diamond was there.

"It looks good on you," I said. "Is it the right size?"

She nodded. "Actually, can I shower?"

"Uh, yeah," I replied, her question having caught me off guard. We both sat slowly. "I doubt Jeff is up yet, so don't worry about…" I glanced at her state of undress. "I mean, make yourself at home. I'll go set out some towels."

"Thanks," she said.

I climbed out of bed and hurried out of the room. I made sure the bathroom was semi-presentable, set a clean towel and washcloth on the counter, then ducked back into the hall, nearly running into her.

"Sorry," I mumbled.

She smiled. Her hands were full, presumably with her clean clothes, and then a small toiletry bag.

She turned and walked into the bathroom as I held my breath until she'd closed the door. She hadn't put on any more clothes, and looked sexier than ever in her underwear in the light of day.

"Damn," a voice said behind me.

I turned to see Jeff's eyes nearly bugging out of his head.

I rolled my eyes, trying to pretend I wasn't just as discombobulated by her amazing body. "I thought you were still asleep. Don't you dare tell her you saw that," I warned him.

We both walked into the kitchen.

"Damn," Jeff repeated.

When Jessica joined us in the kitchen, she had changed into her worn-looking cut-off jean shorts and a tee shirt. It was loose-fitting, but the slinky material clung in all the right places. She wasn't wearing makeup, and her thick hair hung loose in damp waves across her shoulders.

Jeff and I were seated at the table eating and I swatted him, hoping to encourage more subtlety on his part.

"Jessica, this is my roommate Jeff."

She smiled warmly, although her expression was still distant. "Nice to meet you," she said.

I noticed she was fidgeting with something small in her hands just as she turned to me and spoke again. "I think there's a tracking device in my phone. Do you have a garbage disposal?"

I reached for the object she was holding and saw it was the SIM card from her phone. And then I realized Aiden must have sent her another message, showing he knew she was with me. Crap. I knew I had to come clean.

"No, Jess, sorry, I should've told you. He kept texting you last night, so I just let him know you were here and you were safe. I didn't tell him anything else."

I braced myself for yelling, or possibly even tears, but instead she remained calm and distant.

"No, I'm certain there's a tracker. But I guess it doesn't matter."

Jeff eyed me suspiciously as Jessica wandered towards the counter.

"We've got cereal, toast, fruit," I began.

"I can make myself some toast," she said. "You sit."

Unsure of what else to do, I sat.

Jeff shoveled a large bite of Captain Crunch into his mouth, still eying me warily. "You guys both look a little tired," he said with a sly grin. "Not much sleep last night?"

I glared at him. Jessica had placed a slice of bread in the toaster and had wandered into the living room with a pear in her hand, looking out the window.

"Seriously man, if you had her in your bedroom and got any sleep at all, you'd have to be insane," he said, his voice quiet.

I shook my head. "She's had a really shitty week," I explained, certain that was the truth without knowing the details myself. "She's not normally like this."

"Is she normally hot?"

I rolled my eyes again.

Jeff glanced over at her again. Suddenly, as she reached up to take a bite of her pear, his expression changed. "Holy shit dude. Whose fiancée is she?"

I followed his gaze and saw that her ring was very prominent from that angle, especially as it caught the sunlight from the window. "Uh, I guess mine," I said awkwardly.

Now Jeff looked impressed and confused.

"I had no idea you…" he began, and then he stopped, surely remembering the other girls that I'd brought back to our apartment since we moved in a few weeks ago.

The toaster binged loudly as it ejected the toast. I stood and walked over to Jessica. Her back was still towards me, so I placed my hand on her shoulder.

She swiveled around quickly and nearly hit me before stopping herself. She squeezed her eyes shut, then opened them slowly. "Sorry. I guess I'm a little jittery."

"A little? Jessica, you've got to talk to me. I need to know what happened."

To my surprise, she nodded. "Yeah, sure." She took another bite of her pear. "Let me finish this apple and we can talk."

I hesitated. "Um, Jessica, that's a pear."

She glanced down and frowned. "Right. Silly me." She casually ruffled my hair with her hand then returned to the kitchen, slathered some peanut butter on her toast, and sat down beside Jeff in my old seat.

She gave him a quick once-over, her eyes pausing on his thick biceps visible beneath the short sleeve of his tee shirt. I tried to recall how much, if anything, I'd told her about Jeff, but it was clear from her visual assessment that she knew by now, if not before, that he was a hockey player.

"So, I guess congratulations are in order," he said, gesturing to her ring.

Jessica smiled. "Thanks."

"When did this happen?" he asked.

"Um, well, I guess…" Jessica turned to me.

"It's a long story," I said. "And we're not really telling people yet, so…"

Jeff nodded, finished his cereal, and stood abruptly, appearing uncomfortable.

"It was nice meeting you," he said on his way out.

JESSICA

I forced myself to chew the second bite of toast before pushing the plate away. I wasn't hungry, and the peanut butter was sticking to my throat and gagging me.

I turned and noticed Lucas staring at me. "Not hungry?"

I shook my head.

"We can go out for breakfast if you want something different," he offered. "Or I could just go pick something up."

I glanced down at the stupid SIM card from my phone.

"Jess, you have to eat something."

I knew without looking at Lucas that he was concerned about me. I could tell I'd lost weight, but I really didn't have my appetite back yet. "Do you have anything to drink?"

He stood quickly. "Yeah, sorry. Water, coffee, beer, soda, um…" he paused to rifle through a cabinet. "Here, green tea." He didn't wait for my answer before popping a mug of water in the microwave with the tea bag.

I accepted the mug once it was ready and wrapped my hands around it firmly. Even though the room was already fairly warm, the heat of the steaming liquid felt good against my fingers.

"What do you have planned today?" I asked casually.

Lucas laughed. "Nice try." He motioned for me to follow him back to his room.

I glanced around at the generic décor, realizing suddenly the place looked more like a hotel than an apartment. Aside from the hockey gear and random articles of clothing strewn about, it didn't look like a bachelor pad at all.

"Did your mom decorate this place?"

Lucas shook his head. "Furnished short term apartment. Perk of the team. Jeff and I each need to find our own place, but we have until fall to do it. I'm thinking about a unit in this building, though. Good location."

I sat on the bed and took a few slow sips of the tea.

"I want to help you, Jessica, but I don't know what to do. You jump when I touch you, you keep zoning out, you don't know apples from pears, and last night you couldn't stop shaking."

"I just need some time," I said.

"Should I not have told Aiden where you were?"

I shrugged. "I'm sure he already knew. I mean, maybe not that I was with you, but he had to have known the address. I was serious about the tracker in my phone."

He frowned, still pacing in front of me. "But are you hiding from Aiden? Is he who you're afraid of?"

"I'm not," I began. I stopped, sipped my tea, then set it on the nightstand. "I don't think he's going to come after me or anything, if that's what you're asking. But I don't want to see him ever again."

Lucas' eyes narrowed. "Jesus, Jessica, what did he do to you? You have to tell me. I'm imagining all sorts of shit, and I'm going to assume the worst unless I know for sure."

"He didn't touch me, Lucas."

He seemed to consider this. "Swear to me that Aiden did not hurt you at all."

"He didn't," I said. I glanced down and sighed. I felt I owed Lucas an explanation—as truthful of one as I could muster. But I also didn't need him rushing out to kill Aiden and get himself killed instead, which is exactly what would happen if I told him everything. "Well, obviously we are not together anymore. It didn't end well, to say the least. So emotionally, I'm a little hurt, but physically, well, he personally has never laid a hand on me."

"Why is he tracking your whereabouts? Was he trying to keep you from leaving?"

"No. I think he's just fine having me out of his life. But I suppose it's for my protection, not just to stalk me," I explained.

"Protection from whom? Or from what?"

I sipped my tea again. "I don't know. Nothing, I think. Just a precaution."

"Did you have a fight, you and Aiden?"

I frowned, uncertain of what he meant. Plus I was getting dizzy from all his pacing. "Sit down," I ordered.

Lucas sat. "I don't mean to pry. It's just, you break up with him and then show up here and…" He placed his hand on my shoulder.

"It's okay. It's a fair question," I said. Then I tried to find the best way to describe what happened with Aiden. "It wasn't one fight. It was, I don't know. Lots of disagreements, just one little thing after another all piling on top. And then, something happened that made it clear I don't fit in with…people like him. I never will. I don't want to get into the details."

I sighed. "I finally figured out that Aiden is not the person I thought he was and that there was no future for us anyway. And I realized I wanted everything you mentioned before, you know, when you," I fiddled with my ring to avoid saying "proposed."

Lucas nodded.

"He knew it was over between us, but I didn't tell him that I was leaving or where I was going, so he was just worried about me. Now that he knows I'm fine, I don't think we'll hear from him anymore."

"I can talk to him, Jessica. I can tell him you don't want him to contact you anymore," Lucas offered. "You don't have to throw your phone in my garbage disposal."

I shrugged. "It was just an idea," I said. "He doesn't want me in his life any more than I want him in mine."

He shifted his hand from my back to my thigh and rubbed back and forth with his thumb, just firmly enough to avoid tickling me.

"I hate to be the worst guest ever, but I'm exhausted. Do you mind if I take a nap?"

I caught Lucas frowning before he kissed my forehead. He didn't say anything, so I stretched out on his bed. But he didn't move.

I squeezed my eyes shut, hoping he'd take the hint, but he didn't.

"Jessica, if Aiden didn't physically hurt you, who did?"

"I don't want to talk about it, Lucas. I can't...I just want to forget."

He winced and I realized too late that my answer confirmed I was, in fact, hurt.

"I don't need to know what happened now, but I need to know who did this to you."

I reluctantly sat up. "Why?"

"Why what?"

"Why does it matter who hurt me?" I paused before answering my own question. "It doesn't. It's over now and I just want to move on."

"Of course it matters. Jessica, I need to know so I can..."

I gave him a second to finish before cutting him off. "So you can what- kick their asses? Beat them up?" I paused, and his face told me I guessed right. "Yeah, well, don't worry. You're too late."

Lucas frowned again. "What do you mean? How am I too late?"

"The guys that hurt me are gone," I said, struggling to catch my breath.

"How can you be so sure? Jessica, I just want…"

"They won't be back. They're dead, Lucas. Okay? Are you happy?" I saw through blurry eyes that he wasn't happy, but now I was pissed and it was his fault. He should've just let it drop. "Aiden killed them with his bare hands. I saw it all. So yeah, you're too late to get vengeance on my behalf and you don't have to worry about them coming after me again."

I was shaking and sobbing, but suddenly overcome with nausea, too. I turned to the side, clenched my hands over my mouth, and dry heaved, thankful I hadn't eaten much. When my stomach relaxed, I let my head drop onto my lap, still unwilling to look up. I felt Lucas' hand on my shoulders but wisely, he shut up. I cried until I didn't have any tears left, and then I curled up on the bed and slept until nightfall.

CHAPTER THIRTEEN

I ran eight miles then polished off nearly half a bottle of bourbon while pacing in front of the fire. It was, for the present, enough to keep me from throwing my phone into the flames. I had wanted to hear from Jessica. No, I had needed to hear from her. I told myself I only needed confirmation of her welfare, but as the text from Lucas provided that and simply incensed me further, I was lying to myself.

I needed true closure. I needed her to understand I hadn't meant for things to happen the way they did. And I wanted her to forgive me. But deep down, I knew she never would, and I wished I could say that didn't matter.

When I'd agreed to leave the cottage for the night, I was terrified something bad would happen. Without me keeping watch over Jessica, I worried her condition would deteriorate, or she'd be kidnapped again or injured by someone else. But in all of my anxiety, it hadn't occurred to me that Jessica would use my absence as an opportunity to leave on her own volition, without even saying goodbye.

Yet she had.

My sister, father, and all of the guards present confirmed that Jessica voluntarily left the house in a cab headed for the bus station. She'd spoken with my father, of all people, before she left. He said she realized there was no future for the two of us and that she was just going to get hurt over and over again as long as we were together. Ouch. His impression was that she wanted to say goodbye, but thought it would be easier for both of us this way, with a clean break.

Apparently, she had been very clear that she did not want to see me again.

Ever.

I hadn't believed him at first. I returned to the cottage, looked for signs of a struggle, and interrogated every last guard. I refused to return to London until I heard from her, and she didn't respond to any of my texts or calls. And then, finally, Lucas had texted me from her phone.

I should've been thankful that Jessica was safe and that she was with someone who could protect her and someday make her happy. I'd always known she belonged with Lucas, and while I thought I loved her as much as one could love another, I'd never had the strength to actually push her to him. Now, I had inadvertently sent her to him. If I were a good man, I would've been relieved. It was for the best. I knew that to be true. If anyone else actually said that to me, I'd probably punch through the wall, but that didn't change my realization of its accuracy.

Now I was free to concentrate on my people. I could ascend to the throne with a clear heart and focused mind. I would have no loyalties stronger than those I held towards my own clan. Someday, maybe I could marry an elf woman, ideally someone whose company I at least enjoyed, and I could create my own legacy of bettering the world. Meanwhile, Jessica could live the simple, human life she craved, with the happiness she deserved and the safety most humans took for granted.

An abrupt clanking startled me. I turned to see my father eying me disapprovingly.

"Wallowing doesn't become you, Son," he said. "And time to recover from heartbreak is a luxury kings can't afford. That's one of the reasons we recommended the arranged marriage to start with. It isn't that we have something against love, but we do realize how important it is for our leaders to be without romantic distractions."

"Did you need something, or are you just here to lecture me?" I snapped.

His eyes narrowed but he simply handed me an envelope.

I accepted it with a snarl, noting the seal had already been broken.

"We received this letter last night. Marius wasn't sure what to do with it. In light of the current situation, it seems irrelevant. But as I pledged transparency to you, I thought you should know."

He bowed his head and stepped out of the room, shutting the door behind him.

I rubbed my brow tensely then tugged the paper out of the envelope. It was a formal letter to my uncle from the leader of the southern clan. They expressed their regrets at what had happened to Jessica and disavowed any involvement. They said in light of the circumstances, they'd accept the testing Jessica's captors had performed and agreed that she was approximately 74% pure blood elf.

I skimmed the rest of the letter. They apologized for doubting her heritage but expressed surprise that our clan would endorse a leader planning to marry an elf with less than 100% pure blood. I froze. My eyes scanned back up the page. Seventy four percent, it had said. Seventy-four? How was that possible?

I wadded up the letter, certain a copy had been made regardless, and tossed it into the fire with sufficient force to knock several large embers out of the stone encasement.

"It was the blood."

I swiveled around to face my sister, whom I hadn't even heard enter.

"We gave her so much blood that it overwhelmed the human blood in her system. And because of her own natural elf blood, the blood we gave her remained in her system longer than it otherwise would have."

I swallowed, realizing she was answering the question I hadn't asked aloud.

"If it's any consolation," Cordelia continued, "that number also means she didn't feel as much pain as a human would. She healed quickly and felt her injuries mostly as an elf would, which is far better than any human with no elf blood would have fared in her situation."

Instead of retorting in anger, I considered her words, and I actually did find some comfort in the knowledge that Jessica hadn't suffered as extreme of pain as I'd imagined. Still, she'd been terrified. And alone.

And it was all because of me.

"It doesn't make it any easier, but you always knew this wouldn't last," Cordelia said, teetering dangerously close to one of the many sentiments which would have provoked violence in me.

"Send someone to confirm her injuries have healed."

"They have. I saw to that before she left."

"Send someone now!" I bellowed. "Elgin should do it. She knows him." I sighed. "And have him give her one last injection of blood, just in case." I envisioned the scenario in my head, realizing she wouldn't easily trust an elf giving her an injection after what she'd been through. "Have him leave the blood for Lucas to give her later, actually. But I want assurance that she is fully healed."

My sister nodded, acknowledging my official command, although I saw in her eyes that she judged my orders ridiculous.

"Is that all?" I asked, ready to be alone again.

Her lips parted hesitantly. I stared patiently, willing her to speak sooner rather than later.

"I'm pregnant," she said finally.

That, I hadn't expected her to say. I quickly put together the clues of the last few weeks—her excessive fatigue and Elgin's sudden preoccupation with her wellbeing. I should have figured it out sooner.

I eyed her stomach warily. "So you've got my successor there," I said.

"Perhaps," she replied. "Though it feels more like a girl."

"How would you know?"

Cordelia smiled. "I guess I wouldn't. We'll know for sure in a month or so. Until then you can tell yourself it's a boy, if that brings you solace."

"It does," I said.

She gazed out the window. "If I have a boy, do you suppose he is doomed to be as miserable as you are?"

I offered her a smile at that. "It hasn't been all terrible," I reminded her. I stepped forward and offered her a gentle hug. "Congratulations, dear sister. I'm very happy for you and Elgin. And I'm sure father is thrilled."

"We haven't told him yet."

I was honored that she told me first. Or perhaps that was simply protocol since she was, potentially, carrying the king who would follow my reign. "Thank you for telling me now."

She shrugged. "I figured you could use some good news."

I nodded, and she left.

Lucas

I stayed with Jessica until I was certain she was asleep before sneaking out of the room. I would've gone mad lying there beside her, with nothing to do but give in to the horrific visions in my mind of what possibly happened to her to make her this scared. Besides that, I was starving. I didn't want her to freak out, so I planned to grab some food then set up at the desk in my room to study. Not my favorite way to spend a Saturday, but I didn't see Jessica waking in the mood to go hit the clubs, and I might as well be productive.

Jeff was in the kitchen making himself a grotesquely large sandwich that made my mouth water. He held the loaf of bread out to me and I accepted it with a grin and began to make my own sandwich. All in all, Jeff was a great roommate, which was sheer luck since the team had basically stuck us together while we hunted for our own places to live. He was the same age as me, about the same level, and was a nice guy. He was Canadian, so I assumed he wouldn't agree with my parents' conservative political views, but I was grateful just to have an English-speaking roommate since so many of the new guys were from Eastern Europe.

"So, how long is Jessica staying?" Jeff asked cautiously after we'd both sat at the table and begun eating.

I cringed, suddenly aware I hadn't even asked him if he minded having an extra person around the apartment. "I don't know, man. Sorry. I didn't even think to check with you first. When she showed up, I…"

Jeff's chewing slowed and he eyed me warily.

"I didn't really know she was coming. Obviously. We had, uh, been on a break. There was another guy before me and he…" I felt my face grow warm at my struggles to explain the current situation and Jessica's behavior without revealing anything too private about Aiden or anything that would get back to either Jessica's family or my own. "Well her ex was not good for her, I guess is a nice way to put it. So she's not herself right now. I can't kick her out when she's like this, but I know you didn't sign up to have two roommates, so Jess and I can head to a hotel until my place is ready."

Jeff took a moment to piece together what I'd said. "No man, you're fine here." He shrugged. "I mean maybe check back in a week or two, but I don't mind the extra company for now."

I exhaled the tension I'd been holding in my chest. "Thanks. I'll understand if you change your mind down the road." I ate a bite in silence before speaking again. "She's pretty easygoing normally. Nothing like any other girl I've ever met. No nagging, not high maintenance, no drama." And hot as hell, I thought, feeling my body react to my vision of her curled up in my bed. "But we really want to keep this low key for now. We haven't had a chance to tell our families yet, so…"

Jeff nodded. He was no stranger to the hassles of the sudden publicity we were experiencing now that we'd been drafted. "Better not have her wear that rock in public yet," he cautioned.

I nodded, concerned about that same issue and frankly, still perplexed as to why Jessica insisted on wearing it when we hadn't really even talked about us since she returned.

"You headed out tonight?"

"Yeah."

"Have fun," I said. "I've got a bunch of work to catch up on for my classes."

"Nothing says Saturday night like homework," he jabbed, standing and dumping his plate in the dishwasher.

I studied for three straight hours before Jessica woke briefly, showered, pretended to watch part of a movie with me, then went back to bed. That time, I was ready to sleep, too. When I awoke in the morning, she was still asleep. I had never seen a human sleep as long as Jessica had the past few days. It couldn't be normal, but then, I wasn't sure having her awake and distant or crying was any better.

After I showered and made myself an impressive omelet, one of my few culinary achievements, I settled back in at my desk for more studying. I was taking three distance courses this summer, and assuming I took two more the following summer, I'd be able to graduate, albeit late. I hadn't expected the school to be so willing to accommodate me like this, but I guess potential fame was a powerful negotiating tool.

Online courses were not my strong suit, though. I'd never been the best student, and face-to-face accountability had historically been my primary motivator. Without that, I struggled to convince myself to do the work. But now, with nothing else to do, I supposed I would make up for lost studying time.

I felt a hand on my shoulder and jumped, removing my headphones as I turned to see Jessica. She smiled softly, sleepily brushing her hair out of her face. My stomach tightened. She was really so incredibly beautiful when she smiled. It took all my self-control not to pull her onto my lap and kiss her. Her tank top strap slid off her shoulder, truly revealing nothing more than was visible before, but it was enough to eviscerate my so-called self-control. I tugged her hand so she was on my lap, careful to position her closer to my knees so she didn't know exactly how much I wanted more from her right now.

"How did you sleep?" I asked.

She shrugged, absentmindedly twirling a strand of her dark hair. "I guess good. I don't know why I'm so tired. I should be caught up on sleep by now."

"Well, I'm caught up on homework for the century," I joked.

Jessica gazed at the textbooks I had scattered about the desk. "I'm really proud of you, Lucas. Not many guys can make this whole pro hockey dream come true and still graduate."

"I'm a lucky guy," I said, for altogether different reasons. Jessica was quiet. "Are you hungry?"

She shook her head.

"You need to eat at some point."

"I will," she promised. She stood slowly, but before I could feel disappointment at the absence of her body against mine, she stretched slightly. The move was both adorable and incredibly sexy. I glanced down at the ring I'd given her to avoid staring at the inch of her waist exposed as her shirt lifted upwards.

"What do you have planned for today?"

"I have to go in and talk to the coach and do some interviews this afternoon, but that's it." I paused. "But Monday through Friday we have our normal practice."

"What's that schedule like?"

"Not too bad, since it's the off season. Got to be there before 9, then we meet as a team, do weights, get our gear, then we skate. Then stretching, recovery, massages for the guys who aren't rookies, late lunch, showers, you know. Then more meetings. I'm usually back by 3."

"Why don't the rookies get massages?"

"We could, but we'd have to go last. I'd rather head out early and pay for one on my own time."

She nodded knowingly. "Is it hard going from top dog to being the new guy?"

I considered the question. I'd been terrified of that all spring, actually. I'd been the best of anyone I'd played with or against for so long that I hadn't even known how it would feel to suddenly be surrounded by guys with more skill than me. "It hasn't been as bad as I thought. The other guys are all cool, and basically they're really nice to the new guys as long as we aren't too cocky." I laughed. "And it would be really hard for me not to be my usual cocky self if I weren't surrounded by guys who are way more talented than me. So, really it's a good thing."

She frowned. "So you're really not the best?"

I laughed, shaking my head. "Not even close. The worst part is no one even talks about things I do well, it's all about my potential, like I have the 'potential' to handle the puck well or my speed has 'potential.'"

"Can I come watch sometime?"

I cringed. "You might distract me."

Jessica laughed. "You mean you actually have to concentrate now? Wow. How the mighty have fallen!"

We took a short walk later that morning. Jessica didn't talk any more about Aiden, but she did seem more like her old self, so by the time I was getting dressed up to go meet with the coaches, I felt okay about leaving her.

I pulled on a shirt and began fidgeting with the buttons. Jessica came in behind me and took over, her fingers deftly fastening all of them and securing my tie quicker than I ever could have. I forced myself not to think about where she might have gotten practice dressing men in business attire.

"Looking good, LJ," she said.

"You said nobody was allowed to call you that," Jeff whined.

"She can call me whatever she wants," I said.

Jessica smirked, which I found reassuring.

"You're sure you'll be okay?" I asked her.

She nodded. "I feel fine. Maybe I'll challenge Jeff to some poker," she said loud enough so he could hear.

"Game on!" he shouted back.

"See? No worries. Kick ass tonight." She raised on her toes and kissed me. It was brief, but unexpected. I had a funny sensation about the kiss, realizing we might have that exact moment again and again before every one of my meetings or interviews. I smiled.

"Do I even want to know what you're thinking?" she asked.

I shook my head. "I'm just glad you're here," I said.

JESSICA

After Lucas left, Jeff and I launched into a game of poker. We took a break to try to figure out dinner options, but when I confessed that I could only make grilled cheese or spaghetti, Jeff started laughing.

"Wow, so you're a shitty card player and you can't cook?" he teased.

I shrugged. "Yeah, I don't know what Lucas sees in me."

"Eh, I think you've got a certain girl-next-door quality."

I sat back down with my drink, grinning. "That could be because I literally am—or was, anyway, the girl next door."

"For real?"

I nodded. "Lucas and I grew up together."

Jeff appeared to be inspecting me. "That explains it."

"Explains what?"

"I can't put my finger on it, but he's just different with you than how he is with..." Jeff stopped talking and instantly paled.

I licked my lips calmly. "Different from how he is with other girls?"

Jeff didn't answer. "I'll order pizza," he said, standing up.

"It's alright Jeff. I already know he's been seeing other people."

Jeff turned hesitantly.

"Has he told you anything about us?"

"He never mentioned you before you showed up on our doorstep," he said apologetically.

"Yeah, I don't blame him. Our history is complicated. Lucas proposed back in May, when I was leaving town with another guy. I told him I needed to think about it."

Judging from Jeff's expression, he was shocked. I hoped I hadn't revealed more than Lucas wanted him to know.

"Lucas and I have a lot of history together, but we both also have some other people in our past. What matters, though, is that we both want the same future."

We resumed our small talk on lighter subjects until Lucas returned. He changed out of the suit as soon as he got home, which was sort of disappointing since the unfamiliar sight of him all gussied up was a total turn on.

He was about to join us for a hand of poker when he paced past the window and paused.

"Uh, Jessica, I think you have a visitor."

I turned and followed Lucas' eyes to the window. I gazed down and immediately spotted Elgin. As always, he was dressed in black from head to toe, despite the sweltering heat, and he stood nearly two feet taller than anyone else on the sidewalk.

"Shit," I murmured. "What is he doing here?"

"Is that your ex?" Jeff asked, mouth agape.

I shook my head dismissively.

"I'll go see what he wants," Lucas offered.

"No. I'll go," I said, scanning the room for my sandals.

"You're not going alone," Lucas said.

I laughed. "What are you going to do?"

Jeff laughed too. "She's got a point, man. That guy is gigantic."

Lucas remained undeterred.

"Fine, but stay in the lobby," I instructed.

We were both quiet in the elevator down. When we reached the lobby, Lucas planted a good luck kiss on my forehead and then, as promised, remained by the window while I went out into the steamy night air.

"Hi, Elgin," I said casually, as though he were an old friend. Despite everything I'd been through—or maybe because of it—Elgin didn't scare me. His treatment of me had always been professional and unemotional.

He bowed his head politely, his long black hair swinging down over his face. "Good evening, Miss Grove. Mr. Eklund asked me to check your safety and welfare."

"Aiden wanted you to spy on me." I translated, keeping my distance. "He should pick a different stalker then. You don't exactly blend in. Anyway, you can report back that I'm just fine, no thanks to him. And that he can stop tracking my location. It's kind of creepy."

"I will relay your message to him, miss, but that is a concession he is unlikely to make."

"Is that all?"

"No. You haven't said how you're doing."

"I said I'm fine. Aiden knows I'm staying with Lucas now."

Elgin's eyes darted back and forth nervously. "I am supposed to confirm that your injuries have healed."

"They have."

"My orders are to confirm it."

"What, like see it?" I shook my head. "No. I'm not flashing you on a busy street."

"I'll escort you around the corner where it is more private," he said.

"If you try to take me into the alley and start messing with my shirt, you have about ten seconds before Lucas is out here."

"Doing what?" he asked with a chuckle.

I sighed and stepped closer to the wall, just out of Lucas' line of vision. I held out my arms first, showing him the front, then back, and then turned quickly and lifted my shirt to reveal my back. I spun back to face him and let him see my stomach. "That's all the confirmation you're getting," I said, smoothing my shirt back down and stepping back where Lucas could see me.

"That is adequate. Thank you for cooperating. I'll let Mr. Eklund know." He paused. "Is there anything else you'd like me to relay to him?"

"I'd like him to leave me alone," I paused. "I have a chance to be happy now if he stops interfering. I just need some distance."

He nodded professionally. "I will tell him. But you should know that he has ordered a guard to watch you."

I frowned, not having noticed anyone lately. Of course, I hadn't really left the apartment much either. "Is that necessary? Am I in danger still?"

"We have heard no specific threats. It is a general precaution."

I shrugged. "Is Aiden back from London yet?"

"No. He is scheduled to return this week."

"Well, goodbye."

I started to turn and he grabbed my arm.

I glanced at him, slightly panicked, and he reached into his inside jacket pocket. He placed a small makeup-style bag in my hand. "Cordelia asked me to give this to you. She said to have your," his eyes flicked down to my engagement ring and widened, "Your friend administer the injection."

I yanked my hand free, realizing it was too late to hide the ring. "Why? I'm healed."

"She said to give it to you regardless. If you'd like to speak with her directly, that could be arranged."

"No," I said. "I'll have Lucas handle it tonight."

I returned to the building, aware that Elgin was still watching me.

I let Lucas wrap his arm around me as we rode the elevator back up to the apartment, then insisted I wanted to get ready for bed. Alone in Lucas' room, I unzipped the pouch and confirmed it contained a single vial of blood, presumably Aiden's, and no notes or other personal effects. I shoved the pouch to the bottom of my suitcase, having no intention of injecting myself with a physical reminder of Aiden. Then I grabbed my pajamas and went to the bathroom to shower and wash the day away.

Seeing Elgin reminded me of everything I had left behind. I was still so confused. At night, I'd have dreams of wonderful times I'd shared with Aiden, then I'd awaken and remember the brutal reality of my life with him. I had made the right decision by coming to Lucas. Everything would be okay now. It was just going to take a little more time.

CHAPTER FOURTEEN

Jessica clammed up again after she spoke with Elgin. I couldn't hear what they'd said, but the old Jessica was gone when she'd come back into the apartment with me. She was back to the quiet, distant version of herself that had showed up at my apartment days before. She assured me Elgin would not return again, that she wasn't in any harm, and that Aiden was still out of the country. I hadn't realized she'd come back to the States alone.

I went to bed at the same time as her, even though it was earlier than my norm. I figured the extra sleep wouldn't hurt on a Sunday night. As I climbed in bed beside Jessica, she inched closer to me. I kissed the back of her shoulder and she tensed, relaxing again slowly as I draped my arm around her body and pressed my torso against her back.

"My alarm goes off at 7:15," I said. "I should leave by 8:30. Will you be okay alone while we're gone?"

"Yes," she whispered. "I'll probably just sleep. Or read."

"You can do some of my homework if you're bored," I joked.

I felt her back vibrate with a slight chuckle.

"When will you tell your grandma you're back in town?"

"I don't know," she said. "I know I need to soon, but I just feel so safe here. And I can't tell her I'm back and not go see her."

"Yeah," I agreed. "I can drive out with you next weekend if you want."

"Maybe."

I hesitated about what I planned to say next, but I knew it had to be said. "Jessica, now that I'm with the Blackhawks, I do get some publicity. I don't have any stalkers or major paparazzi followers yet, but it's possible I'd get my picture taken in public."

"If that happens, I'll just tell my grandma right away that I'm back," she said. "It's not like she'd see the pictures anyway. She doesn't read sports news or tabloids."

"Yeah. But the ring…"

Jessica was quiet.

"They asked me in one of the interviews earlier about my personal life. Apparently, some people think I'm quite the hot commodity."

Now Jessica giggled. "I read online that you're the sexiest recruit in years."

I winced, having read that exact article. I'd never denied that I had been blessed in the looks department, and I happily accepted the positive attention it had brought me from the ladies, but seeing it in print was awkward, especially when I knew my mother read every word written about me.

"Anyway," I continued. "I was vague in my answer. I figured you don't want random people to know about us before we talk to our families, but no matter what I say, the ring is a big giveaway."

"You want me to take it off," she said finally, her voice distant.

"No. Well, maybe in public. Just until we've had a chance to get our stories straight."

"What story?"

I was now deeply regretting bringing this up. I felt like a total girl, waiting until we were cozy in bed to raise a serious discussion topic. "Jessica, your grandma knows you left the country with Aiden, doesn't she?"

"No, not exactly. She knows I was studying abroad. And I told her that his family does some business there so he'd come to visit."

"Did you tell her you broke up?"

"No."

"Well, don't you think she'd react better if she knew you broke up with him before she learned you're engaged to me?"

Jessica was quiet.

"Normally people break up with one person, then date a new person before agreeing to marry the second person."

"You knew I was with Aiden when you proposed," she said.

"I know. And I'm not complaining. I just…I want to make sure you see how this might look to other people. If you tell your grandmother you're engaged, she's going to assume you're marrying Aiden." I paused. "Jessica, we never even dated."

"Dating is for people to get to know each other. I already know you, Lucas."

I stayed quiet. I was flustered. I knew what I meant but apparently didn't know how to express it. Why had I even started this discussion? Well, I suppose I knew the answer to that. I wanted her to tell her grandma that she broke up with Aiden, that she realized her whole relationship was a mistake and that she was really in love with me. And then maybe a few months after that she could start wearing the ring and tell her grandma we were engaged.

Mostly, I wanted her to act like we were newly engaged. I wanted her to want to tell her friends and family about me. I wanted her to be all over me all the time. I wanted to feel like she actually wanted to marry me as much as I wanted to marry her.

"Lucas?" Jessica's voice cut into my thoughts.

"Hmm?"

"What are you thinking?"

I exhaled silently. "I was thinking that maybe you don't really want to be engaged right now and you're just using it as an excuse so you don't have to go back to your real life."

"Oh. Ouch."

"I don't mean it to sound harsh, Jess. I just want you to know you can stay here with me anyway. You don't have to wear the ring or pretend you want to marry me."

Jessica turned onto her back so I could see her face. "I like wearing the ring. I'm really uneasy lately, and I keep having these nightmares. And as soon as I wake up, I feel this ring. It reminds me that I don't need to be scared anymore because I have you, and I know you love me and that you'll take care of me and that we can have this happy life together."

I tried to think of a response but my mind was blank.

"I don't want to date you, Lucas. I like that we're already comfortable with each other and that we already know each other's annoying habits." She paused. "And I will tell my grandma sometime. I just don't feel ready to come back to reality yet."

I let my hand relax against her stomach and stared into her eyes. In the dark room, all I could see was the slightest sparkle around her pupils. Her hair silhouetted her face in a way that reminded me of a famous painting and I was again, stricken, with wonder at how effortlessly gorgeous Jessica was.

I saw her blink a few times, then she brought her face forward and gently kissed my forehead. Before she could pull back completely, I moved my hand to cradle her head and pressed my lips against hers, holding her gently in place. There was no hesitation as she kissed me back, turning towards me and gripping my hip with her hand as she parted her lips for me. For the first time, I believed what we had was real.

JESSICA

I briefly woke when Lucas kissed my forehead on his way

out the door Monday morning, but then I fell back asleep until mid-morning. After I woke, I took a long walk, checking out my surroundings constantly and convinced there was not anyone following me despite Elgin's words. I bought a salad for lunch and picked at it while watching trashy daytime TV and then was surprised to see Lucas home shortly after 2 o'clock.

He smelled clean and masculine, suggesting he'd showered after practice, but he headed straight for the bathroom, flicking on the tub faucet. He was walking awkwardly, the way he always did after back to back games in college, so I suspected he was sore. He dumped a full bag of store-bought ice into the tub, changed into his swim trunks, and carefully lowered himself into the tub.

"Care to join me?" he teased, wincing from the ice.

I couldn't believe he was actually sitting in a tub of ice. I wondered how badly one must hurt for full body ice to actually feel better. He hadn't shut the door, and I assumed Jeff would be home soon since they'd been together, but I still had to wonder about the swimwear.

"Is that for my sake or Jeff's?" I asked, gesturing to his suit.

Lucas grinned. "Neither. It's to keep my balls warm."

I laughed at his bluntness. "Won't you get pneumonia?"

"I won't stay in long." He hesitated. "Although some hot coffee or tea might help."

I hopped up to go get his drink. When I returned with it, his eyes were shut but he still looked pained.

"I thought summer practice wasn't supposed to be hard," I said. "You said the focus was recovering from the season and maintaining skills."

"Well, yeah, for the regular guys. They don't have anything to prove. My future contracts hinge on my performance at training camp in a month and I need to hone my skills and get as fit as I can before the season starts. But I also need to make sure I fully recover each day so I don't hurt my performance once the season starts."

I shook my head. "I cannot believe you actually did it. You are a professional athlete. Playing for your favorite team. How does that even happen?"

"Lots of hard work, dedication, and sacrifices," he said in a silly voice I knew was imitating his old college coach. "And a lot of luck."

I shook my head and gave him privacy for the rest of his torture. He took a hot shower right after the bath and then convinced me to do yoga with him until Jeff came home.

On Tuesday, I intended to follow the same routine as Monday, but was surprised by a woman barging into the kitchen as I was drinking my tea in the morning. The noise of a key in the door had terrified me, but once I saw her, and registered the surprise on her face, I concluded she was likely harmless.

She dragged a vacuum cleaner in behind her and placed a tote of cleaning supplies on the counter. Either she had a very convincing costume or she was, in fact, the cleaning lady.

"Hi, I'm Jessica, um, Lucas' friend. He forgot to tell me you were coming this morning. I can get dressed and get out of your hair if you prefer."

She seemed to like the idea of me leaving, so I quickly dressed and then grabbed Lucas' laptop to head to a nearby coffee shop. I'd been checking email on my phone, but the laptop would work much better. Plus Lucas had given me the login for their grocery account and asked me to add anything I wanted to the list and place the order for grocery delivery.

I supposed the fact that the guys had a cleaning lady and grocery delivery explained why they hadn't yet starved to death or run out of clean athletic shorts. I settled in with my hot cocoa and a fruit salad and quickly finished email and the grocery order when I noticed a word processing document was open at the bottom of the screen. I clicked on it out of curiosity and found

Lucas' term paper for his composition class. Clearly it was a rough draft, since it was awful.

I found myself correcting typos as I skimmed, but by the time I finished reading, I realized I still had over an hour before I could expect the cleaning lady to be done with the apartment. So I went back and did more intense revisions, keeping his basic ideas but rewriting some portions more than others. When I was done with that, I corrected the footnotes and citations, then fixed the formatting. I saved my completed work as a separate document, in case Lucas didn't like my edits, then headed back to the apartment.

When Lucas returned home, he repeated the ice bath, but this time I had a hot coffee waiting for him from the start. And while he was bathing, I mentioned the cleaning lady's arrival.

"Shit, I'm sorry, Jessica. I forgot to warn you she'd be coming. I hope it didn't freak you out," he said.

I shrugged. "It was fine. But she wanted to work alone so I went to a coffee shop. I brought your laptop."

"That's fine."

"I noticed your composition assignment," I began.

He groaned.

"When is that due?"

"Well, there's not exactly a firm date. It's the last assignment for that class, but it's the main one. Since it's a correspondence course I really have until August to finish, but I started it a few nights ago while you were sleeping. I fucking hate writing though. As soon as I turn it in, she's just gonna flunk me and then this whole damn class will be a wash."

I blew out a breath. "I might have done some revisions."

"On my paper?"

"Yeah. I was bored, so I read it, and then I made a few basic corrections, but one thing led to another, and now it's sort of done. I'm sorry. I didn't mean to meddle."

Lucas was quiet for a moment and then he laughed. "Are you saying you finished my paper?"

"Well, yes."

"How is it now?"

I shrugged. "I don't know. You can read it. I don't want to toot my own horn but I think it's pretty good. Maybe not A plus but at least a B."

"And you're apologizing?"

"It's your paper. I should have minded my own business. I just felt bad because you are working so incredibly hard, physically torturing yourself at work and then coming home and trying to finish this coursework and taking care of me on the side. And then here I am watching crappy TV shows and sleeping all day. I had to find some way to pull my weight."

Lucas smiled. "Jess, you don't owe me anything. I love having you here. And you know I'm not miserable when I'm playing hockey. Yeah, it hurts, but it's a good hurt. I like it." He sighed, and I saw the steam from his breath rise off the ice water. "I don't want you feeling like you have to do my homework to earn your keep. You can't screw with your lofty moral code just because you feel bad for me."

I frowned, not fully sure what he as saying.

"You're not a cheater, Jessica. You know you play by the rules."

Now I realized what he was saying. "I don't think it technically counts as cheating. You wrote the paper, I just did some revisions." I sighed. "But I get what you're saying. I should've just left it alone. I'm sorry, Lucas."

He laughed again and lifted the drain on the tub. "No, Jess, I was dreading finishing that paper. Don't apologize for saving me hours of torture trying to finish it up. My only concern was that you'd feel guilty about the slight ethics violation."

He stood slowly from the water, his muscles still all tensed from the cold and his swim trunks clinging to him. I bit my lip as he flicked a piece of ice off his chiseled torso then turned quickly, aware I'd been gawking.

I swallowed hard. "No ethics concerns. I'll give you some privacy while you warm up."

I left the bathroom quickly, nearly bumping into Jeff who was just now returning home. Apparently, Lucas was leaving early to come check on me. When Jeff said he could've stayed another hour to get a professional massage, that gave me another idea of how to repay Lucas for letting me stay with him.

I'd seen massage oil on his dresser a few days before, and while I'd tried to block thoughts of what alternate uses he might have found for that product, it seemed relevant now. When Lucas returned to the bedroom, his towel tied around his waist, I offered him a massage.

"I know I'm not as strong as your professional masseuses, but unless you're worried I'll make things worse…" I began.

Lucas shook his head, grinning. "I would take that risk any day." He reached into his dresser drawer and pulled out a pair of boxer briefs and I quickly turned, not ready to see the full Monty. When I glanced back, he was holding his towel loosely around his waist again. "Where do you want me?" he asked, clearly proud of his phrasing.

I shrugged and pointed to the bed. There weren't really a lot of other options. He sprawled out on his stomach, tossing the towel onto the floor. I stood beside him, squirted the massage oil into my hands and rubbed them together to warm it. Then I began kneading the tight muscles in his back. I started on his lower back, then worked along his legs, realizing they took quite a beating at practice. Lucas was quiet at first, but groaned a few times as I reached spots on his thighs where I could actually feel small knots in the muscle.

"Can you do my shoulders?" he asked a few minutes later.

I squirted out more massage oil and complied with his request, but the angle was all wrong, so I climbed onto the bed and straddled his body. I kept myself raised on my knees at first, careful not to put any weight on his back.

Lucas opened his eyes and craned his neck around to see me, smiling when our eyes met. "This isn't exactly how the pros do it, but I'm not complaining," he said.

"I'm not hurting you?"

"God no," he groaned.

My arms were starting to tire, but I felt motivated to continue every time I reached a tight spot and could actually feel the muscles loosen as I massaged them.

"Should I turn over?" he asked suddenly.

"Sure," I replied absentmindedly, not fully processing what he'd asked until he'd swiveled onto his back. The motion threw me off balance so by the time he was in position, I was resting with my full body weight on his groin. He didn't appear to mind, so I ignored the potential awkwardness of the position and poured more massage oil onto my hands and began rubbing his chest.

"Are your muscles this tight every day?"

"Pretty much," he said. "Although they tell me this is nothing compared to how I'll be feeling come February."

I swallowed, torn between my appreciation for his chiseled body and my unease at how much pain he was putting himself through on a daily basis. I felt him watching me for a moment, and then his eyes drifted shut. I rose back onto my knees to reach the tops of his shoulders and the sides of his neck, then glanced down.

A large bulge had appeared below Lucas' midsection and his boxer briefs were straining to contain the, uh, new development. I quickly averted my eyes but couldn't help gazing down again. I tried not to linger on it, or at least not to be obvious, but it was just so pronounced. I'd felt it pressing against me before, so it wasn't like I hadn't known he was well endowed, but this was the first time I'd actually seen it in the light of day, albeit still covered by the thin material of his boxer briefs, now being pushed to their limits. I willed myself to shut my eyes before he realized what I was gawking at, but apparently my attempts at subtlety failed.

Lucas cleared his throat. "Sorry about that. I promise that doesn't happen when the sports therapists do this." He chuckled. "Although they don't straddle me either."

I smiled, poured more oil on my hands, and began to massage his chest again. I felt his eyes on me and knew I was blushing. I realized the entire massage could've easily been construed as foreplay, which had not been my intent. As spectacular as Lucas' perfect human form was, sprawled out beneath me, glistening from the oil, I was not in the mood for sex. I was admiring his body, sure, but almost in the way I'd appreciate an amazing work of art.

Something was seriously wrong with me. I had a supremely sexy, muscular man half-naked beneath my thighs, clearly ready to satisfy my every whim and I wanted none of it. It wasn't that I didn't appreciate it, because I did. I was the luckiest girl on earth right now. I knew that. Lucas was sweet, funny, honest, caring, smart, successful, and as of late, I guessed, rich.

Besides all that, he wanted me. I didn't doubt for a second that he would love me and cherish me and take care of me as long as we both lived. He was definitely the man for me. I was certain. He had to be. I just hoped my body would get on board and realize that quickly.

Lucas reached out and squeezed my hands. "You must be getting tired," he said, sitting up and scooting me further down his lap to avoid direct contact with the still-protruding appendage.

I felt my cheeks grow warm and turned away, suddenly uncomfortable by the close proximity and the intensity of his stare. Lucas gently nudged my face back towards his with a finger and kissed me softly.

"Thank you," he said. Then he lifted me off his lap and scooted off the bed, keeping his back to me while he retrieved a pair of shorts and began to dress.

Lucas

Having Jessica around was exhausting. I should've felt better rested than ever before, since she had taken over large chunks of my homework and waited on me hand and foot when I wasn't at the rink. But mentally, I was a wreck trying to decipher her moods. She seemed more like her normal self as the days went on. She was starting to be chattier, and she only woke me once or twice each night with what I assumed were nightmares. She never seemed to fully wake during the episodes that left her thrashing around, shaking, crying, and often yelling out, but I assumed these sleep disturbances were responsible for her continued fatigue during the day.

She didn't speak of Aiden at all, aside from a few mumbles in her sleep. And she seemed more comfortable with me. But I still wasn't confident that her heart was actually in this whole engagement thing. We kissed often, but in the way I imagined old married couples kissed. I caught her checking me out a few times when I was shirtless or changing, and I was pretty sure she went out of her way to touch me more than necessary, but when I tried to initiate anything serious, she quickly grew distant.

I was stumped. I didn't know if this was because of whatever shit she'd gone through with Aiden, if she was still hung up on him, or if she just didn't want me. And I supposed there was the possibility that this was normal. I really hadn't had a relationship since high school that started with kissing and grew more physical over time. Generally, when I met a girl I was interested in, we'd have sex the first night. If that was fun and I was still interested, we might go out a few more times. Being with a girl and not having sex was new to me, and very, very confusing.

By Friday, I was ready for a casual night at home, but I had a few frat brothers in town this weekend and had already made plans to go out with them. I ran it by Jessica, assuming she'd have no interest in joining, but she quickly agreed to come. As we got dressed, I started stressing about the ring. Obviously, she couldn't leave it on, but I really didn't want to risk an argument by asking her to take it off. Thankfully, as soon as she'd combed her silky, long hair, she slid the ring off and stuck it in a drawer.

"All ready," she said, her voice casual.

I bit my lip as she spun around to face me. She was wearing a short black skirt and flimsy shirt that revealed an inch of her hips above the skirt. It was so sexy and yet so not her style.

"Where did you get that outfit?"

She blushed. "Claire picked it out. Do I look okay?" She turned towards the mirror with uncertainty.

"Jessica, you look sexy as hell. I don't think you can even go out in public like this without hoards of men flocking to you." I stepped up behind her and wrapped my arms around her waist, my heart fluttering as I made contact with the strip of bare skin of her midriff. I tilted my head towards her neck, breathing in the feminine, fruity smell of whatever crap she used to make her hair so shiny and soft, then brushed the hair out of my way and planted a slow, soft kiss on her warm flesh.

She squirmed against me, clearly ticklish, and I released her, solely out of concern that I would attempt to lean her over the dresser right now and have my way with her.

The bar where we were meeting the guys was close, so we walked. Jessica had met these guys before, and normally I didn't worry about her holding her own while I chatted it up with people, but tonight I stayed close to her side. She was still fragile after her whole ordeal, and she wasn't used to drinking a lot. Mostly, though, I knew I just didn't want her out of my sight while she was dressed like that.

She was drinking vodkas with cranberry juice, which, thankfully, I convinced the bartender to make extremely week, and she was sipping them, not chugging. But as she polished off the second one and sent me to get a third, it was obvious she was looking for a total release tonight. I couldn't blame her. After everything she'd been through, it was a wonder she hadn't tried to get wasted every night.

I sat at the bar with one of my former brothers chatting about their fall schedule and starting to feel the tiniest bit of nostalgia for the frat house that would soon be filling with all my friends while I was still here in Chicago. Jessica left her drink with me and went to the bathroom with some girl one of the guys was dating. Just as I started to worry that she'd been gone too long, I spotted the girls in the center of the dance floor.

As I watched Jessica singing the lyrics to the song while dancing, the relief was overwhelming. She finally seemed back to normal. That girl—the one smiling and dancing without the slightest concern for what others thought of her—that was my Jessica. Every aspect of the moment felt like before, well, except for the drinking. I had only seen Jessica drunk once before, and this seemed to qualify.

Just then, she stumbled to the bar and reached for my hand. "What are you doing? You can't just watch, you've gotta dance!"

I barely had time to set my beer on the bar before she dragged me back to the dance floor. She looped her arms around my neck and swayed back and forth to the music. Her smile was contagious, but it wasn't like I stood a chance anyway. Every guy in the club was drooling over her just from sight alone, and I was close enough to be overwhelmed by her tantalizing scent and the touch of her silky shirt, smooth skin and soft hair.

I leaned closer to say something, but before I could speak, she kissed me. It was a short, sloppy kiss, but it was enough to drive me wild.

"You're drunk," I said, when she pulled away.

She shrugged and squeezed my butt with both hands. "Maybe.

But you're hot," she said, her big brown eyes sparkling.

I laughed. Jessica swiveled around so her back was to me, pulling my arms around her waist, grinding against me as she moved to the music. I kissed the side of her neck and let my mouth linger beside her warm, salty skin.

"Are you ready to get out of here?" I asked when I knew I couldn't stand it any longer.

She grabbed my hand. "I thought you'd never ask."

The walk back to my apartment was too short to sober her up any, and by the time we reached my room, Jessica was all over me. She pulled my shirt over my head and I leaned her against the door, kissing her until my lips started to tingle with numbness. I stepped back slightly, and she unzipped her skirt, letting it fall to the floor.

I was already breathless and my entire body ached for her, so I followed suit with my pants. She smiled, giving me all the reassurance I needed. I pressed her into the bed and slid my hand over her legs, relishing every inch of her smooth, bare thighs, before working my way up the front of her shirt and over her breasts.

A slight moan escaped her lips as my fingers grazed across her lacy bra. I kissed her harder, then paused with my face less than an inch from hers. "I love you," I said. For some reason, I'd been certain she'd say it back. But she didn't.

Instead, she nudged me off of her and climbed on top of me, her gorgeous bare legs straddling mine.

"You are so sexy," I murmured, and she smiled. I sat up part way to kiss her, but she quickly pushed me back onto the bed, still kissing me. After a moment, she sat up again and slipped her own shirt over her head.

I swear I felt my pupils dilate as my heart skipped a beat. I'd seen Jessica in various states of undress over the years, but never this close, in nothing but a lacy bra and skimpy thong. It was the most beautiful vision I'd ever experienced. I wished she'd stay still longer, just to let me enjoy the moment, since I knew within a matter of minutes this would all be a memory and I'd never again get to enjoy the first time with her.

Instead, she leaned over me again, her kisses growing more frantic. Her mouth worked its way down to my chest before returning to my neck. I returned the favor, licking, kissing, and sucking at her neck. She squirmed and smiled, still ticklish, I realized. I reached for her breasts again and she moaned.

I placed my hands on her hips and slowly slid them around to her back and under her bra strap to unfasten it. Suddenly, Jessica arched away, her entire body tensed.

I froze.

She climbed off of me and backed slowly away to the corner of the bed, silently.

I sat up, totally confused. "Jessica? What's wrong?"

A second later, I heard a whimper and realized she was crying. I crawled towards her and pulled her in for a hug. She clutched at the covers, wrapping the blanket around her.

"Are you okay? Did I do something?"

"I'm sorry," she mumbled, crying and shaking.

I sighed and squeezed my eyes shut, willing my body to relax since it was now clear that nothing was going to happen.

I waited until she stopped trembling before asking a second time what was wrong.

"Nothing," she said. "I'm fine."

"Yeah, clearly," I replied, unable to keep the annoyance out of my tone. "It's cool, Jessica, I'm fine, too. Thanks for asking."

"I said I was sorry."

I sighed, feeling like a complete jerk already. "I know. I didn't mean that. I just want to know what's wrong. One second you were all over me and the next you're completely repulsed by my touch."

"I'm sorry," she repeated.

"Me too," I said, standing and grabbing an extra blanket. "I need to cool off. I'm going to take a shower and then crash on the couch."

"Please don't," she said, her voice panicky.

"Don't what—shower?"

"Don't leave me," she said.

I sat reluctantly at the foot of the bed. "I just need to understand, Jessica. I feel like you're sending me mixed signals, and it's killing me." I thought about everything for a minute. "Jessica, you know how much I want you. So when you act like you feel the same way and then..." I sighed, then tried a different route. "I don't think you really want to marry me."

"Lucas, I didn't mean to make you feel that way. I just need some time."

"Are you sure that's all? Because you don't have to marry me, you know. You can choose not to be with Aiden or me. I'll still let you stay here. I'll still keep you safe. Hell, I'll even still snuggle with you at night. But you've got to be honest with me. Stop getting my hopes up for nothing."

She was quiet for an unusually long time. "I do want to marry you. I swear I'd tell you if I'd changed my mind."

I should've found her response reassuring, but I didn't. "Jess, you do realize if you're going to marry me, you'll have to sleep with me eventually, right? I mean, I can overlook the fact that you don't really cook or clean, but I'm not cool with a chaste marriage. This is my first, and hopefully only, engagement, and yet it's the longest I've gone without sex since high school. That isn't right."

"I just need time, Lucas."

I nodded, not that she could see me in the dark. I already felt like a total dick, but I had a right to know what was going on in her head. I climbed back into bed. "Come on," I said quietly.

She slowly crawled back beside me and curled against my chest. I sighed and waited for her breathing to slow down, signaling she was asleep.

CHAPTER FIFTEEN

The next morning, my phone buzzed with a text just as I was waking. I'd only been back in the US for two days, and I'd flown straight into Los Angeles for a meeting, so my sleep was on an even more erratic schedule than usual. I glanced down at the text with measured disinterest but fully roused when I saw it came from Lucas.

All it said was, "We need to talk."

I sat abruptly, my stomach lurching. What could have happened to Jessica? She was supposed to be safe with Lucas. I clicked to call him immediately. While the phone rang, I stood and paced the floor anxiously. It went to voice mail, and I hung up, barely resisting the urge to leave an irate message. Instead I typed back a quick reply.

"Is Jessica okay?" I asked.

"Yes," came his reply.

I started to relax, then realized it might not be him replying. Why hadn't he answered when I'd called if he was readily available to text. "How do you know?" I asked, followed quickly by "Why didn't you answer my call?"

"She's asleep right next to me, so I can't talk now. But we need to talk later. I have some questions. I don't know what the time difference is wherever you are so tell me a time when we can talk and I'll get out of the apartment then."

My stomach didn't feel much better at the thought of Jessica sleeping beside Lucas, but I tried to ignore the unsettled feeling and focus on the rest of his message. I was flying out in a few hours, so honestly now was about the only time I could talk until my flight landed. I was about to tell him that when I rethought the whole plan.

"I'm in LA now, flying back to the Midwest tonight. Let's meet and talk in person tomorrow. 3 p.m.?"

His response took longer than the last texts, but he finally replied. It said, "Okay, but you're just seeing me, not Jessica."

"Fine," I replied. "Text me the location."

He replied with an address, and I went to tell Elgin the change in plans.

THE NEXT AFTERNOON, I WAS SEATED AT A BURGER RESTAURANT near the Chicago River. I spotted Lucas approaching and quickly noted he looked the same as always, though perhaps a little more muscled than I remembered. He was smirking as he approached, which didn't surprise me. He nodded as he saw me, then sat.

"Is she okay?" I asked, not trusting his earlier response via text.

"Yeah."

The casual tenor of his voice made me question his intentions in meeting me. A waiter approached and Lucas ordered a burger and fries.

"Did you just call me to gloat?"

"No," he said, sipping his water. "But I guess that means your creepy bodyguard shared the happy news with you?"

"Don't expect me to congratulate you."

"I wouldn't dream of it."

"I can't say I was completely shocked," I admitted, instantly regretting saying it aloud. "She kept that ring with her all spring. It was like she was just waiting for me to give her a reason to leave."

"She told you about the ring?"

I shook my head. "No, actually. But I saw it."

"Ouch," he said with a smirk.

I glared at him. "I told you before, it was always Jessica's choice. What I want is for her to be happy."

Lucas frowned.

"What?"

"I just find it hard to believe that you even care about her happiness. You clearly scarred her for life."

"Elgin said she seemed like her normal self."

"Elgin was wrong. Nothing about her is normal lately, and that's why I wanted to talk to you."

"What do you mean? What's wrong with her?" I tried to hide the panic in my voice, but I almost didn't care.

He shrugged. "She's not herself. She doesn't eat. She's always tired. And she has these nightmares, where she wakes up screaming. She'll seem totally normal for a few hours and then just start crying or freaking out." He paused. "She started shaking when I touched her back last night."

"So help her feel better," I snapped, nauseated by the thought of him touching her. The only thing worse than knowing she chose Lucas to comfort her was the realization that he wasn't taking care of her like I would.

"I'm trying, but I don't even know what happened," he said.

"She didn't tell you?"

Lucas shook his head then lowered his voice. "She told me what you did. How you… killed those guys. She's terrified of you now, you know."

I winced. "You would've done the same thing."

"You don't know me."

"After what they did to Jessica, they're lucky I made it quick," I said.

"What did they do?"

I shook my head. "If Jessica wanted you to know, she'd tell you."

A long, exaggerated sigh escaped his lips. "I can't help her if I don't know what happened. I've been trying, but it's clearly not working. She needs to talk to someone."

"Then find her someone to talk to."

"Like a shrink? Sure, she can tell them how some elves ruined her life. I bet the doc will be really sympathetic, I mean, after they hospitalize her for being completely insane."

I took a deep breath. He seemed to have a point. I glanced around to make sure no one was within earshot, then leaned forward. "First off, it wasn't supposed to happen like that. We were trying to work out a clandestine deal that would convince the other clans to leave our people alone even if I took Jessica as my wife. No one was supposed to hurt her." I shook my head. "It was supposed to be the solution to all of our problems, a way that I could still be with Jessica without abandoning the throne."

"So what went wrong?"

I paused as the waiter brought Lucas' food. As soon as we were alone again, I continued.

"We thought we were setting them up, and they fell into our trap all right, but then they played us like fools. They tricked me and our other senior officials into leaving with most of the security force and while we were gone and distracted, they took her."

"What do you mean 'took her'? Jessica?"

"Yes, Jessica." I was growing annoyed by his thick-headedness. "They kidnapped and tortured her. It took us over two days to get to her."

Lucas looked nauseous. "Why didn't you call me?"

"There was nothing you could have done. I had all of my men on it. Obviously."

He swallowed audibly. "What do you mean by torture?"

I inhaled sharply. "They were experimenting about the effects of elf blood. They would," I paused to search for the right word. "They did different things to hurt her to see how the blood would heal her."

Lucas pushed his hamburger away. The expression on his face told me I was correct, that he would've reacted exactly as I had. Somehow, that didn't make me feel any better, though.

"What did they do?" he asked.

I shrugged. "They started small, cigarette burns, shallow flesh wounds, then they moved on to bigger things. They..." Even remembering it was making me sick. "When we found her, her entire back was cut up, like they were carving it slowly."

"Her back," he repeated. "She doesn't like being touched on her back, on the bare skin."

I tried to ignore the implications of Lucas' statement about her bare skin. "Why would Elgin say it was all healed if it weren't?"

"There is nothing on her back. She doesn't even have scars. I checked."

I swallowed my disgust at the image popping into my mind of Lucas poring over Jessica's body searching for clues to her injuries.

"Good," I mumbled finally.

"Just because the cuts have healed doesn't mean she has," Lucas snapped.

I frowned. If he was trying to make me feel guilty, it was unnecessary. I was acutely aware that I was responsible for all of her pain, that I was the one to blame for everything.

I sighed. "I'm well aware this was my fault, Lucas. As is Jessica," I added.

Lucas raised an eyebrow. "She knows it was your shitty plan that landed her in that mess?"

I nodded, then clarified, "But that wasn't how the plan was supposed to go. If it hadn't gone horribly awry, she would've been fine. I never authorized anyone to hurt her. I said they could come to my house in London with their own medical personnel and draw her blood samples and test them independently. That's it."

Lucas stared at me for a long, hard moment. "Do you know how many times she got hurt because of you?"

"Yes," I said. As if I could somehow stop replaying each horrific incident in my mind. As if I wasn't overwhelmed with disgust every time I even looked at myself after what Jessica had gone through because of me.

"You still love her, don't you?" Lucas' tone suggested he was confirming the fact, not accusing me of everything.

"I'm not going to try to get her back, if that's what you're worried about."

"But you still love her," he said.

I sighed again. "Yes. I will probably always love her. I don't think I will ever love anyone the way I loved her." I paused. I omitted the fact that, since I had to marry someone else in less than a year to take the throne, it was best that I not worry about love ever again anyway. "But I assure you I will leave her alone. You won her fair and square. I screwed things up for her too many times. I had so many chances and…" I shook my head. "She's better off with you."

Lucas took a long sip of his drink, still eying me warily. "The thing is, I distinctly remember telling you that I would kill you if you ever hurt her again. And here you are, admitting you did just that."

I chuckled.

He cocked his head to the side. "You think that's funny? I don't even think you'd defend yourself. You wouldn't touch a hair on my head because you know anything bad you do to me would just hurt Jessica more."

"You have a good point, Lucas. But unfortunately, I have two bodyguards within twenty yards of me at all times, and they don't share my concerns about protecting you for Jessica's sake. If you touch me, they'll crush you like a bug before you even have a chance to inflict an injury that'll take me more than an hour to heal."

He smiled. "Well, you can call off the dogs. I wasn't going to try anything anyway. If you love Jessica like you say you do, I think living without her, and knowing what you did to her, is more punishment than I could dish out anyway."

With that, he stood up and left.

He was correct, of course. And as I sat there lamenting all the questions I didn't get answered, I realized he didn't have the slightest idea how truly miserable I was.

JESSICA

"Look, Jess, I feel like a complete jerk about the other night," Lucas said shortly after returning home from a mysterious errand with a massive bunch of flowers.

I gazed at the excessively large bouquet again and nodded. "Clearly."

"I didn't mean to make you feel bad for not having sex with me or to guilt you into doing it."

I smiled politely, unsure of how to respond.

"I wasn't mad because you stopped," he continued. "The thing is, I want you to want me."

I giggled now, the song lyrics instantly popping into my head. He rolled his eyes.

"You've got to understand, though, Jess, I've been fantasizing about sleeping with you for a decade now. When we got that close and then stopped, it threw me for a loop, I guess." He paused. "If you need to wait longer, fine. I get that. But I got the impression you didn't want to sleep with me. And I guess I'm really not okay with that."

"Lucas, everyone wants to sleep with you."

"You're not everyone."

I raised an eyebrow but didn't answer.

He sat down. "Okay, so am I forgiven or not?"

"There's nothing to forgive."

"I was an insensitive prick."

"I'm hard to put up with sometimes," I replied.

He seemed to consider this. "Well, I have a confession then. I saw Aiden today."

"Why? Where? How?" I was so confused. I hadn't even known Aiden was back in the country.

"I'm sorry for going around you, but I knew you didn't want to see him and I couldn't think of any other way to find out what happened to you."

"Wait, so you called him?"

"I asked him to meet me."

I felt tears forming in my eyes again and I squeezed them away. I wanted to be pissed now, not weepy. "I would've told you myself when I was ready."

"When would that have been? Jessica, I'm trying to help you, but I don't feel like I am. I thought if I knew that I could…"

I glared at him. "What? Tell me, Lucas. Now that you know what happened, how do we fix this? Go ahead. Make me feel better. I'm waiting."

He didn't say anything, so I stood up. I turned to leave when suddenly Lucas grabbed me and pulled me close. "I'm sorry, Jessica."

I let him hold me until I stopped feeling angry at him. I didn't know what I felt about anything anymore. I started to pull away and he stopped me.

"What?" I asked.

"I would have killed them too," he said.

I wasn't sure why he told me that, since I already knew that. Maybe he wanted me to know he wasn't that different from Aiden, even if that wasn't in his best interest for me to realize. But he was different from Aiden. And Lucas hadn't killed them. Aiden had. And if I'd been with Lucas all along, none of it would have happened.

I caught Lucas staring at me. "You okay?"

I nodded.

"Are you hungry yet?"

I shook my head.

He was clearly exasperated. "You have to start eating again someday, okay?"

I was tempted to make a wisecrack about him needing to decide which was more important to him, me eating or having sex, but I refrained.

Lucas

After I told Jessica about my meeting with Aiden, she spent the rest of the afternoon on her own, staring at the same page in a book she was pretending to read. I gave her a couple hours to regroup, but then approached her again. I needed to get to the bottom of everything that was bothering her before I forgot everything I had learned from Aiden.

A smarter man would've just let it drop, but I had to know, had to understand her logic. I personally thought the fact that Aiden's life put her in a position where she could even be kidnapped and tortured was more than enough reason to dump the man and never look back. But what I didn't understand was why now? What had happened to drive Jessica to reach that conclusion now when she hadn't before? She'd already told me that she was kidnapped and shot once before—because of him. Frankly, that sounded more horrifying than this ordeal, and yet that whole thing had somehow brought her back into his arms. Then, when his fiancée's family tried to—again—kidnap her, and Jessica ended up breaking her arm, she once again forgave Aiden.

So why now? Was the third time he nearly got her killed truly the charm?

"Jess, I'm sorry for bringing this up again, but I need to understand. You told me about all the other times you were hurt because of Aiden, but each of those times you forgave him. How can you be so certain you'll never forgive him now?"

She fiddled with the engagement ring I'd given her, apparently understanding why I was curious. "I just am. But it's a moot point anyway," she said. "Even if I forgave Aiden, he doesn't want me back."

I tried to hide my shock. Was that seriously what she thought? Had she stayed with me most of the summer just because she didn't realize she could have him? "What makes you think that?"

She shrugged.

"Jessica, he still loves you. He actually said he'd never love anyone the way he loved you." I cringed at my own confession as I saw her expression soften.

"He did not."

"Yes, he did."

"Well, it doesn't matter. He made it very clear that if he had to choose between his kingdom and me, it wouldn't be me."

"He gave me the impression he wouldn't have to choose." I shook my head, hating that I felt compelled to tell her all this. But I couldn't relax with Jessica until I was positive she was over Aiden. "And I think you're wrong. I think he would choose you. I sure would," I added.

"Yes, you would," she agreed easily. "That, I believe. But Aiden, no. He had the chance, and he didn't choose me. I don't think I could forgive him for what he did anyway."

"Because he..." I hesitated, "killed those guys?"

"No. I'm glad they're dead. It was terrifying to see. I never—I never realized there was that side to Aiden, I guess. I wish someone else had done it and that I wasn't there. But no, I'm not the angelic girl you think I am. I wanted them dead."

"I'm glad they're dead, too," I added. But now I was even more confused. "Then tell me what Aiden did that was so unforgivable because, from talking with him, it seemed like he had mostly clean hands in all of this."

Jessica crossed her arms in front of her chest. "Why are you so determined to make me like him?"

I paused, wishing I knew. On some level, I accepted that I was just a good guy and I wanted her to be happy. In an ideal world, she'd be happy with me, and we'd have tons of sex, but if that wasn't going to happen, I still wanted her to be happy. I couldn't deny the way Aiden looked when he'd talked about her. That dude was miserable. And as much as I hated losing, if I was going to lose, I'd like it to be to someone who loved her at least as much as I did.

But even more than that, I needed reassurance. If she really chose me, I needed to know it was because she wanted me, not because of some misunderstanding with her ex.

"Stop changing the subject," I said.

"I thought he told you what happened," she retorted.

"He did. But I want to hear from you what exactly he did that you can never forgive."

She swung her feet back to the ground and turned to look me in the eye. "Lucas, he let those guys hurt me. I saw the paper that authorized them to test my blood. He signed it."

"He didn't mean for you to get hurt. He told me that, Jessica."

She shook her head, and I saw more tears in her eyes. "It was his stupid idea. All of it. He may not have wanted me to get hurt initially, but he was the one who decided it was okay. He realized the only way to keep his stupid job without having to let me go was to ship me off to a group of psychopathic terrorists. He was the one who did it without even telling me."

She paused to catch her breath before continuing, her voice growing louder and more disjointed with each word. "I trusted him and he let me be flown across the Atlantic in a cargo hold, chained to the floor and wondering if I was going to be left for dead when they finished torturing me. He didn't even warn me. He treated me like a piece of property and then acted like I should just get over it once the scars were gone."

"Jessica," I whispered, pulling her close. She'd gone quickly from calmly obstinate, to softly weeping, to full-blown sobs. Although hearing her perspective of what she'd gone through was so gut-wrenching that I nearly cried, too. "Jessica, is that what you've thought all this time?"

She kept crying in lieu of answering.

"Jessica, if he let those guys do that, why would he then kill them?"

She didn't answer.

"Seriously. If they were just doing what he told them to do, why would he kill them?"

"Because he's a violent psychopath," she replied.

I squeezed her even harder, then released, worried I'd actually break her if I held her any tighter. "Jessica, you have to talk to Aiden. I don't think...you're not going to get over this until you stop blaming him. You're never going to be able to trust anyone again until you realize he didn't mean to hurt you."

"But he did," she said. "He said he loved me, then he hurt me."

"No, Jessica. I saw his face when he was talking about this, when he told me that he agreed to let them come to his house and draw a blood sample and that was all. He never meant for them to take you or to hurt you. I really don't think he was lying."

"His father told me he signed off on it," she said. "And even if he hadn't, he left me. I was unconscious and still in shock and he ditched me at some random family friend's house in Tennessee and flew back to London without even telling me."

I frowned. "That just doesn't make sense. You've got to talk to him and try to figure it all out. At least call the guy."

She seemed to consider this, then shook her head. "I couldn't tell anything over the phone. I can't read people without seeing their eyes."

"Okay."

"And I don't want to see him in person. It might, I don't know. It might bring up all the bad memories."

"Are you scared of him still?"

She shook her head. "No. I never thought he'd hurt me himself. It just, well, terrified me to know that he would use me as a pawn."

"But I don't think he did, Jessica."

"It doesn't matter," she mumbled.

I wished I agreed with her, but, from my vantage point, Jessica's chances of recovering from this betrayal—whether perceived or actual—did not look good. And the fact that the person she thought had betrayed her was the last man who claimed to love her…well, I had to assume that wasn't good news for her ability to trust me or any other man in love with her.

CHAPTER SIXTEEN

JESSICA

I slept terribly that night, waking twice, drenched in sweat and shaking. Lucas seemed surprised that I was awake, but not the slightest bit shocked that I was having such awful dreams. I hadn't realized how often, or how bad, they'd been, and now that I did, I felt guilty for disrupting his sleep when he needed it so much.

I still couldn't figure out why he was so concerned that I was wrongly blaming Aiden for his role in the hell I'd been through, but somehow his attempts to lead me back to Aiden were actually making me feel more connected to Lucas. Lucas was being so sweet and so patient with me that it really made me wish I felt ready to be the kind of fiancée he deserved.

On Monday, I decided to take a small step in that direction. I called my grandma, and while I didn't come clean about most things, I did casually mention that Aiden and I weren't dating anymore and that I'd been talking with Lucas a lot since I left. Then I took it one step further and told her that my return flight was scheduled to land in Chicago and that I planned to spend a couple days with Lucas before driving home with him. She accepted it all in stride, so I was confident that when I did see her in a couple of weeks, I could tell her Lucas and I were dating, and then shortly into the semester I could fess up that we were engaged.

Lucas returned home later than usual Monday, having stayed after practice for a massage. He seemed pleased when I recapped my phone call with my grandma to him, and then he insisted he had had an epiphany during his massage.

"I think one would help you, too," he insisted, clearly ignoring the skepticism I was sure my face revealed. "How do you feel about a massage?"

I grimaced, the thought of some stranger touching me horrifying.

"No, sorry, not a professional one. I mean, would you let me give you a massage?"

I considered this, and didn't find anything too offensive, so I agreed.

"Good. I'm going to go take another extremely long shower so I'm less likely to molest you later, and you should eat something. Anything, okay? Then we'll meet up in my room."

I laughed at his shower comment, but nodded.

A half hour later, Lucas called me into his room. He had changed into a pair of khaki shorts after his shower and his dark hair still glistened with moisture. Candles were lit and music was playing softly in the background. The overhead light was off, but he'd left a lamp on so the room wasn't too dark. A bottle of massage oil sat on the nightstand.

"Wow, you actually put some planning into this," I said. Then I hesitated, "Unless you just happened to have this stuff on hand."

He laughed. "Yeah, right. I nearly stole the candles just to avoid having to face the cashier and pay for them. I'm pretty sure I've officially lost all street cred."

I smiled.

"Okay, so technically you're supposed to strip down to your underwear. But you can start however you feel comfortable."

I hesitated.

"No funny business, I promise. But the oils could stain your clothes," he said.

I cautiously stepped out of my shorts, feeling surprisingly comfortable with him watching me. Then I unfastened my bra and slipped it off without removing my tank top. I sensed some disappointment on his part when he realized I wasn't taking my shirt off, but he hid it well, instead motioning for me to lay down on my back.

He threw a blanket over my stomach and arms then crouched by my legs.

"Close your eyes," he instructed.

I heard him pour the oil onto his hands and jumped a little as he touched my legs. He froze for a moment before beginning to rub it in. "Okay?" he asked.

"Yes."

"Do you remember the sixth grade camping trip when we snuck away from the group and ended up getting poison ivy?"

I smiled. "You mean the time when you tricked me into leaving, got us totally lost, then tripped and knocked me into the patch of poison ivy? Yeah, I remember."

Lucas laughed. "Is that what happened? Hmm. Anyway, that was fun." He started to massage my arms. "What about the canoe trip in seventh grade?"

"You flipped our canoe."

"But then I saved you," he said.

"True. And you went back for my shoe."

"I was quite the hero," he teased.

We reminisced for a few more minutes before he asked me to flip onto my stomach. I complied, and he began massaging the backs of my legs.

"I think we should build a tree house someday," he said. "I mean, when we have kids."

I smiled, remembering all the good times we had shared in his tree house. It had always been my safe place. When I first moved in with my grandma, Lucas had taken me there and told me that he went up in the tree whenever he felt sad or scared. He claimed it really needed a girl's touch. So I had helped him decorate it, in my ten-year old way, and then I went there, too, whenever I was sad.

Sometimes, I'd go there alone, and sometimes, he'd join me. It was like he'd always known when I needed to be by myself and when I could use a friend.

We kept talking, sharing memories of the tree house, and he moved to my arms again. After a few more minutes, he paused.

"Can I take off your shirt?" he asked tentatively. "I'll stop as soon as you want."

My heart pounded nervously, but I agreed. I raised up to my elbows and he carefully lifted my shirt up without touching my skin. I relaxed back onto my stomach and bit my lip nervously.

When his hands first touched my back, every muscle in my body tightened. I forced myself to lie still, reminding myself that it was just Lucas touching me. Breathing deeply, I focused on the sound of his voice. He was still talking about fun times we'd shared in the past, but by now he had reached high school.

"Do you remember how pissed Katie was when I invited you to the homecoming dance?" he asked, jolting me out of my thoughts.

I smiled, remembering it very clearly. Katie, who the whole school knew had a crush on Lucas, was also the captain of the cheerleaders and the school drama queen. She was the homecoming queen and he was the homecoming king, so the whole school was surprised when he didn't take her as his date.

"Why did you do that?"

"Seriously?" He stopped massaging for a moment, kneeling on

the bed beside me to work from a different angle. "Because I wanted to go with you. I liked you."

I considered this. "What do you think would have happened if we'd started dating then?"

"Hmm…you mean instead of you making me wait seven more years and then agreeing to marry me without ever having a real date?"

I smiled.

"What's the fun in that?" He rubbed his hands softly over my back now, kissing me softly between the shoulder blades. "Some things are worth waiting for," he said.

I felt my muscles tighten again as he kept kissing my back. His kisses were gentle and soothing, but I couldn't shake the feeling of vulnerability.

Lucas sensed my discomfort and resumed the massage instead. "I hate that you jump when I touch your back."

I sighed, but before I could answer, he continued.

"I don't mean to be critical, I just wish I could make you comfortable."

"I know. You just want me to want you…and your hands," I said with a giggle.

He didn't answer for a while.

"Can I ask you something?" he finally said.

"Yes."

"Does it still hurt? Your skin looks perfect, but I didn't know…"

"No."

"Why your back? Aiden told me you were…that you had injuries all over, but it seems like your back is the most sensitive."

He was right, although I hadn't really thought about it before. And now, he was rubbing both hands all over my bare skin on my back and I was fine. "I think maybe because I couldn't see. I never knew exactly what they were doing to my back. I could watch the rest, so I saw what it was and could guess how long it would last, how bad it would hurt, but with my back…" I felt tears forming in my eyes.

"Jessica, I'm so sorry," Lucas said, climbing onto the bed beside me. He kept rubbing my back with one hand while resting on his other. "I'm so sorry you went through all that." He pressed his lips firmly into my shoulder, then worked his way slowly down my back.

"You're safe now, Jessica," he said. "And I want you to remember this, from now on, whenever someone touches you, I want you to remember this feeling, me rubbing your back, kissing your perfect skin. I want you to feel safe."

He kissed me more, and I felt something cooler than his lips dampen my skin.

"I love you, Jessica. No one will ever hurt you again," Lucas repeated, and I realized he was crying. "You are safe with me."

"I know, Lucas," I said, rolling to face him. I placed my hand on his cheek and gazed into his damp eyes. They seemed lighter than usual now, more blue than green, and his long eyelashes were clumped with tear drops. I kissed each of his eyes gently, then moved to his mouth, my lips slowly meeting his. His tongue tentatively reached for mine, and we gradually increased the intensity of the kiss.

His hand was still on my back, lightly tickling my skin as he moved with each kiss, but it no longer bothered me, at least for the moment. He slid his hand closer to his body, stopping abruptly when he reached the side of my breast, as though he'd forgotten it was bare.

I opened my eyes and met his intense stare. "I love you, Lucas," I said.

He smiled so wide he could barely keep kissing me. "Oh, Jessica," he murmured. "You are perfect."

I WOKE UP THE NEXT MORNING FEELING COMPLETELY RELAXED AND well-rested, but a bit disoriented. I supposed that was the downside of all the travel we'd done lately. I couldn't remember what day it was or what our plans were. I assumed it was still early, despite the sun peeking in through the cracks between the blinds, since Aiden was always an early riser.

I slowly peeled his arm off my waist and rolled towards him to glance at the clock. I jumped when I saw that it was Lucas, and not Aiden, draped over me like a blanket. I froze again, hoping my sudden movement hadn't awoken him. Clearly I needed to gather my bearings before talking with him.

Luckily, Lucas was still asleep. But as I gazed at his peaceful face, it all rushed back to me like a flood. I smiled at the realization that I'd gone several minutes without remembering the awful things I'd been through lately, and I wondered how long it would be until I could keep those memories at bay for an entire morning. I trusted it would get easier with time, but for some reason, it was the first day I'd even seen the potential to someday feel peaceful again. Obviously, that was Lucas' doing. His patience and his love for me had fixed whatever was broken inside.

I snuggled closer to his arm and exhaled slowly with a smile. I meant what I'd said the night before. I did love Lucas. I was certain I would always love him. And now that I'd accepted it, something about that awareness was extremely comforting.

I just wished I knew how long it would take before I no longer felt the same way about Aiden.

Lucas

I'd had a really good night with Jessica. I could tell we'd made some progress at working through all the shit that had been bogging her down lately, and she'd told me she loved me. Not in the friend sort of way she'd said it before, but in the actual romantic partner for life sort of way. So yeah, I was in a pretty awesome mood at practice the next morning.

Jessica had texted that she was by the pool, so when I got home, I changed into my swim trunks and went to find her. The rooftop pool wasn't too crowded, but even if it had been, I'd have spotted her right away. She was stretched out on her stomach on a lawn chair, a dark brown bikini the only thing covering her skin. Her eyes were closed, so I stared at her perfect, perky ass for much longer than otherwise would've been appropriate. Then I adjusted my swim trunks and approached her slowly, careful not to startle her.

When she saw my feet she smiled and turned. My eyes drifted down to her breasts, which were tumbling out of the top of her bikini. I swallowed audibly and Jessica giggled.

"You've seen me in a bathing suit before, Lucas," she said, gesturing for me to sit in the chair beside her.

"Yes," I agreed, but the last time, I couldn't picture exactly how soft the skin on the sides of her breasts truly was. And I didn't know what she tasted like or how smooth her lips felt against mine.

"Lucas?" Jessica cleared her throat.

"Yep. Sorry. Just thinking about your ass again," I said with a grin.

She swatted me playfully and sat up, offering me sunscreen. I nodded and let her massage the lotion into my back and shoulders.

"I could return the favor," I offered.

"I'm good, thanks," she said.

We sat beside the pool and talked for a while, then got in the pool and played. Seeing Jessica frolic and relax in the water was refreshing. Everything felt normal and calm. Then she paused by the edge of the pool and offered me a strange half smile. I was about to kiss her, when she spoke.

"I think you're right about Aiden," she said.

My stomach muscles clenched.

"I want to put everything with him behind me, completely, but I just have so many questions still, and I think it'll be easier for me to move on once I have answers."

"So you want to call him or go see him?"

"I need to talk to him in person. I just can't read people over the phone. If he's going to lie to me, well, let him lie to my face."

I nodded. "Okay." I looked at her expression, trying to decipher whether she was trying to break off our "engagement" or what, and I came up blank.

Finally, she spoke. "Lucas, is that okay? It was your idea, so I just thought…"

"Yeah, no, you should go."

She nodded, then started to climb out of the pool. I followed and we towel-dried ourselves in silence.

"Will you call him?" she asked suddenly. "To set it up?"

I must have look confused, because she explained.

"I'm sorry if that puts you in a weird position. But I don't want him to get the wrong idea about things. I just want some answers so I can stop replaying it all in my head. I don't care whether he still has feelings for me or not, so I don't want him even trying anything."

"Oh," I said, realizing I had been completely misinterpreting things. "Do you want me to come with you?"

She considered this for a minute. "That might be awkward."

I agreed, but I wasn't too thrilled about leaving her alone with him either.

"Have him meet me someplace busy and public. And tell him not to touch me at all." She shook her head. "The last thing I need is to get totally freaked out and scream like a crazy woman in public."

It felt weird to call Aiden, but I did it. I would've preferred texting, but the guy had completely panicked the last time I'd done that, assuming something was wrong with Jessica. I hoped he wouldn't answer, but, of course, he did.

We cut through the preliminaries pretty quickly and I told him Jessica was willing to talk with him. Before he could get too excited, I clarified.

"She has no interest in getting back together with you. She asked me to set this up and she told me to set the ground rules."

"Ground rules?" he repeated.

"Yes. All she needs to hear is the stuff you told me. She still thinks she was some pawn in an elaborate scheme you arranged and it's really messing with her head to think that someone could actually do that to another person."

"But I…"

"Don't interrupt," I chastised. "I don't need to hear it so save it all for her. Keep it brief and to the point. She doesn't need all the emotional mumbo jumbo and you're not allowed to hit on her, flirt with her, or touch her at all. No hugging, not a pat on the hand, nothing. Got it?"

Aiden chuckled.

"I'm dead serious, Aiden. Jessica finally seems more like herself and if you come on all strong and fuck with her head again, I will kill you, guards or no guards."

He agreed, and we settled on the details.

CHAPTER SEVENTEEN

AIDEN

I saw Jessica approaching from over a block away and couldn't help but stand as she drew closer. She froze, several feet away, and stared back at me. Her expression was blank, but her heart was racing. At first, that reassured me—her pulse was always through the roof when we were intimate or even kissing. But then, I realized that fear had the same effect on her. I sat, concerned I was too intimidating on my feet.

She inched closer, still gazing at me with uncertainty, then took her seat.

I nudged the large drink across the table to her. "It's that strawberry tea with coconut milk you used to like," I said, although the Pepto-Bismol color of the beverage had probably already told her that. She accepted it, but didn't sip any. I wondered if she still liked it. Maybe she had a whole new summer drink now and I didn't even know. I considered the millions of other things that had probably changed in her life that I was now completely unaware of.

"I would hug you, but Lucas gave me some pretty strict ground rules," I said, hoping to put her at ease. She looked decidedly tired, but that didn't make sense since Lucas claimed she slept all the time. She'd definitely lost weight, too, and not in a good way. Her tee shirt looked baggy on her and gave me a sense that she was frail, which had never been the way I'd seen her before.

"Are you doing okay?" I asked after another long pause. "I know you've been...I mean, I talked to Lucas. He seemed concerned about you. I hope he's taking good care of you, and..."

"He is," she interrupted, her eyes narrowing.

I inhaled slowly, savoring her still-familiar scent, but with a sense of depressing nostalgia. Seeing her in front of me, the loss was overwhelming. I had been missing her for weeks, mourning her absence from my life every waking moment. I'd assumed being near her would ease the pain. Instead, it was worse. It was a sharp reminder of what I'd done, and of how much I'd lost.

"You're returning to school in the fall?" I asked.

She nodded.

"But Lucas—he's..."

"He signed with the Blackhawks. He's already begun training with them."

"So he's not finishing school," I concluded. Her face twitched and I instantly regretted being so nosy. It wasn't my business what Lucas was doing. Although I wondered how he would take care of her when he was traveling all around the country playing hockey. And surely there were still hoards of women fawning over him.

"He's taking classes this summer via correspondence. His plan is to take more next summer. That will give him enough credits to graduate. The school is letting him finish that way, given the circumstances." She licked her lips anxiously. "He only has a one-year contract for now, and then he's technically a free agent, but as long as he plays well, he thinks they'll keep him around and give him a longer contract once he proves himself."

I wasn't sure what to say to that. I had known Lucas was the star player at our large university, but it hadn't occurred to me that he was professional-athlete good. I wasn't sure how I felt about that.

Jessica raised her hand to her mouth and timidly nibbled the tip of her thumbnail. I frowned, never having known her to be a nail biter before. Noticing my disapproval, she quickly moved her hand to her cup. She slowly lifted it and wrapped her lips around the straw. I watched her sip, mesmerized for a full minute. Then I realized she was keeping her other hand—her left hand—wedged firmly between her knees. I opened my mouth to ask if she was injured, then remembered what she was actually hiding—the ring. The symbol that she no longer belonged to me, that she had moved on, whereas I likely never would.

That depressing thought reminded me of my actual purpose in seeing her today. It wasn't just to torture myself, although clearly it was having that effect. I was here for her, to make sure she could actually move on fully and not be permanently traumatized by my shortcomings as her boyfriend.

"I'll get to the point," I said. "Lucas said you were…frightened."

Her face remained expressionless.

"I know what they did to you. I mean, I realize I don't understand what it was like for you, how terrifying and how painful, and I hate that. But I know generally what you went through. And I can't imagine it's been easy to put that behind you. I can't change what happened," I shook my head and gazed at the sky, exhaling hard. "God knows I would do anything to be able to go back and do things differently—to keep you safe, but I can't."

I paused and sipped my almost-empty coffee before continuing. "I'm not going to sit here and pretend like it wasn't my fault, because it was. I'll live with that guilt for the rest of my life. If I hadn't gone to Russia—if I'd stayed with you that morning. If I'd met up with you after your exam…"

My voice trailed off. I'd gone over the scenarios countless times in my head. There were dozens of instances when I could have made a different choice, followed a different path, and she would've been fine.

I was doing a terrible job of making my point. "You weren't a pawn, Jessica. I never wanted you to get hurt. What happened to you—that hadn't even crossed my mind as a possible result of my actions."

She frowned. "Then what happened?"

"We had done some testing," I began, noting her grimace at the word. "I did sign off on that, but nothing invasive. We took willing human participants and gave them significant quantities of elf blood and then drew samples from them to see how long the elf blood remained in their system. No one was hurt. No one had negative side effects."

I paused, realizing I still hadn't told her what we had figured out, that she was part elf. I'd debated telling her that the last two days, ever since I'd learned I'd have a chance to talk with her, but I kept reaching the same conclusion. There was no reason for her to know. It wouldn't help her move on. It wouldn't make her happier. If anything, it would just confuse her and raise more questions than it answered.

"My father and I decided that if everyone— even Marius — believed you were part Elf, they would accept you as my queen. Then we could marry without it inciting an uprising or civil war, or worse."

"So it's possible then," she interrupted. "For an elf and a human...I mean, if there are part elves..."

I nodded. "Yes. Although not as many studies have been done on the safety or details as I'd like, but it's definitely possible. There was a period in our history where it was greatly opposed, though. There's still a group that doesn't support it."

She sighed, clearly flustered by this revelation. Apparently adequately distracted by my words, she reached for her drink with her left hand. The gleam of the stone caught the sun, reflecting the bright light. I'd seen the ring before, but never on her, of course. I didn't want to gawk, but I couldn't take my eyes off it. She followed my gaze to her hand, blushed, then tucked her hand back under her thigh.

I returned to my story, wishing I could erase from my mind the vision of his ring on her graceful finger. "We didn't want to outright tell the other clans you were part elf because we knew they wouldn't believe us, so we leaked some supposedly private emails and documents discussing it. One of them was the paper showing I'd authorized the testing on you. It wasn't even a real order, though, just something we'd drawn up so it could be intercepted. We knew the other clans would want to do their own independent testing to confirm what we claimed, even if they thought we were planning to keep it a secret. And we weren't sure how soon they'd find our leaked information and move on it, so that's why we started you on the blood right away."

I paused and frowned, nauseated even thinking of the horrific turn of events.

"In my mind, we'd keep you on the high doses of blood for a few days probably, and then they'd come to us, asking for confirmation and we'd be ready. In reality, they came to us immediately, maybe suspecting we had leaked the papers. They wanted to test you right away, before we had a chance to do anything to alter the results. I hadn't planned to fly to Russia early that morning. I wasn't even sure it was about you, but as soon as I got there, it was clear that it was. I thought it was a legit meeting, not a set up. The leader of the eastern clan wanted to send an ambassador back to London with me. He was going to draw your blood when we arrived. It was supposed to happen in our house."

I shook my head and exhaled.

"I had so many times when I wanted to talk to you about it, and we kept missing each other. I was going to ask you before letting him touch you. If you didn't want him to draw your blood, I wouldn't have let him. I was supposed to be there with you, holding your hand." I swallowed hard. "That was what was supposed to happen. That was all I thought would happen."

Jessica cleared her throat. "I don't understand. If what you're saying is true, then what went wrong?"

"Everything. They never intended to test you at our house, under my supervision. They read our leaked papers and knew only that they wanted to kidnap you. The trip to Russia—they didn't need us to go there, especially not all of us. It was a trick to distract us and to make it easier for them to get to you without me or my guards around. It worked."

My breathing sped up and my mouth ran dry. I hated reliving that day, but I had to do it, for her. I told her how we'd questioned the ambassador, that we'd determined he was unaware of his leader's evil plot, and how we'd finally learned where she was and what they were doing. And then I explained that we'd learned their clan's already-cruel plot had been undermined by an even more evil group who hated half-bloods and took it upon themselves to torture her rather than just inflict simple injuries and draw blood.

"Why didn't you just tell me about all of this from the start? What you and Ivar planned to do?"

Why hadn't I? "I don't know. I really don't. Things were just so… strained… between us. I wanted to make you happy and I didn't want to drag you on the rollercoaster of ups and downs when I thought I could get us to a decent solution."

"And after? You let me think…your father told me you authorized what they did!" Her voice raised, and I could tell she was struggling to hold back the tears.

It pained me to see her trying to stay so strong when she was clearly hurting. God, I wanted to touch her. I'd have done anything to be able to hug her and hold her tight until she trusted me and believed everything would be okay. "I didn't know what you thought. I saw that you were frightened of me and I wanted to give you space."

"Aiden, I watched you kill people with your bare hands. And I was disoriented."

I frowned. "What exactly did my father say to you?"

"He said you hadn't meant for them to take things so far, but that I needed to calm down because you were the one who authorized it all and that it made you look bad to have me so worked up." She struggled drawing in her next heavy breath. "He also said that you were out of ideas. He told me that was your last-ditch attempt to help me fit in to your world. He said you had been so stressed and miserable the weeks before because you knew everything would always be a challenge with me in your life. He told me you regretted getting involved with me. He said you were weak and felt guilty and wanted to leave me but didn't have the strength, and that the best thing I could do for you would be to walk away and not look back."

"None of that is true," I said. "I swear it."

She wiped her eyes, that damn ring catching the sunlight again. "You left me and went back to London while I was still in shock. What was I supposed to think?"

I shook my head. "No, I stayed in Tennessee for days after you left, hoping you'd come back. My father told me you wanted me to leave and then, when I did, he said you rushed out to a bus station. He said you'd be better off without me. I didn't mean..." My voice trailed off.

My father had obviously told us both what he wanted us to believe. But at some level, he was right. Our relationship was completely illogical, and I kept hurting her. "I was only thinking of you. I know what I was feeling then couldn't even compare to what you were, but I was a mess. I had been totally lost when you were gone, and the guilt from knowing you were suffering again because of your connection to me...it nearly killed me. I never meant that I wanted you to leave."

She nodded. I couldn't be positive if she believed me, but I hoped.

I was furious. I hadn't known my father had said all of that, but it shouldn't have surprised me. His focus was ensuring a smooth transition in leadership and maintaining our family's role in the empire. Surely he saw what he said to Jessica as a harmless white lie to get her out of my life for good. I didn't doubt my father thought I was better off without Jessica, even though he was clearly sorely mistaken.

"Lucas said you still…loved me."

I tried not to let the shock register on my face. I couldn't believe he'd told her that. "Jessica, I will always love you."

She nodded. "He told me you said that, too. But also that you promised not to try to convince me to come back to you."

"I did. But not because I don't want you. I've been miserable without you."

Her face softened and I wondered if she was noting that this sentiment matched my haggard appearance. "Then why?

"You're better off with Lucas."

She finished her drink and began fidgeting with the cup, knocking the ice from side to side with her straw. I realized we had said everything that needed to be said, but I was stalling, desperate to keep her in my presence longer. I stared at her unabashedly, carefully memorizing each detail of her appearance as this likely would be the last time I'd ever see her.

Finally, I sighed. It wasn't enough. Even if I sat here and stared at her for the rest of the day, the whole week even, I wouldn't have gotten my fill of her and walking away wouldn't be any easier. I needed to just rip off the band-aid.

"I should let you go," I said, before I could talk myself out of it. She seemed surprised by my statement but didn't protest. She scooted her chair back slowly.

"Jessica," I said as she started to stand. "I really do want you to be happy. I need to know that you're going to be happy."

She gazed at me sadly. "I will be," she said, her voice not altogether lacking in conviction. "And you deserve to be happy, too.

You're a good man." She picked up her cup and turned abruptly, tossing it in a nearby waste bin before slowly walking down the street. I watched her until she turned the corner, then stared down at my empty coffee cup, wishing it were filled with liquor.

JESSICA

I wandered around downtown for over an hour before heading back to Lucas' apartment. If I had my own place, I probably would've just gone straight home, crawled in bed, and bawled my eyes out until a day or two had passed and I started to feel better. As it turned out, though, the fresh—albeit humid—air and exercise were somewhat cathartic.

I tried to convince myself everything I'd learned was good. Aiden had confirmed what Lucas had said, and there wasn't a doubt in my mind about his honesty. He hadn't sold me out to a terrorist group to be their test dummy, and he wasn't glad to be rid of me.

He looked awful, actually. And while I wanted to take solace in that fact after what I thought he'd done to me, it mostly just made me sad. What a crappy turn of events where we both ended up miserable. I hadn't had the guts to ask him about his future plans. Well, I assumed he still would become king in a year, but I didn't ask whether he was to be married to someone else, too. I wasn't even sure which answer I'd prefer.

It didn't matter anyway. Soon, although we hadn't exactly picked a date or narrowed down the timeframe at all, I was going to be Mrs. Lucas Jackson. Did people still say that? I wasn't sure. Jessica Jackson had a nice ring to it, though it would have suited me well in the porn industry, too. I could go by JJ for short. I giggled. JJ and LJ, what a pair we'd be.

My phone buzzed with a text from LJ right then. I chastised myself for not checking in with him earlier. He must've been worried out of his mind.

"Sorry," I texted back. "Aiden left an hour ago. I'm walking around, clearing my mind."

"You ok?" came his reply.

"Yes."

"Code word," was his next text.

I giggled. When I'd promised to text him as soon as I was done meeting with Aiden unless I was kidnapped my elves, my own joke hit a little (okay, a lot) too close to home. I'd totally freaked out. I wasn't scared of Aiden, but... Anyway, Lucas gave me a code word so he'd know it was actually me texting and no one else. Somehow that actually reassured me.

"Fried chicken," I texted back, adding an emoji of a chicken leg to brighten up my code word text.

He replied with a thumbs up.

I wandered around for another hour or so before the heat started to exhaust me and I headed back to his apartment. As soon as I opened the door, a delicious smell wafted out. Lucas and Jeff were lounged in front of the TV with large buckets of fried chicken beside them on the sofa.

I burst out laughing, the sight so unexpected and amusing that I totally forgot how close to tears I'd been seconds before. Lucas joined in the laughter, leaving Jeff eying us both warily.

"I got a craving," Lucas explained when I finally calmed down.

I wiped my eyes, having laughed so hard I cried. I could tell Lucas was trying to gauge my mood by the way he was staring at me, and I really did owe him a recap. But I didn't want to get into it now. So instead, I met his eyes, smiled, and then wedged myself between his broad thighs and the arm of the couch. I tilted his bucket of chicken towards me and grabbed a leg.

"Thanks," I said, taking a big bite.

I was about halfway through with the leg when I noticed both Jeff and Lucas gawking at me.

"What?" I asked.

"I thought you were a vegetarian," Jeff said.

At the same time, Lucas said "You're eating."

I smirked at both of them. "I am not a vegetarian and I always eat."

"You've had nothing but toast and tea since you got here," Lucas said.

He was exaggerating, but I guessed I hadn't been eating much. My stomach had been a mess as of late and I was almost afraid to eat anything too tricky to digest because it would just come back up if I started to think about what I'd been through.

"I guess my appetite is back," I said. To make my point, I grabbed another piece of chicken and took it with me as I went to the kitchen. I couldn't eat with an audience, and all that walking around in the midsummer heat had made me thirsty.

Lucas

I watched Jessica as she made her way back to the kitchen. Seeing her eat that chicken was the hottest thing ever. It was so typically Jessica. She was never the type to avoid junk food, and she wasn't one of those girls who wouldn't pig out in front of guys. Whatever had happened with Aiden, that was a good sign.

I turned back to the TV and realized Jeff was staring suspiciously at me now.

"When's she due?" he asked.

"Do what?" I rummaged in the bucket to see if there was another wing.

Jeff laughed. "I can't believe I didn't figure it out sooner. It all makes sense now. Her sudden arrival, becoming your fiancée out of the blue, the never eating, the weird mood swings, and the creepy way you watch her like you're afraid she's going to break."

I frowned. "No clue what you're getting at."

"Alright man. That's fine. Although I didn't tell anyone your engagement secret so I should have earned your trust about the whole pregnancy thing, but whatever."

"Pregnancy?" I nearly choked on my chicken. "You think Jessica is pregnant?"

He eyed me skeptically.

"Jessica is not pregnant."

Jeff clearly didn't believe me.

"Seriously. She's not. I already told you I proposed a while back but then we were on a break and she went through some serious shit. She's just now starting to get back to her normal self." I shook my head and stood, realizing I should go check on her anyway. "Dude, you can't go around calling every chick who eats a chicken leg pregnant!"

I rounded the corner to the kitchen and saw Jessica sipping a coke and then licking her fingers. I came up behind her and wrapped my arms around her in a bear hug.

"How did it go?"

"Good, I guess." she said, taking another swig of her soda. "He confirmed everything you said, so I guess I can go back to trusting humanity, or whoever."

I tilted my head to the side, wanting more detail, but she wasn't forthcoming. "How did he seem?"

She shrugged. "Not great, really." She paused, chewing her lip. "He was furious about what his father said to me. I got the impression Ivar used what happened as an excuse to try to drive us apart."

"So he wants you back?" I interpreted, feeling the adrenaline kick in.

"No, Lucas. He followed all of your rules."

My jaw tensed. She had set out the rules, so why did it now feel like she was blaming me? "Did you talk about anything else?"

Jessica looked pensive for a minute. "Not really. I guess he asked about you some. But mostly he just explained to me in detail what he had been trying to do and how it went wrong and led to me getting kidnapped. It wasn't him, or anyone in his family, who arranged the kidnapping."

I nodded. That all seemed good, as did she. "And now you're eating."

She shrugged then grinned mischievously. "I was hungry. And for some reason fried chicken sounded good."

I smiled back. "Jeff thinks you're pregnant."

"What? Tell him I'm not."

"I did. I don't think he believes me. Or he thinks you just haven't told me yet."

She frowned.

Suddenly, a realization hit me. Just because she and I hadn't been intimate didn't mean she wasn't pregnant. I didn't know for a fact that she'd had sex with Aiden this spring, but if I were a betting man, I'd have bet the ranch.

I cleared my throat awkwardly. "Jess, you're sure, right? That you aren't pregnant?"

Her eyes widened and she looked at me as if she couldn't believe I had the nerve to ask her that. In my defense, it would've explained some things.

"Lucas, unless you've taken some liberties while I was asleep…" she began.

"Not by me!" I interrupted, struggling to keep my voice at a whisper.

Her expression changed as she realized what I was implying and any doubts I had about whether she and Aiden had done more than sleep in their bed were quickly cleared.

She turned her back to me. "No. I'm not pregnant, Lucas."

CHAPTER EIGHTEEN

I spent the evening with Lucas and Jeff, then excused myself for a walk at dusk. Lucas offered to come, but I declined, insisting I'd stay within a block or two and would return before dark. His concern for my safety was both sweet and annoying, but I knew I'd enjoy more freedom with Lucas than I ever would have with Aiden. Had I not left when I did, well, he'd probably have me locked in a tower somewhere in Eastern Europe for my own protection.

With Aiden, I never would have had a chance at normalcy. I'd always be surrounded by people serving him and I'd probably never see my friends or grandma. And while I believed my parents would have wanted me to be happy above anything else, I couldn't shake the feeling they would've been disappointed in me for giving up my dreams of being a teacher or for basically abandoning the woman who'd raised me. No, this was definitely for the best.

I stopped abruptly outside the drug store. I glanced around furtively, unsure of whether I was looking for Lucas or spies from Aiden's kingdom. When I spotted nothing suspicious, I stepped inside. I quickly located the aisle I needed and waited until the only other customer in that aisle walked away before approaching the products. I don't know why I was so embarrassed. No one knew me here, and it's not like I was a teenager still. A woman wearing an engagement ring buying a pregnancy test wouldn't raise any eyebrows even in our small hometown, let alone in Chicago. So why did I feel so naughty?

I didn't actually think I was pregnant. I mean, surely I'd know if I were. I'd feel different, somehow. But Lucas' question reminded me of a fact I'd been ignoring since I'd returned to the states. My period, which was due the day after I'd been kidnapped, had never come. My memories of Health Education class told me logical explanations for this included the stress I'd been under and the fact that I wasn't eating. But given that this was the first time since I'd officially become a woman that my cycle didn't arrive like clockwork, I couldn't help but panic.

I'd thought about having Aiden's baby before, but in all my fantasies, we were actually a couple, he hadn't almost gotten me killed, and his father wasn't plotting to keep us apart. I'd also pictured myself raising a baby with Lucas before. I could actually see most aspects of that fantasy matching reality, but I'd never wanted to raise Aiden's baby with Lucas. I could never do that to Lucas, anyway. Not that Aiden's family would let me, anyway. If I were pregnant with his child and they found out, which they inevitably would, I was certain that would have pretty drastic ramifications for my life, since the baby would theoretically have some level of royal pedigree in their world.

I purchased a name-brand double pack and stuck the clear plastic bag inside my purse, walking back to the apartment much quicker than I'd walked there. Lucas eyed my purse suspiciously, probably wondering why I'd even brought it along on a walk. But he didn't comment, so I excused myself to the bathroom.

Three minutes later, I had a clear answer.

I was not pregnant.

I exhaled a sigh of relief, refusing to waste another moment on the what-ifs. I shoved the used test back into the package with the other test, reasoning that I would take the second one for confirmation in a few days if I still didn't have my period. Then I wadded the bag up in my purse and went out to rejoin Lucas and Jeff.

It wasn't long before we decided to head to bed, Lucas being in the habit of trying to start the week well rested. I decided to take a shower, and I changed into my pajamas and twisted my hair into a long damp braid before returning to Lucas' room. When I entered, he was on the bed, holding the pregnancy test.

He didn't have the deer-in-headlights expression I'd expect from someone who just got caught snooping and that bothered me.

"You went through my purse?"

"You said you weren't pregnant. You went behind my back to buy a pregnancy test?"

Touché. I sat beside him. We were quiet for a moment. Finally, I spoke first. "I didn't think I was pregnant, but I decided I should make sure. It didn't make sense to stress you out more before I knew for certain. And now I know I'm not. The test was negative."

Lucas nodded. "You were acting weird when you returned from your walk. I was worried about you. It occurred to me you could've been meeting with Aiden or one of his henchmen and I didn't want you to get hurt."

He looked sincere enough. I nodded, which was going to be the extent of my forgiveness.

"How long have you been holding that?" I asked, gesturing to the test stick in his hand.

He laughed. "A few minutes. I wanted to make sure I read the result correctly, and then I sort of got hung up on the implications of what it means that you even had to take a test to be sure."

"What?"

"Virgins don't have pregnancy scares," he explained.

"Oh. Right." I paused. "Well, it's not like I'm going to be your first either."

"But hopefully my last?" he said with a sweet smile.

I squeezed his free hand. "You know I peed on that," I said, gesturing to the test stick. He dropped it back into the bag and shook his head, laughing.

AIDEN

I'd been home for three days when I heard my father's voice in his study. I dropped my pen and hurried down the stairs. I had assumed he was talking on the phone, so I was surprised to see my mother and Genevieve with him. My mother started to greet me warmly but halted a few feet away when she saw my expression.

"Mother, Genevieve," I nodded, curtly acknowledging them both. "Father and I need a moment alone." I stepped into the study and shut the door behind me. As I turned to face my father, all the rage I'd bottled up boiled to the surface.

"Do you think I'm a toy?" I asked. "Do you consider yourself my puppet master, orchestrating my life in whatever way suits you?"

My father appeared bemused.

I slammed my hands on the desk, but he didn't move. "Damn you!" I stood and paced around the room. "I saw Jessica earlier this week. Did you think I wouldn't find out?"

He sighed and calmly sat behind the desk. "What exactly do you think I was hiding?"

I shook my head. "Don't play games with me. Not anymore. I know it's because of you that Jessica left. You told her I authorized them to kidnap her, to torture her. What were you thinking?" I exhaled hard, aware that my voice was shaking with anger.

"What was I thinking?" he repeated. "Perhaps I thought what

happened to her was awful, but that it could have been a lot worse. It was only a matter of time before your relationship resulted in her death. And in the meantime, your feelings for her prevented you from doing the job you've been preparing to do since birth. I gave you an easy and clean way out. You should be thanking me."

I lunged forward, clenching my hands into tight fists to resist strangling my father. "Thanking you? Are you mad?"

"Clearly," he replied, rolling his eyes.

Before I could formulate a response that didn't consist of a string of curse words, he continued.

"I did what I thought was best, Aiden. I realize you don't agree with my methods, but any rational person would see the outcome is ideal. You are going to be a king of the elves. You have no business jeopardizing our way of life because of a crush on some human."

I opened my mouth to argue but he raised a hand, shushing me.

"And as to your earlier question, no, I do not seek to be your puppeteer. I am a soon-to-be-retired director of security. You are the king-to-be, the chosen and trained leader of our kind, not to mention an adult. Do you have any idea how embarrassing it is that I still have to treat you like a child? That we even continue to have these discussions? Do you assume you'll simply wake one day and feel like a ruler?"

He paused, but not long enough for me to understand his point.

"Because right now, Aiden, I don't see it. I don't feel like I'm being chastised by a ruler I just disobeyed. I don't see you writing me up for suspected treason for having chased away your would-be queen with lies about you. No, what I see is an impudent, defiant child upset that things didn't go his way."

I swallowed the bitter metallic taste rising in my throat. "You want me to treat you like a subject and not like my father?"

He shrugged. "I want you to act like a leader, for once. Like a man. I want you to take responsibility for your own life, to make your own decisions, and not to leave me to piece together solutions for your problems that you may not like."

I stared back at my father, suddenly feeling more tired than angry. He was right. Our dynamic needed to change, and that was up to me. He gazed back at me expectantly, looking altogether too cozy at my desk.

"Fine." I said, inhaling sharply. "Then get out. I don't want to see you within five miles of me unless you are with Marius, and even then, you are not to speak to me unless specifically instructed to do so. Once I am king, I will have you arrested if you come anywhere near me. Do you understand?"

For a moment, I questioned whether my father had heard me. But then he smiled sardonically, nodded once, and left the room. He escorted my mother out of the house without a word, and Genevieve simply shook her head sadly at me and followed after them.

I focused on my breathing for a moment, and then poured myself a drink from the crystal decanter on the table adjacent to the desk. I sipped the drink slowly, wishing the burning liquid would drown out the pain in the rest of my body, and then I threw the decanter against the wall, watching as the liquid dripped down the wallpaper onto the tiny shards of glass on the floor.

JESSICA

The next week flew by. I could finally say I felt like myself again, which was a relief. Classes would start again in less than a month and my grandma was expecting me home in just over a month. I'd taken the second pregnancy test and it was also negative, so I told myself it was time to move on completely with Lucas.

We'd been kissing and touching more the last few days. Of course I found Lucas attractive, and while the way he cared for me so tenderly was probably the main turn on for me, even his excessive confidence was starting to seem sexy. He hadn't pressured me for sex at all, but I knew it was time. I just needed to get it over with.

Not that I thought it would be bad. Sex with Lucas would surely be very, very good. I enjoyed kissing him and couldn't deny that my body reacted well to the ways he touched me. And I didn't doubt he had had lots of practice. It was more a mental block. If I slept with Lucas, my relationship with Aiden was really and truly over for good. I had no intention of becoming intimate with Lucas and then letting anything come between us, and I wasn't going to be one of those girls who still had occasional improper thoughts about an ex while in bed with her fiancé. Once Lucas and I sealed the deal, that was it. The relationship was real.

We were supposed to go to a bar with some of Lucas' teammates and other local friends Saturday. So, I planned that as the night I would finalize my official engagement with Lucas, so to speak. I selected a slightly more conservative outfit than the last time we'd gone to a bar, knowing I would feel like the hottest girl in the club regardless of my outfit as long as I had Lucas at my side. And I thought I was all ready to head out when Lucas awkwardly gestured to my ring finger.

I removed the ring, feeling slightly annoyed, albeit inexplicably so. But then, Lucas kissed my bare hand, a gesture which tempted me to suggest we ditch the bar and take things to the next level right away, before I lost my nerve. But I didn't. I wanted a few drinks in my system first, just to help me relax.

"My grandma thinks I'm flying here later this week, and I figured I'd tell her we are dating when I call her after I'm supposed to arrive here."

"How do you think she'll react?"

"Are you kidding? She loves you. She'll be thrilled. Compared to…" I stopped myself, and rephrased. "You are the person she always wanted me to end up with."

He smiled. "I always knew your grandma was a smart lady."

"Will you tell your parents we're dating when I tell my grandma?"

Lucas appeared to consider this briefly. "Nah. I don't share many details like that with them. They'll hear it all from your Grandma Betty anyway. Besides, I'm pretty sure they think we've been dating on and off again for years."

I laughed, since I'd gotten the same impression from his mom, too. I distinctly remembered times when I'd come over to hang out in high school and she'd insisted we keep the door open. In retrospect, that all made sense.

The bar was already bopping when we arrived. Lucas started a tab and we finished our first round of drinks at a table before heading out to the dance floor. I enjoyed being surrounded by so many happy, energetic people, and it was fun watching Lucas in his element. It felt very reminiscent of our early college days when I'd tag along to parties with him and have a blast even though he was really the only person I knew. Lucas had one of those enigmatic personalities that just made everyone like him. We danced through several songs, and then I offered to grab our next round of drinks while Lucas chatted with some of the other players who'd come out tonight.

I made my way to the bar and waited while the bartender mixed the drinks. Exhausted, I sat on an empty barstool. As I gazed back towards our table, I saw that two women had descended upon Lucas like vultures.

I laughed at the predictability of it all, then watched more closely. They seemed to know him, or at least the taller one did. She flipped her hair casually behind her ear, grinning, then leaned closer to say something. When Lucas replied, she laughed uproariously, although I doubted whatever he'd said truly merited that response. She licked her lips and pushed her fingers against his arm playfully when she spoke again.

I turned back to the bar, unable to watch any longer.

"We call them hockey groupies," Jeff said, startling me as he sidled up to the bar beside me. "They're at all the games and have taken a particular interest in some of the newer guys."

I smiled politely. "Oh, I figured."

"He hasn't slept with either of them, if that's what you were wondering."

I nodded, although I hadn't even considered that as a possibility. I definitely felt a pang of jealousy, but something about the sensation was unfamiliar.

"Lucas has always been like that," I finally said. "If he's alone for even a second, single girls flock to him and fawn over him."

"Must be rough," Jeff joked.

I shrugged. "I think it gets old for him sometimes. In high school, he'd bring me to events just so he didn't have to deal with all the flirting. When he had a date, even if it was a fake one or just a friend, girls seemed to back off."

Jeff frowned. "That must have been confusing. For both of you."

The bartender slid our drinks across the bar as I considered Jeff's words. Confusing was precisely the term for it, but not for what went on between Lucas and I in high school because I never questioned our relationship then. Until recently, Lucas was always a friend to me. Now, since I felt jealous watching other girls flirt with him, I knew that had changed.

Except…the more I thought about it, the more inexplicable it was. I wasn't jealous of the way Lucas was interacting the girls. I was jealous of the way they were responding to him. I envied their feelings for him, the way they effortlessly felt a strong physical attraction.

I brought the drinks to the table slowly, but Lucas was visibly relieved when he saw me. He gazed up at me and smiled as though he hadn't seen me in years. Since the taller girl had taken my seat, he stood immediately, offering me his seat and kissing the side of my head in case there was any remaining question about his feelings. The girls took the hint and politely left.

"Friends of yours?" I teased.

He smiled. "Sorry, I would've introduced you, but you scared them off."

"Hardly," I replied. "The way you look at me scared them off."

"What way is that?"

I hesitated. "Never mind."

Jeff returned to the table and the discussion progressed to sports. I tuned out.

By the time we walked home, it was late. Jeff had already left, so Lucas and I trudged back alone. He wrapped his arm tightly around me, a gesture which hampered my ability to walk quickly, but was nonetheless appreciated since the temperature had dropped significantly from the afternoon when I'd chosen my outfit.

"You're quiet," he observed.

I glanced up and smiled at him, but didn't answer.

"Is everything okay?"

I nodded.

Lucas laughed uneasily. "Okay, care to tell me what's on your mind?"

"I was just thinking about those girls earlier. The ones that came over while I was getting our drinks."

"Candy and Brandy?"

I giggled. "Those aren't their names."

"Might as well be. Does it matter?" He kissed my cheek.

"I guess not."

"Well, sorry. They aren't my type. I wasn't flirting."

"They were, though. Especially the taller one."

His arm dropped from my waist. "Jessica, I can't really control what other people do."

"I know that. I'm not mad, Lucas."

Now he was quiet. "Okay, I'm stumped then." He finally admitted. "What's wrong?"

"It's hard to explain."

"Try."

I shivered, and he placed his arm around me again. I snuggled closer to his strong body, already regretting what I was about to say. "Do you have any idea how many girls want you?"

Lucas laughed.

"I mean, really. There are probably dozens of girls on campus alone who will literally be crushed when they learn you're off the market for good. And when you start playing in games this fall and the whole world knows who you are, there will be thousands of women pining over you."

"I think they'll survive," he said.

"But, I mean, there are women who probably daydream about your big muscles and that sexy grin, women who get goose bumps just from you talking to them."

"What's your point, Jess? This is getting weird."

I took a deep breath. "I don't think we should get married."

Lucas didn't break his stride. "Because you're concerned about the masses of young women who will die from sorrow at me being taken?"

"No, because I'm not one of those girls."

"Huh?"

"Lucas, I love you, but not that way. Of course I find you attractive. I'd have to be blind not to notice how hot you are. And I would be lucky to spend my life with you, but you should have so much more. You deserve to be with someone who is obsessed with you, someone who craves your touch all the time, someone who thinks about you every night when they fall asleep."

I turned to him, but his expression never changed. We were nearing the apartment, though, and his pace did slow.

"Lucas?"

"Yes?"

"Say something."

He stopped, turning to face me. He pulled me close, wrapping both of arms tightly around his back, and kissed my forehead. "Okay," he whispered.

"Okay what?"

He breathed a laugh. "Okay, we won't get married."

I frowned and pulled back enough to see his face. "What do you mean?"

Lucas rolled his eyes, but offered a half grin. "Isn't that what you just said you wanted? I'm saying okay, we won't get married. You can keep staying with me longer if you want, or I can drive you back home tomorrow, or even to campus if you prefer."

I was still confused. "I know you've put up with a ton of crap from me lately and I owe you everything, but I don't think we should get married now or ever." I sighed. "I know you'd make me happy if we were together, but I just don't feel that spark, and you deserve someone who does. I'm being serious, Lucas."

"I know," he said.

"Then why are you reacting this way?"

Lucas smiled. "Jessica, you know I love you, and I probably always will. You're my best friend, and unlike you, I do feel a spark between us." He paused to kiss my forehead again. "But I know you don't feel that way. I'm not the idiot everyone thinks I am. It's been fun pretending, but I never thought you were in love with me in that way. You never looked at me the way you did Aiden, anyway."

He sighed. "I figured you just needed some time to come to this conclusion on your own."

"So you never planned to marry me?" His reaction had caught me so off guard that I wasn't sure what to think now.

"My proposal was sincere. I wanted you to choose me, but you didn't. And the offer still stands. If you want, we can still get married, or hell, we can just pretend to be engaged a little longer, too. But no, I didn't think you'd go through with it," he said. "Why do you think I asked you to take off the ring when we went out together? Or why I didn't want to tell people?"

I nodded. It all did make sense now. Of course Lucas wasn't an idiot. He wasn't so lovestruck by me that he couldn't see how I really felt.

Lucas chuckled. "You are the only woman who has ever slept in my bed and not tried to have sex with me."

I shook my head, trying to dismiss any visions conjured up by his comment.

"And the only woman who has ever called out another guy's name in my bed," he added.

I felt my cheeks redden. "I did?"

He shrugged. "You were always asleep."

Lucas hugged me again, and I realized how much I was going to miss being this close with him.

"What do we do now?"

"Well, I vote we head up to the apartment, have a quickie, get some sleep, then figure out the next step in the morning."

I shoved him playfully. "So you aren't kicking me out?"

"You can stay as long as you like."

"Thanks. I think I should go home by next weekend, though. I haven't seen my grandma in a while and that's when she's expecting me anyway."

Lucas nodded and guided me towards the building.

We were both quiet as we got ready for bed. After I changed into my pajamas, I went to the bathroom to brush my teeth. When I returned, Lucas was already in bed. I hesitated, unsure of what the protocol was, but he patted the bed beside him. I crawled in slowly, and he immediately scooted closer and draped his arm over me.

He kissed my bare shoulder before laughing.

"What?"

"I was just thinking that this is the weirdest breakup ever," he said.

"Oh. I was just thinking how much I was going to miss this."

"Jessica, we can still be friends. I'm glad we got to spend this last month together, but there's no reason things can't go back to the way they were before when we're back at school."

"Does that mean you'll still come over for sleepovers?"

"Something tells me Aiden would find that uncomfortable."

My muscles tensed at mention of his name.

"You are going back to him, right?"

"No," I said quickly. Then I sighed. "I don't know. I don't know what I'm doing at all. I don't know that I'll ever see him again, actually."

Lucas was quiet for a moment. "Stay the week and figure it all out. I'll drive you home next weekend."

"Thank you," I said, gazing back at him. "You really are the best. Whatever woman does end up with you is very lucky."

Lucas didn't answer, and I drifted off to sleep.

CHAPTER NINETEEN

Sunday was awkward, with neither Jessica nor I really discussing what we'd decided the night before. Even weirder was that neither of us mentioned it to Jeff, and I couldn't tell if he even noticed she wasn't wearing the ring anymore.

On Monday morning, Jessica got up early and attempted to make me breakfast before I left for practice. It was a short day with yoga at the end. I cut out early, assuring my coaches I'd get all my stretching in later.

Jessica was lounging on the balcony when I returned. She had a book on her lap but was gazing off in the distance instead of reading.

I tapped on the glass. She slid her feet off the chair facing her and turned to me, smiling warmly.

"You're back early," she observed as I stepped outside.

I nodded. "I bailed on stretches. I figured we could talk. And do yoga. I promised my coach."

She frowned. "You don't really do yoga, do you? Is that code for Kama sutra or something?"

I wiggled my eyebrows seductively. "No. We do honest to God

226

literal yoga every fricking practice in the summer. The older guys swear by it, too." I sat across from her. "Really, in the spring, when I first started training with them, they were all walking like ducks their muscles were so tight. Now they're all limber and ready to start again."

"So this is when your practices really amp up again?"

"Yeah. Training camp is just over three weeks away, so we'll start pushing it now. Those of us that have something to prove will push it more than others."

"You're amazing, Lucas. I know it's got to be hard going from top dog to little fish in big sea or whatever, but you have real talent and you're smart and hardworking. The team would be lucky to have you and they're going to see that."

"Have you been saving that pep talk all summer?"

She made a face at me and I laughed.

"Seriously though, Lucas. Even though you are the cockiest boy I'll ever meet, sometimes I worry you don't see how truly awesome you are. And not just at hockey. Don't let anybody ever brush you off as a player. You are a sweet and generous and caring and sweet..."

"You already said sweet," I interrupted.

"Well, you're just so fucking sweet," she said.

I eyed her suspiciously then tasted the liquid in her cup. Jessica never swore except when she was drinking, but this beverage tasted like regular old iced tea.

"I'm not drinking!" she insisted, reading my mind. "I'm just nervous. I feel like there is so much unsaid between us and everything is going to change when I leave."

"Nothing has to change, Jess."

A small tear escaped her eye. "I'm going back to school and you won't be there. You'll be here, playing hockey, living your dream, whisking other girls off their feet with your dashing good looks and untoppable sweetness."

"Untoppable?"

She smiled. "Yes. As in 'can't be topped'."

I shook my head. "You don't have to go."

"Yes, I do. I've got school. I need to see my grandma."

"Go visit your grandma and come back. You can go to school somewhere around here."

"And live where?"

I gestured to the apartment.

"Yeah, as your live-in friend who's a girl? That would go over well with your dates. Especially when they get to squeeze in between us in bed."

I laughed. "I'm moving to a two-bedroom soon. Or you could get your own place in the building."

"Yes, because I actually have millions in lottery winnings I forgot to tell you about," she teased.

"I have money, Jessica. Plenty of it. And once the season starts, I won't have any time to spend it on cool stuff, so I might as well…"

"No," she said with a smile, rising from her chair and moving to sit on my lap.

She casually draped an arm around my neck. I wrapped my arm around her back to hold her steady. I was grateful she was mostly on my leg and not centered directly on my lap because, even though I knew she was not coming on to me now, I couldn't stop my body from reacting to the feel of her perfect thighs pressed against me.

We were quiet for a moment, and then I asked her what I really wanted to know. "You seemed surprised last night, when I asked if you were going back to Aiden. Had you really not considered that, or were you just not going to tell me?"

She stiffened, and I immediately regretted asking.

I hadn't meant to stress her out, but I needed to know. I had it in my mind that if we both were on the same page about why she was leaving and where she was headed next, it wouldn't change things. But if she told me she was going back to school to enjoy single life and then went back to Aiden a week later, I might resent her. I didn't want that. Engagement or not, I loved her. Maybe more in a best friend way than a lover, but I didn't think I'd feel like me if I couldn't still love Jessica.

"I'm not trying to keep anything from you, Lucas. I had very different plans for last night that didn't involve ending our engagement, but when I saw those girls throwing themselves at you...I guess it finally clicked for me."

At least she was being honest. She'd always told me I would be the first to know if she decided she didn't want to marry me, and I had no reason to question her. But I also felt I had a right to know if she was leaving me for someone else. "So you haven't thought about Aiden? Not just if you'll go back to him right away, but ever?"

"I honestly don't know. I don't think he's good for me. But I feel... lost without him."

Ouch. I hadn't expected her to admit that part. I had thought I'd been doing a better job than that at keeping her happy.

"It's nothing to do with you," she said. "In other circumstances, if I weren't so messed up now, this would be my utopia. I would be lucky to have this life. I am lucky, really. But it's me. I feel like something is missing from me right now and I don't know if it's because of Aiden, but I do know I care too much about you to keep playing house with you while I'm still figuring myself out."

She shifted to the side, and I helped her swing her legs over my other leg so she was fully across my lap. She rested her head against my chest, and I inhaled the sweet fragrance of her hair.

"God, you smell good," I mumbled.

She giggled then sniffed loudly. "You do too, actually," she said, slightly surprised.

"I showered at practice," I said. "And thanks for the skepticism there."

I pulled my arm tighter around her and enjoyed the sensation of her body against mine. Geez I was pathetic. I was going to miss this too. What kind of a guy is sad about losing the long conversations and snuggling in a relationship? I hadn't had sex with anyone since Jessica came to stay with me. I should be missing that, not thinking about how I'd survive without the scent of her strawberry shampoo on my sheets. Well, I was missing the sex, I decided. But with Jessica. I hadn't even thought about doing it with someone else since she came back.

"You still there?" she asked suddenly, interrupting my internal monologue. "Whatcha thinkin' about?"

I laughed. "You don't want to know. It might hurt my untoppable sweet guy ranking."

"Uh-oh, thinking dirty thoughts are you?"

I narrowed my eyes at her. "How did you know?"

Now Jessica laughed. "LJ, I'm sitting on your lap. Unless you have some sort of a weapon in your pocket..." Her voice trailed off.

I figured a lesser man would start blushing right about now. But it didn't bother me. She already knew I had the hots for her. "So let's get back to the discussion at hand. You were about to tell me how you like me too much to keep spending time with me."

She giggled and sipped her tea.

JESSICA

My last week in Chicago was good. Lucas let me come watch one practice, and I loved it. I appreciated it in the same way I had enjoyed my last week of classes in high school. I had attended many practices before, but knowing that one was likely the last, it took on special meaning to me. I felt Lucas start to distance himself a bit, which was understandable. He no longer kissed me anywhere on my face and he gave me a lot more privacy when I was changing.

In a way, things had simply reverted to how they used to be

between Lucas and me, back when we were nothing more than close friends. To me, that was comforting, since my biggest worry about ending our engagement was that I'd lose him altogether. But at the same time, I couldn't fool myself into believing nothing had changed. I knew I'd gotten Lucas' hopes up again, and that this time, we weren't likely to bounce back.

We were driving back to our hometown Saturday morning, which would give Lucas one night with his family before returning to Chicago. Friday night we went out for our last dinner together. He chose the restaurant, a Japanese steakhouse where we both ordered hibachi meals they prepared on the giant cooktop at our table. It was a fun and distracting way to spend our last night together, but when we returned home, I knew we needed to talk.

I changed into my shorts and tank top then sat on the edge of the bed while he threw a few items in his bag to take home with him. I had packed earlier, although it hadn't taken me too long since I was just repacking everything I'd brought with me. As Lucas tossed one last tee shirt in his bag and zipped it shut, I sighed.

He turned to me, a forced smile on his face, and I lost it. I'd been worried that I'd get weepy, but instead it was a full out sob. Luckily, Lucas already knew I was crazy, so this probably didn't damage my reputation in his eyes.

"Jess, please stop crying," he pleaded. "You're breaking my heart."

His concern for me simply made me more sorrowful.

"Jessica, this isn't goodbye. There is no reason to be sad. We're still friends. I'm still going to be right here whenever you need me. And we both knew you'd be leaving soon anyway to finish school."

I managed to pull it together, wiping my eyes with my thumb. "I know. I'm just really going to miss seeing you every day."

"Me too."

I took a slow, deep breath, then reached into my purse and retrieved his ring. I held it out for him to take, but he shook his head.

"Lucas, you need to take it. We're not getting married now, so I shouldn't keep it."

He pushed it back into my hand. "Jessica, keep it. I got it for you. It's not like I'd ever give it to anyone else anyway."

"You could sell it."

"I don't need the money."

I frowned. I really wanted to keep the ring to remind me that this month had really happened, that there was a time when I had allowed myself to pretend I had a shot at a normal, happy life with a wonderful man. But I couldn't.

"I can't, Lucas," I said. "You will never know how much this summer meant to me, how much I appreciate everything you've done for me. I am pretty sure I will always love you, and I'm certain that marrying you wouldn't have been a mistake for me." I paused, trying to regain composure and swallowing back more tears. "But you deserve more. You can do so much better than me, and as long as I hold onto this ring, we are both going to think in the back of our minds that this—us—is a possibility. And you can't be my fallback option. It isn't fair to you. Besides, if I keep the ring it's just going to remind me of what I'm missing and the fact that I can never have you."

Lucas rolled his eyes. "Never say never, Jessica."

I shook my head. "No, this is it, Lucas."

I leaned forward and kissed him, intending it to be a brief, soft kiss, but lingering a little too long and opening my mouth when his tongue pressed forward. By the time I pulled myself together and ended the kiss, my hands were in his hair and we were both flushed.

"That has to be our last kiss, Lucas. We have to go back to being friends now." I licked my still-tingling lips. "You are going to be completely fine without me. You are going to kick butt at training camp and have an awesome time playing pro, and you will be too busy with all the girls who actually put out to even think of me."

"Jess," he chastised sadly.

I continued. "But I'm going back to school, and I'm going to be all alone. I'm not going to want to date anyone new because I'm too scared to get hurt again and because no one could possibly compare to you anyway. And when I'm feeling all alone and hopeless about my future, I can't have you in the back of my mind as an option. I'll never take a chance and actually live my life that way. And you have wasted enough of your life waiting for me to come to my senses."

Lucas was quiet for such a long time that I almost thought he was going to cry. Instead, he took the ring out of my hand and set it on his nightstand. "You're never going to be alone, Jessica. Even if we aren't together, I'll always be there for you. I want you to talk to me. Don't be a shitty friend when school starts up again, okay?"

I smiled, and we both lay down for bed.

Neither of us spoke for several minutes, but I could tell Lucas was just as wide awake as I was. Finally, he broke the silence.

"Jessica?"

"Yes?"

"Will you do me one favor?"

"Yep."

"If you do end up going back to Aiden, will you let me know? I mean, if you end up screwing the entire college hockey team in your first week back, it's okay to spare my feelings and not tell me about that, but if it involves him, I just...I think I'd feel better hearing about it from you." He paused. "Unless you don't think that's fair."

"No, Lucas, of course I'll tell you. You deserve to know."

He was quiet again for a minute. Then he said, "It's pretty convenient that you're leaving right before I move. Dumping a guy just so you don't get stuck packing boxes is a low blow," he teased.

I giggled, and eventually, I fell asleep.

Lucas

Dropping Jessica off at her house was the hardest thing I'd ever done, hands down. We'd already said our goodbyes, and her grandma was watching from the living room for her, so there was no time for anything. I guess there was nothing left to say anyhow, but I still felt like shit as I watched her walk into her house with her grandma, wave, and then shut the door.

I tried to keep it together for my parents that night, but it was fucking miserable being in the house next door to Jessica and not knowing if I'd see or hear from her again before I left. As it was, she dropped by Sunday morning to say goodbye, and although my mom was in the room with us, that actually made me feel a little better. When I got back to Chicago Sunday evening, all I wanted to do was drink until I didn't give a shit about anything. But of course, I couldn't do that because I had practice Monday.

Instead, I worked out my angst on the ice. I increased my reps in the weight room, picked up my speed on the treadmill, and put every ounce of passion I had into my effort in the rink. Every day I came home and felt like I was going to die. I was physically, emotionally and mentally spent. So I focused on recovery and I forced myself to sleep a lot. And then I got up the next morning and killed myself all over again.

It paid off. I soared through training camp, actually improving all of my stats from where I'd been at the start of "recovery" season. My coaches and teammates alike noticed and appreciated my effort, and I knew I was in. I told myself it didn't matter that I'd lost Jessica because I had achieved my other dream.

Since the first time I won a hockey match, back before I could even tie my shoes, I'd been obsessed with the Blackhawks, and I'd consistently dreamed of playing pro hockey somewhere ever since. Not only had I gone pro, but I was on my favorite team. That should've been enough.

As soon as the regular season begun, I'd started getting a lot of publicity and a lot of positive attention from females in town. It turned out that single, English-speaking professional hockey players with all their teeth were a pretty hot commodity. I enjoyed the compliments and brushed up on my flirting skills, but I never actually took it further than that with any of the girls I saw while out and about. I told Jeff I worried about getting a bad reputation if I had one night stands now that people actually knew who I was, but deep down, I realized it actually had more to do with Jessica.

She held true to her promise and kept in touch. At first it was mostly text messages, where we could hide our expressions and keep everything light and friendly. And then there were a couple of brief phone calls. But neither of us could pretend nothing had changed between us, and that just sucked.

CHAPTER TWENTY

Jessica

I had never before been so grateful for classes to start again. It had been great seeing my grandma, but staying in our house right next to Lucas' childhood home made it difficult to forget about him. Even on campus, where we'd spent so much time together, there were memories of him. But for every single thing on campus that reminded me of Lucas, there were two to remind me of Aiden. Returning to campus reopened all my old wounds from the breakup with Aiden. I knew why I wasn't with Aiden or Lucas. But understanding why didn't make me miss them any less. Claire was amazing, of course, pulling all the tricks out of her "get over the guy" bag, and my class load was insane since I was graduating at the end of the semester so I'd be able to student teach in the spring.

Once classes began, I threw myself headfirst into my studies. I promised Claire I'd at least look for cute guys in my classes by mid-September, and maybe try to flirt with one or two by Halloween. But so far, I was failing miserably. I was so focused on my course work that I really couldn't even say if there were guys in my classes, let alone whether they were cute or single.

On a mid-October afternoon, I started out of the history building while still trying to wedge my notepad into my backpack. I had probably overdone it on the books when packing my bag this morning. I figured I wouldn't leave campus until after my final class, which meant I'd have almost three full hours throughout the day to study. Therefore, I needed extra books.

But apparently I also needed extra arms to carry the extra books. Just as I successfully squeezed the notepad between my education textbook and my iPad, my sociology book slid out the side. I winced right as the book should have hit the top of my foot, bare aside from the minuscule strap of my flip flops, but the contact never came.

I pushed my hair out of my eyes to see Oliver standing before me, holding the book. "Oliver," I said, like a moron.

"Jessica," he replied.

"What are you doing on campus? Didn't you graduate?"

"Med school."

Oh, right. I remembered that now. But I had assumed he'd attend somewhere else, probably abroad. "Here?"

He nodded and followed me to a nearby bench, where I plopped my backpack down so I could properly organize it. He handed me the book once I was about to zip the bag.

"Thanks." I pulled my hair behind my ear and saw Oliver's eyes widen. I quickly swiveled to see if a bug or something was behind me. "What?"

"Your ring," he mumbled, still eying my hand.

I wasn't sure what to say to that.

"Is it being cleaned?"

I tried to think of a snarky comeback, but my mind was blank. "I'm not marrying Lucas."

"Does my brother know this?"

"I don't know. Doesn't he have spies everywhere?"

"What happened? With Lucas?"

"How is that your business?"

Oliver frowned. "I guess it isn't, unless you're not with Lucas because you figured out you don't love him the way you love Aiden. And it's probably none of your business that Aiden is still a miserable wreck and is refusing to marry anyone before becoming king." He picked up his own bag and started to walk off.

My stomach churned. I wished I could unheard what he'd just told me, and I tried to convince myself it didn't matter. My resolve lasted about four seconds.

"Oliver, wait up!"

He quickly turned and grinned.

"I'm not with Lucas anymore because I don't love him the same way I loved Aiden. Is that what you wanted to know?"

He nodded.

"Is Aiden in town now?" I bit my lip as soon as the words left my mouth. What if he were? Was I actually prepared to see him without Lucas waiting in the wings with a code word and a bucket of chicken?

"No. He avoids this place like the plague. He's a mess now, though. He's in some epic fight with our father, Marius can barely stand him, and he boycotted Genevieve's wedding because she tried to set him up with a date." He paused. "He literally banished Father."

"But he has to be married...soon, right?"

Oliver shrugged. "Theoretically, yes. But he's rejected every contender they've brought his way."

My breath hitched in my throat. What did that mean? I heard the large campus clock chime 3 p.m., which meant I only had five minutes to get to my next class. Shit.

"I have to get to class," I said. "But if Aiden ever comes to town to visit you or anything, he could call me if he wants to catch up or something."

Oliver raised an eyebrow and waved as I scurried off.

I slept terribly that night, second guessing why I'd even said that to Oliver. Besides, I was sure Aiden wanted nothing to do with me after I'd made him as miserable as Oliver seemed to think he was.

But the next day, Aiden called. He said he'd be in town in two days. Inexplicably, I invited him over to "catch up" when he was in town. And then, of course, I'd remembered my promise to Lucas. I didn't want him to think I was keeping anything from him, so even though I was just going to talk to Aiden, I figured I should tell him. I called him the next day, and I casually threw it in the middle of the conversation. I hoped Lucas would understand it wasn't at all a big deal.

The day after that, the knock on the door came promptly at 8. I took one last slow, deep, soothing breath and then opened the door.

"Hi," I said, totally thrown off my game by the fact that Elgin was standing right beside Aiden. "Come in?"

"We're good," Aiden said to Elgin. He stepped inside my apartment and Elgin positioned himself beside the door, which I shut and locked.

"He's not going to shoot Claire if she comes home early or anything, right?"

Aiden smiled. "I think she'll be safe."

I had forgotten how that smile made my knees weak. I quickly headed towards the kitchen. "Beer, wine, soda?" I called to him, assuming he was still in the living room. I turned to wait for his answer and jumped. He was right behind me.

"Sorry," he said. He pointed to the bottle of rosé on the counter, which happened to be my favorite.

I nodded.

"Corkscrew?"

I handed it to him, then grabbed two wine glasses from the cabinet, inspecting them and swapping one out for a less dingy-looking one.

Aiden poured the wine and offered me a glass. I inhaled

deeply, enjoying the sporty scent of his aftershave that I loved so much.

"Thanks. Cheers," I clinked my glass to his and then felt completely mortified. I took a large sip of my wine, wondering why my nerves turned me into a babbling fool.

"To what are we toasting?"

I said the first thing that came into my tiny brain. "Old friends."

His eerily bright blue eyes locked with mine. I saw a hint of a smile cross his face and suspected it had something to do with the way my heart started pounding when he looked at me.

"When, exactly, were we friends?" he asked, walking back into the living room. He paused by a picture on the wall. Claire and I weren't big decorators, but we'd managed to hang a few things up.

I sighed. "You make me flustered."

"I see that."

He turned and walked towards me. I froze, suddenly over-whelmed with the desire to rip off his shirt and touch every inch of his perfectly sculpted chest. What the hell was wrong with me? Why was Aiden suddenly a walking aphrodisiac for me?

"Do you want to sit?" he asked.

I sat. He positioned himself at the other end of the couch.

"How are classes?"

"Good." I told him everything I was taking, the names of my professors, and a few other random tidbits. I felt myself relaxing the more I chatted about innocent, unimportant things like my course load or my student teaching plans for next semester. The fact that I took a sip of wine every other sentence might have had something to do with it too.

"How is, um, the political life?" I asked awkwardly.

"Frustrating," he replied, standing suddenly. He retrieved the bottle of wine from the kitchen and returned to the couch, refilling our glasses. "The more involved I become, the more opportunities I find that actually excite me. But then everything just leads to a series of closed doors and I end up running in circles and changing nothing."

I wasn't exactly sure how to respond to that so I changed the subject.

"Did you really skip your sister's wedding?"

He stared down at his wine glass. "It was a bad time for me. I regret not attending. She understands."

"Do you like her husband?"

Aiden nodded. "Gregor is one of my trusted advisors and a good friend."

"Oliver also said you and your dad aren't really getting along," I fidgeted with the stem of my wine glass.

"He shouldn't have lied to you. Or me. He treated us like pawns in a game."

"I'm sorry," I said. "You know why he did it, though."

"I do. And that doesn't excuse his actions."

"But he's family. And that's really all you've got," I said, not intending my words quite as harshly as they sounded.

My comment caught Aiden off guard. He stared at me a moment, just long enough for me to fall captivated by his smooth, full lips. Oh how I missed those lips.

"What happened to Lucas?"

I gazed down at my wine again, as though it were the most fascinating thing I'd ever seen. "Nothing. He's doing great. Still in Chicago, you know, playing hockey. We talk all the time. Just last night, actually."

He laughed softly. "Touché."

I realized how my words must have came across and quickly clarified. "We aren't engaged anymore. I returned the ring."

Aiden placed his fingers on the tip of my knee. "Why?" His voice was soft but deep, and painfully raw.

I took a breath and actually thought before speaking. "Lucas was exactly what I needed. And I still think I would've been happy with him."

"But…?"

"He's my best friend. We didn't have that spark."

"You weren't attracted to him?"

I smiled. "No, I was." I omitted the fact that I still found Lucas incredibly attractive. And that I googled him daily now that he occasionally made the news for his hockey. "But I never *had* to have him. It was a rational love, not a passionate one."

Aiden opened and closed his mouth twice, clearly uncertain of how to respond.

"Did you miss me?" he finally asked.

I giggled, clearly at my limit on the wine now. "Of course I missed you, Aiden. I mean, even when I thought you agreed to let them do all that awful stuff to me, I still wanted you. And once I learned the truth, it was just harder."

"What was harder?"

"To remember why I wasn't with you."

I heard him swallow. "And why was that?" he asked.

"Because we don't make sense," I said. "Our relationship isn't rational at all."

Aiden glanced to the door suddenly, as though he'd heard something. "What time did you say Claire would be back?"

"Probably not till 10," I said, looking to the clock above the microwave and seeing it was already five after ten.

Aiden was at the door in a flash. I followed and saw Claire stepping out of her car, eying our front door warily. I waved at her cheerfully so she wouldn't think she was walking into a home invasion. The sight of Elgin positioned at the front door could be a tad unsettling.

"I want to see you again," Aiden said to me. "We have more to discuss, don't we?"

I hesitated. There was not a doubt in my mind that if I'd been left alone with Aiden for another ten minutes, I would've pounced on him and had my way with him. It had clearly been too long since I'd been with a man in a non-platonic sort of way and I didn't know if I could trust myself to be alone with Aiden. I'd agreed to see him because I wanted to know how he was doing, not because I wanted to rile up all my feelings for him again. Nothing good could come from me seeing him again.

I became aware that I was nodding in agreement with Aiden's statement, despite my brain just deciding it was a bad idea.

"I'm at the house with Oliver this week. No one else is there." he said. "I can pick you up tomorrow evening, after you've had a chance to study?"

I nodded again.

"I'll call you," he promised. He stared at me again with those stunning blue eyes, drawing me closer to him until he turned abruptly, nearly causing me to stumble over the door stoop. "Evening, Claire," he said casually.

Elgin followed Aiden to the car and I turned back to Claire. Her jaw dropped, leaving her mouth hanging wide open. She looked at me, then at the black SUV pulling out of the parking lot, then back to me. And then she fanned herself.

"I had always wondered what they mean in books when they say some guy's look is smoldering. Now I know. That, my friend, was smoldering. You have some serious explaining to do."

I exhaled the pent up sexual tension out of my body and shut the door, collapsing against the door and sinking down to the floor. I focused on my breathing until I was no longer panting. Claire plopped on the floor beside me.

"He wasn't supposed to still have that effect on me," I finally said.

"What effect is that? The one that had you seconds from yanking your panties off when I interrupted?"

"Yes," I said dryly. "Thank you, by the way, for coming home when you did. The last thing I need is to hook up with my ex."

"Uhhh why?"

I stared at her. There were so many obvious reasons I wouldn't even know where to start explaining.

"He obviously wanted you, too," Claire said.

"You think?"

"Oh yeah."

I shook my head. "Doesn't matter. Can't happen. I just wanted to catch up with him and get some closure so I can move on."

Claire was frowning. "I still don't get why you are so against a hook up with him. For starters, hooking up with exes is the best kind of hook up. He already knows what you like, and it doesn't raise your total number of guys you've been with."

Hmm. I wasn't too concerned about my number. If anything, it was too low. But I wasn't ready to raise it just yet anyway.

"Second," she continued. "Whatever happens, it's all good, and you're no worse off than before. Either you're still broken up or you get back together."

"We can't get back together. We already tried that and it didn't work."

"You never told me why, though."

"It's complicated."

Claire smiled. I hadn't realized how much I'd missed her company when I was in London and Chicago.

After a moment of silence, she asked about Elgin. I tried to brush him off as a friend of Aiden's who just came by to give him a ride home.

"So what are you going to say when he calls?" she asked as I finally picked myself off the floor and went to wash out the wine glasses in the kitchen.

"Well, we didn't really finish chatting about everything, so I'm going over to his house tomorrow night. He's just calling so we can confirm the time."

"Jess!" Claire shrieked so loud I thought she saw a spider. "You cannot go to his house with him if you don't want to sleep with him."

I started to protest and then realized that she was right. *Crap.* Why had I agreed to that?

CHAPTER TWENTY-ONE

AIDEN

I had barely arrived home when Jessica sent me a text message insisting we go out to dinner instead of talking at the house as we'd planned. I called her to discuss and she acted very strangely about it. I told her I'd prefer to order in, what with the hassle of the security detail seeing and hearing my every move out in public, and she said it wouldn't be a date, as though that was my hang-up. She even offered to pay. Since *that* was clearly why I wanted to stay in.

Oh well. Whatever she required to feel comfortable was fine by me. All I knew was that I needed to see her again. I pulled up outside her apartment a little before 7. Elgin let me drive, but he was in the backseat. Apparently, following us in a separate car posed some sort of security threat. Once we arrived at the restaurant, though, he would be waiting outside, whether he liked it or not.

I unfastened my seatbelt to walk up to the door, but Jessica, who had apparently been watching from the window, rushed out. Her thick, dark brown hair swayed side to side as she ran, and I longed to feel it between my fingers. I thumped my hands against the steering wheel, disgusted at how quickly my mind turned to mush when I saw her. From the back seat, Elgin chuckled.

"Oh, hush," I snapped.

Jessica climbed in the car. Consistent with her efforts to convince me this wasn't a date, she was wearing jeans and a tank top and carried a zip-up sweatshirt with her. As she sat, I spotted the Chicago Blackhawks emblem on the sweatshirt. *Ouch.* Well, unfortunately for her, she looked amazing in jeans and a tank top. Jessica had one of those bodies that jeans seem to be designed for. She was slender, but with a perky butt. And the tank top showed off her toned shoulders and drew my eyes in to that perfect handhold between her neck and shoulders. Oh how I missed resting my hand there.

"I would've come to the door," I said to her.

She shrugged, shooting me a look. "Not a date," she said.

I suppressed the urge to compliment her attire, instead noting that her hair was longer. "That length looks good on you," I said.

She eyed me briefly, then turned back to the road. Okay, now I was stumped. Why was she avoiding looking my direction?

"Hello, Elgin," she said suddenly, her voice melodic and smooth.

"Hello."

"How's Cordelia?"

"She's uh…" he hesitated. "Well, she's okay. More difficult than usual now."

"Cordelia is six months pregnant," I explained.

"Oh. Wow. Congratulations."

He thanked her, then we were quiet the rest of the drive. Once at the restaurant, we perused the menu. Jessica stared at hers for much longer than necessary before eventually ordering the same spicy chicken wrap and sweet potato fries she ate every time we went to this restaurant. Then we made small talk while we waited for the food.

It was uncharacteristically awkward. Things between Jessica

and I may have never made sense, but they were never before awkward. When our meals arrived, Jessica continued to focus her gaze directly on her food.

I sighed. "Why won't you look at me?"

"I don't want to drop food everywhere," she insisted, glancing up briefly.

I bit back a laugh. "Yes. We don't want you staining your fancy date clothes."

"This is not a date," she insisted. Then she looked up, saw my face, and realized I was teasing her.

"Oh, Aiden," she said.

My gut clenched. I loved the way she said my name. It always sounded like a praise, and I could generally decipher her thoughts based on how she said it. That time, she likely meant it to sound as a rebuke for my teasing, but it didn't come out that way. It came out precisely the same way it did when we were in the bedroom.

At least now I knew why she was avoiding eye contact. Jessica wanted me every bit as much as I wanted her.

Fine. *Game on.*

"I missed you," I said. "I haven't had this in a while."

"Fish tacos?"

I laughed. "No, not the food. This. A conversation with someone who treats me like any other guy and resents me enough to lie right to my face."

She wrinkled her nose at me. "I don't resent you."

"You do. And you told me yesterday you missed me. So I know exactly why you aren't looking at me and, unfortunately, it won't work."

"What won't work?"

"Convincing yourself you don't want me."

"I'm very persuasive," she said, finally making eye contact.

My pulse quickened at the sight of her glimmering brown eyes, delicately framed by the longest black eyelashes I'd ever seen.

"So am I," I replied, reaching my hand across the table and clutching hers.

Jessica stopped breathing for close to a full minute, rendering the pounding of her heart even louder.

"Nothing has changed," she said quietly.

"I have."

She tilted her head to the side. "How so?"

"When you were kidnapped and I didn't know if I'd ever see you again, I realized I didn't care about anything else. What's the point of trying to save a kingdom if it doesn't even let people fall in love?" I paused. "And when you were with Lucas, I was miserable. Not because you were with him, because it actually made me feel a little better to think you might be happy. I was miserable simply because you weren't with me. It turns out I don't enjoy anything when you're not in my life."

Jessica started to speak, then closed her mouth and glanced away. She dabbed at her eye with her pinkie nail.

"I don't want to be the king if I can't have you," I said bluntly, shocked by the instant relief washing over me at finally having said it aloud.

Jessica's face was a nearly unreadable mixture of panic, hope, and something else. The waiter passed us then and she grabbed his sleeve, bewildered. "We need the check," she said.

Then she turned back to me. "We can't discuss this here."

We paid quickly and returned to the car.

JESSICA

The drive back to Aiden's house was awkward, neither of us even attempting small talk due to Elgin's presence. When we arrived at our destination, I noticed an additional security guard outside the house. Aiden and Elgin shared a few words, too quietly for me to hear, and then Aiden whisked me inside the house, leaving Elgin outside with the other guard.

It was strange being back in that house, where I'd created so many memories with Aiden. He went to the kitchen to make us drinks, while I remained in the living room, glancing around at the knickknacks and décor to see how much had changed.

"So you increased security I see," I said.

"Yes," he said without elaborating, handing me a glass of wine. He clinked his glass against mine, winked, and said, "To old friends."

"Is Elgin with you all the time now?"

"Pretty much."

"Are there guards inside the house?"

"Not right now. We are alone at the moment." Aiden turned to me with hooded eyes and I immediately knew the implication of his words.

"Doesn't Oliver still live here?"

"He'll be home later tonight. I'm not sure when." He paused, sensing my discomfort. "We can go upstairs to talk so he doesn't interrupt us."

I nodded, leading the way to his room, careful not to spill my wine on the cream-colored runner newly adhered to the stairs. Aiden followed me with his own glass and the wine bottle. I sat in an armchair across the room from his bed, careful not to send the wrong signal. He smirked, but sat in the chair beside mine.

"You can't give this all up," I said, skipping to the point.

"I can and I would. My people would do fine without me. Marius could continue leading for a few years longer and then perhaps Oliver would be ready. Or someone else altogether, like Gregor."

"Genevieve's husband?"

Aiden nodded and sipped his wine. I caught myself staring at his mouth as he drank, growing thirstier by the second, but not for wine.

"Wouldn't your father be disappointed?"

"Yes."

"You've worked hard your entire life so you could become king. You deserve this."

He furrowed his eyebrows. "I have worked hard, but becoming king feels like a punishment if it means I have to live without you." He swallowed, and my eyes dropped down his strong jaw line to his throat. My chest filled with longing. I struggled to stay focused.

"I don't want to be the cause of you not taking the throne. That's not fair to me. I'd have to live with the guilt and I'd always wonder if you resented me."

"What if I told you I would give it up regardless of what you decide?"

"You wouldn't."

Aiden appeared thoughtful. "No, you're right. If I'm going to spend the rest of my life lonely and full of regret, I need the job to keep me busy. I can't imagine any other position would be quite so distracting from my failed personal life."

I was feeling warm, slightly lightheaded and flustered. He wasn't supposed to say all this. He wasn't supposed to be so… perfect. "We just need to give it time, Aiden. Another year apart, and we both will have moved on. Two years from now, you'll be happy. You will have found someone new, someone like you, and you'll be in love. You'll be so glad you let me go when you did."

Aiden set his wine glass on the table between us and stood. "Jessica, trust me when I say you are wrong. No measure of time will change how I feel for you."

He took my glass from my hands and placed it beside his own before kneeling in front of me. My heart thudded uncontrollably and I was certain if I hadn't been seated, I would have passed out.

"One hundred years from now, Jessica, I will still love you with my whole heart, whether today is the last time I ever see you or whether I spend every day with you until then."

Aiden stared up at me expectantly and my mouth went dry. With him this close, the urge to touch him was overwhelming. I yearned to run my fingers through his hair, squeeze his shoulders or even just trace my thumb along his jaw. I could see how cleanly shaven he was today, I could smell his masculine aftershave, and I could hear his breathing, much calmer than my own.

"I don't know what to say, Aiden," I finally said, tears welling up in my eyes.

Our eyes locked and my knees quivered with desire. "Tell me you miss me," he said, his voice deep and husky.

"I do miss you, Aiden." I reached my hand towards him, cradling his face in my palm. He tilted his head to rest it in my hand, then lowered it to my thigh. We remained like that for several minutes, but with each second that Aiden's head lay innocently on my lap, I found it harder and harder to recall why I was resisting him.

Finally, I said what I'd been thinking for months. My voice came out so softly that a mere mortal wouldn't have heard my words.

"I still love you too, Aiden. I just don't know if that's enough."

Aiden lifted his head and gazed back at me for a moment, rising to his knees. "It's enough," he said. "That's more than enough."

Then he kissed me, hard, on the mouth. The force of the kiss nearly pushed me backwards, but it quickly softened. Within seconds I was parting my lips, making way for his eager tongue. As the kiss deepened, a soft moan escaped my throat, spurring Aiden to lift me from my chair.

My legs wrapped around his waist for support and my entire body trembled with a mixture of excitement and relief. I hadn't realized how much I missed kissing Aiden. Now that I was experiencing it again, I couldn't fathom how I'd survived without the feel of his breath against my cheek, the taste of his tongue against my own, or the tingling in my lips from the pressure of his mouth on mine.

Aiden carried me to the bed and gently lay me on my back, positioning himself next to me. I supposed that was the gentlemanly thing to do, but I ached to feel the weight of his body on mine. His hand cupped my cheek as we kissed, then slowly worked up to my head, his fingers raking through my hair. I followed suit, letting my own hand explore his soft, blond hair, grateful there was still enough of it for me to play with even after he'd cut it short.

He broke off the kiss then and gazed at me in that way that only he could, with a look of pure wonder that made me feel like the most gorgeous woman on earth.

I bit my lip, certain I was blushing, then felt his mouth move to my neck. As his warm lips traced down my throat, I felt a gnawing ache growing in my core. I purred at the numbingly wonderful sensations from his mouth and twisted my body closer to his. I tugged on the hem of his shirt, desperate to feel his smooth skin.

In a flash, Aiden had removed his shirt, leaving me to admire his sculpted abs and perfectly defined chest. He looked bigger than I remembered, like he'd filled out a bit, and I wondered if he'd turned to exercise to deal with his loneliness. I ran my hand up and down his bare side, but it wasn't enough. I needed more. I shifted to the side, and he followed my lead, lifting my top up and over my head before pulling my mouth back to his.

"You are so beautiful, Jessica," he whispered, his breath tickling my ear.

I kissed him harder and rolled onto my back, nudging him over me. Still kissing me, Aiden guided my hands above my head, tracing his hand along my side until I giggled. He released my hands and smiled at me.

"I haven't stopped wanting you Jessica, not for one moment," he said.

"Oh, Aiden," I murmured. "I missed you too."

From that point, we moved quickly, with the rest of our clothes piling beside the bed in a matter of moments. When Aiden finally entered me I nearly cried because I was so happy. I hadn't realized how incomplete I felt without him, and now that we were so intimately intertwined, I couldn't imagine ever being apart from him again.

Our eyes locked as we made love, and after we'd both found our pleasure, I realized my eyes were damp with tears. Aiden wiped them away with his thumb, planting chaste kisses all around my face, and whispered into my ear.

"I love you, too," I said.

We remained quiet and still for a while before Aiden finally spoke.

"I could lie like this with you forever," he said.

"I'm not going anywhere," I promised.

"I wouldn't let you," he replied.

We fell quiet again, and I heard the distant sound of doors shutting and footsteps.

"Oliver's home," he said.

"Should I…"

"Stay," he insisted.

I smiled. I felt so comfortable lying beside Aiden, so safe, so peaceful. At some point, I drifted off. When I awoke later, Aiden was still awake, and he was still gazing at me adoringly.

"Do you ever sleep?" I teased.

"If I close my eyes, I won't be able to look at you anymore. And I'm afraid if I fall asleep, I'll wake up and realize this is all a dream."

We opted instead to shower, together, taking turns sudsing each other up and kissing until we ran out of hot water. We made love again in bed, and then, finally, we both fell asleep.

CHAPTER TWENTY-TWO

I awoke with a start, dreading the sense of loss I was certain would come as soon as I opened my eyes. But then I smiled, sensing Jessica's presence even before I looked beside me. Her breath was soft and even, and her body emanated a warmth that comforted me. I stared at her peaceful slumber and watched her lips curl into a small smile, making me wonder what filled her dreams. She woke naturally a short while after I did, stretching her legs and shifting so she was facing me.

"Good morning," I said, kissing her forehead. I smiled. Yes, I could definitely start each day like this. What happened the rest of the day really wouldn't matter.

Jessica sighed sleepily and burrowed closer. I took that as a hint. I kissed her softly while tracing my hand along her stomach and down her shorts. She smiled peacefully but winced suddenly when my hand reached its destination.

I froze.

"Don't stop," she whispered.

I pulled my hand away. "What's wrong? Did I hurt you?"

She opened her eyes and shook her head, blushing. "I'm fine. Just a little…sore, I guess."

"Sore," I repeated. "From last night?" I was perplexed. We'd made love twice, but I thought I'd been gentle with her. "Jessica, I'm sorry. I didn't mean to be rough."

"I said I'm fine. And you weren't rough," she said, as though the notion were preposterous. "I think it's just been a while."

"Oh," I said, still a tad confused. "I didn't… Wait, when did you and Lucas break up?" I had assumed it was sometime after she returned to school, but I realized now that I didn't know any of the details about how things ended with them.

Jessica lifted her head and eyed me warily, as though trying to gauge my intent. Finally, she plopped her head against my chest and groaned.

"What?"

"Not that it's any of your business," she began, "but the last time I had sex with anyone was last May."

I tried to piece together what she was saying but was struggling. Then, suddenly, it hit me. "You never slept with Lucas?"

"I have been with exactly one man ever, and that would be you," she answered.

I didn't understand. I'd seen him with her—there was not a doubt in my mind that he would've been all over her in a heartbeat. "But you were engaged. You spent the whole summer living with him. Did you have separate rooms or something?"

Jessica groaned again. Clearly this was not her topic of choice, but now that we'd started the discussion, I wanted details.

"Okay, I guess if I'm being precise, I did sleep with Lucas."

My abs clenched.

She continued. "We slept in the same bed every single night for over a month. Usually cuddling. And there was a lot of kissing and, I don't know, some other stuff. But we never had sex." She sat up and stared at me, annoyed. "Are you happy now?"

"Of course I am, Jessica. I know I don't have any right to an opinion about who you did or didn't sleep with. I'm just surprised is all. When I heard you were engaged, I assumed… Well, you know. I don't understand. Why didn't you ever…"

Jessica rolled her eyes. "Why do you think, Aiden? I wasn't over you and Lucas is a really good guy. He would never pressure a woman to sleep with him before she was ready."

I nodded. "Okay. I'm sorry. It's not my business." I rubbed my forehead, overwhelmed by all the developments in the last twelve hours. "For what it's worth, I haven't been with anyone since you either."

Jessica didn't say anything, but settled back against me.

"What time is your first class this morning?"

"Not till noon," she said. "It's my short day."

That was good, since it was already after 8:30. A soft rumble escaped Jessica's stomach.

"I'll go make some breakfast and bring it back up," I said, shimmying away from her.

"No. Stay," she said. "I'm not hungry."

"I can hear your tummy growling."

She groaned. "Fine, but hurry."

I pulled on some pants and went downstairs. I was tempted to make the grand feast she deserved, but my desire to rush back to her side won out so I made her tea and toast and grabbed an orange. I was pleasantly surprised to find Jessica still in bed when I returned.

We made small talk while we ate, but Jessica soon grew quiet. I knew that meant she had something important to say.

"Did you mean what you said about giving it all up?" she finally asked.

I nodded.

"I don't want you to rush into any decisions."

"It's not rushing. I've had months to consider what I want, and I want you."

Jessica blushed and smiled. "I don't think you should abandon your plans to be king, though. I mean, is there some deadline you need to tell them by?"

I laughed. She made it sound like I was considering turning down a nomination to head up the PTO or something, not a birthright to rule an entire nation of elves. "No. We can take as long as we need to decide. I'm done letting anyone else have any say in our lives. You and I will decide if I agree to rule, and, if so, how, and under what conditions."

She smiled and chewed off another small bite of her toast.

It was such a normal, pleasant moment that I hated to ruin it by bringing up the past, but I knew I needed to tell her what my father and I had learned about her ancestry. The longer I waited, the harder it would be. And now that we were back together, Jessica needed to know.

"Jessica," I began, clearing my throat awkwardly. She gazed up at me lovingly, and I completely lost my train of thought for a moment. "There's something else you should know."

Now she looked more serious, and I knew I had her full attention.

"Do you remember our first dinner in London with my father, how he kept questioning you about your great-grand-parents?"

She nodded slowly, clearly curious where this was headed.

"I found out why he was so interested. There was a man by the same name as your grandfather, Fritz. He was an elf, actually. And he left his clan, moved to America, and married a human named Ethel. He cut all ties with our people, but our genealogy charts show they had one child, a son they named Joseph. According to our records, Joseph married a woman named Kathleen. Our charts show the family line ended there, that Joseph and Kathleen died without any biological children."

Jessica swallowed audibly. She was frowning, but didn't yet seem to realize fully what I was telling her.

"We thought this could all be a coincidence, but when we ran blood tests on other humans after they were injected with elf blood, we found that no matter how much elf blood they received, it was completely out of their system within a matter of days. Whenever we gave you my blood, it stayed in your system a little longer each time. There was no such cumulative effect with other humans."

"I don't understand."

"We believe your grandfather Fritz was an elf. And that makes you one quarter elf."

Jessica shook her head dismissively. "Nice try, Aiden."

I reached for her hand. "I'm serious, Jessica. I can show you all the lab results if you want, but there's no other explanation.

She was quiet for several minutes. I knew it would take time for her to think through news this big, so I didn't speak or rush her.

"How long have you known this?" she asked.

"That night of the dinner my father told me his suspicions. We knew for sure soon after. I..."

"You've known for months now that I'm part elf, and you wait to tell me until after we..." she shook her head with disgust as she gestured at the disheveled bed. "This is unbelievable Aiden, even for you."

She jumped up and began dressing quickly.

"Jessica, wait." I reached for her arm, but she swatted my hand away.

"No," she said. "I need time to process this. And I need time to figure out how I feel now that I know that you haven't changed at all, that you still think it is okay to keep things from me." She started out the bedroom door.

"I tried to tell you in London," I shouted, following her down the hall. "You wouldn't answer my calls. And I was going to tell you that night, but you passed out drunk after your final exam. And then I couldn't tell you in the morning because you were gone by the time I returned from Russia."

She picked up the pace as she reached the bottom of the stairs, but I was faster. I grabbed her hands and backed her against the wall in the hall. I hated to restrain her but I couldn't let her leave without explaining.

"I could have told you right after we freed you, but you were so upset then. This would have been just another thing for you to process. And I considered telling you when you were with Lucas, but what would have been the point? I thought you were happy with him. I didn't want to make you question your entire world when it didn't matter anyway."

Jessica shook her head. "Then why tell me now?"

"Because you deserve to know. Because I wish I'd told you the second I found out. Because I'm trying to start fresh, to be completely open and honest with you about everything."

Jessica looked down to the ground. "I need to go."

I released her immediately. "Take my car," I said, gesturing to the keys by the door. "I'll send someone to pick it up later if you don't want to see me."

She snatched the keys and stormed out, wordlessly.

I sighed and leaned against the wall, knocking my head against it twice. Then I looked up and saw Oliver on the stairs. He stared at me for a long moment before silently retreating to his room.

JESSICA

I reached our apartment in record time, apparently having sped. I slowed my pace as I neared the door. I was too sleep-deprived to remember if Claire would be home now, and I was not in the mood to explain my whereabouts last night. I tiptoed through the apartment, bypassing her closed door, hoping she was still sleeping. I changed clothes then headed out for a long walk around campus. I needed to clear my head, and I couldn't do it locked in my bedroom.

It was a gorgeous fall morning. The leaves had reached their peak brightness, filling the trees with bold reds, yellows, and oranges that would soon dry out and fall to the ground. The crisp air kept me alert, but I kept walking for good measure. I forced myself to focus on what Aiden had said and not why he had said it—or how I felt about his timing.

I had no reason to question his veracity. I could see that he did have ample motivation to convince me I was more like him, maybe to calm my concerns about us being together, but I was certain Aiden wouldn't lie to me. Not about this. And being a rather thorough guy, he surely would have verified the accuracy of the records and my blood work. It was odd that their records showed my family's accurate lineage right up until me. If the elves were so on top of this whole record keeping business, why weren't they aware of my birth?

But regardless, there it was. I was one-fourth elf. What that entailed, exactly, I certainly didn't know. I definitely lacked Aiden's super hearing and sight. I didn't need glasses or hearing aids yet, but I was pretty sure my abilities were well within the realm of normal. I also was decidedly not remarkably fast or strong, not that I'd ever really tested out those feats. I guess I did have a good immune system. I really never got sick, and I didn't suffer allergies either.

I thought about my grandma, Ethel. She'd died when I was little, so I didn't have many memories of her, but if what Aiden had said was true—if she, a human, conceived my father with an elf, then it could be done. I could be with Aiden and someday still have children of my own. That was huge. I could pretend it wasn't a big deal and that I'd be happy enough with Aiden to not miss the lack of children in my life, but it would be a lie. I'd always wanted to be a mother, and ever since I'd lost my own parents, my desire to someday have biological children had grown.

I returned to the apartment to collect my books for class. As I scooted into my desk in the poorly lit lecture hall, I finally allowed my mind to focus on the other issue—the fact that Aiden had known this information long before he shared it with me. I suspected I should be deeply disturbed by that. It should bother me that the whole time he was claiming to love and miss me, he was keeping something—something huge—from me.

But really, it didn't.

When I returned home after class, I noticed the black sedan Aiden had loaned me was gone, but just as I started to panic, I spotted a large, white SUV parked directly in front of my apartment. As I approached the door, Aiden popped out of the passenger seat.

"How many cars do you have?" I asked, unlocking my door.

"I don't know. A lot."

I rolled my eyes. "And I assume you took your other car back? Because it isn't in the lot where I parked it."

"Yeah."

I rummaged around in my purse for his keys and dropped them in his hand.

"Can I come in?"

I sighed. "How long were you waiting out here?"

"A few hours."

I laughed. "For someone with an entire army at your disposal, you suck at stalking people. Couldn't you have hacked into the school computers and figured out my schedule?"

His eyes narrowed. "Yes, but I'm trying to respect your privacy."

"Come in," I said, my voice still terse.

He rushed in behind me as though he worried I'd change my mind. "Thank you. Jessica, I just…"

I held up my hand to stop him. "I want to talk."

Aiden nodded.

"You should have told me. I understand all your excuses for why you didn't, but you should've tried harder. You could've told

Lucas if you didn't want to tell me." I paused, dumping my back-pack beside the table and shrugging out of my jacket. "The point is you can't filter what information you provide me. I understand you want to protect me, but you can't do it by withholding information or lying. It isn't your job to decide what I get to know. I am an adult. If we are going to be involved in each other's lives at all, we can't have secrets, no matter what the motivation behind the secret may be."

He gazed expectantly.

"That's all. You can talk now."

"Okay. Well, you're right. I agree with all of that," he said. "And I'm sorry. I realize I messed up."

"Okay. I forgive you."

Aiden frowned. "Seriously? That's it. You just…forgive me."

I blew out a sigh. "Yes, Aiden, that's it. Is that okay with you? Or do you want me to stay mad? I thought about why you kept it from me, and I see where you are coming from. So as long as we're in agreement that it can't happen again, I don't see how it helps to stay mad."

"I love you," he said, stepping closer.

I held a hand up again to stop him. "Just because I'm not mad doesn't mean I'm ready to move forward. I still have a lot to think about. It's just… are you sure about everything you told me?"

Aiden nodded and motioned for me to sit. "Is Claire here?"

I shook my head. Although I hadn't confirmed her absence, she usually had a class at this time, and she was never this quiet when she was home.

"There are a lot of people—my kind—who don't like the idea of elves and humans intermarrying. So, historically, when it happened, there wasn't a lot of documentation." He breathed a laugh. "Ironically, my father and my uncle Marius, our current king, are both big supporters of full integration. Or at least they were, before it got too close to home with our involvement. The more I think about it, the more I think my father had suspicions about you from the start. He was so sure you'd sought me out for some reason, that you knew what we were before I told you. And I could've sworn he looked like he recognized you the first time he saw you."

"But he couldn't have seen me before, could he?"

Aiden shrugged. "Probably not. But if there was documentation of any intermarriage, maybe there was a picture of your mother and father that he saw."

"I don't feel like an elf. All those times you gave me elf blood, I felt different. Wouldn't I just feel that way normally if I were actually an elf?"

"Jessica, you're basically human. The majority of your genetic makeup is human. You just have the tiniest bit of elf blood in you. It isn't enough to be noticeably different. I realize it must be unsettling to learn all this now, especially when your parents and any others who could answer questions about your heritage are gone. But this is actually good news."

I frowned, certain there were some perks to being an elf with special powers like Aiden, but sure that I had no such special abilities. "How so?"

"Well, for starters, the fact that the elf blood we give you has a cumulative effect in your system is good. That means you can feel like an elf if you need to. Or want to," he added. "And it means you could most likely have a successful pregnancy with an elf." Aiden gazed sideways at me as he said that.

"Wait. So you're saying this means we could have kids someday and they'd be healthy?"

"Yes. That is what I'm saying."

I smiled, relieved that he was confirming my suspicions.

"And there's some other related good news, which I don't think you're going to like hearing, but that I need to tell you in light of our new complete honesty policy."

I braced myself, then nodded for him to continue.

"Back in London, when we gave you all those extra injections of my blood, it had the desired effect."

"What do you mean? What was the desired effect?"

"Well, we thought the rival clans would come to the house to test your blood, and we wanted the results to show that you were at least half elf. Granted, nothing turned out the way we intended, but those monsters still tested your blood, and both rival clans accepted their results as accurate."

I turned away, not wanting to think about that time.

Aiden reached for my hand. "Jessica, their tests showed that you had nearly 75% elf blood. By those standards, you could marry an elf without causing too much upheaval."

I tried to swallow the lump in my throat. "So you're saying that because of everything they did to me, there are now fewer obstacles for you and me to get married and have children someday."

He frowned. "Well, yes, but I had wanted that result from tests performed in our home, with your consent. I'm not saying it was a good thing that any of that happened to you."

I nodded. It was just a lot to take in.

We talked for more than an hour, and I still didn't feel at peace with it all. I felt like I needed another sounding board to discuss it all with, but of course I couldn't tell Claire I was part elf or she'd think I was insane. And I didn't think Lucas would be interested in hearing about my increased chances of conceiving Aiden's baby. When I'd called him to let him know I was going to see Aiden, he had acted casual and accepting of it, but he was uncharacteristically sloppy at his game the next day, so I suspected he was far from okay with it all.

"I have to leave town for a few days," Aiden said when it was getting late. "I'll be back on the 31st."

"Halloween," I said, not sure how I felt about him leaving. On the one hand, I'd just gotten him back and was eager to keep him as close as possible. On the other hand, I might have a better chance of sorting out all my emotions without him by my side.

"You could come over to the house," he offered.

"Claire is dragging me to a party that night," I said, refusing to be that girl who bailed on her friends when a boyfriend waltzed back into her life.

"Can you bring a date?"

"Sure, but it's a costume party."

Aiden grinned. "I can dress up."

I was skeptical but agreed. We shared a long kiss goodbye, and then he was gone.

CHAPTER TWENTY-THREE

I called Jessica every night while I was gone. Knowing I'd hear her voice at the end of each day kept me going through the long, tedious meetings. On the last day of my trip, I realized I hadn't yet procured a costume for the party with Jessica, and I didn't want to let her down. After everything we'd been through, she needed some fun. I was always so serious around her, well, and everyone else, so I decided on a costume that would show her I did have a sense of humor.

The next night, I arrived at Jessica's apartment promptly at 8 p.m. I climbed out of the car, eager to escape Elgin's hysterical laughter that had been nonstop since he first saw me fifteen minutes before. Honestly, when I'd thought up the costume idea and sent an assistant out to buy it, I hadn't envisioned it being quite so...comical. But, there I was, wearing striped red and white tights, a long green jacket with a cheap black belt, and, of course, a green stocking cap with a jingle bell on the end.

Elgin rolled down the window, presumably so he could hear Jessica's reaction to my costume. She opened the door and her eyes widened as she bit back a smile.

"What are you?" she asked.

"Isn't it obvious? I'm an elf."

Claire came up behind her. "I could've told you that. Nice costume, Aiden."

Jessica burst into laughter and threw herself into my arms. "You are my absolute favorite elf," she whispered. "I love you."

"I thought you might have a thing for elves," I teased, nudging her back so I could see her costume.

She took the hint, stepped back, and spun around. She was a vision in a long, shimmery white gown. Her hair was pulled over one shoulder in a long braid and a simple silver tiara perched atop her head. I was tempted to rush home to pick up a real tiara for her, but decided that wouldn't coordinate as well with my polyester blend tights.

"I'm a fairy princess," she said, explaining the small glittery wings strapped to her back.

"A gorgeous one at that," I said, kissing her delicate hand.

Claire made a gagging sound. "Jack is meeting me there," she explained to Jessica.

I glanced at Jessica, wanting an explanation as to who this Jack was, but she shook her head mouthing the word "later."

"Well, my brother-in-law is in the car if we're all ready to go," I said.

"The scary dude with the long hair?" she asked.

"Yep, that's the one," Jessica replied, latching arms with her friend.

The ladies rode in the back while I sat up by Elgin. At the party, he insisted on coming inside, and, even though he wasn't in costume, no one gave him a hard time.

We stayed late, then spent the night at my house. I slept soundly, with the satisfaction that I'd given Jessica at least one day of normalcy.

. . .

JESSICA

The next few weeks were a blur of perfection. When Aiden traveled, which was often, I threw myself into my studies. When he was home, I stayed glued to his side. Even though we hadn't been apart that long, I felt like we had so much catching up to do, and I was enjoying listening to all of his political adventures and relearning every inch of his perfect body.

We'd fallen into a glorious routine of spending the night in his luxurious bed whenever he was in town, eating breakfast in bed, and then burning off the breakfast calories until I had to leave for class. It was definitely a ritual I could get used to.

"I could stay right like this forever," I said on one such perfect morning as Aiden shifted his body above mine, pushing me back against the fluffy pillows.

He captured my mouth with a forceful kiss then pressed his lips gently against my ear, tickling me with his breath before whispering, "marry me."

I froze, certain I'd misheard him, but then he breathed a laugh, apparently having perceived my sudden panic, courtesy of his special elfy powers.

"Please?" he added, pulling back enough to lock eyes with me.

God, he was gorgeous first thing in the morning. His chiseled jaw, those vivid blue eyes, his silky full lips, and that soft blond hair, now just long enough for me to run my fingers through—everything about him screamed perfection. And I wasn't even going to let myself think of his gifts that awaited me below neck level.

I realized I was staring at him while he was waiting for a response, but I didn't really know if I'd even heard him right or if it was a serious request. "Aiden, you can't just say that when we're in bed. I thought we were about to..." I was too embarrassed to finish my sentence.

Aiden flashed me a devilish grin and grazed his hand across my breast, eliciting a squeal as a tinge of pleasure shot down my torso. "Oh we are, don't worry." He rolled to the side, keeping me pinned in place with his arm but removing the majority of his body weight from me.

"Jessica, I want you to marry me because of this. Because you want to be with me for me, not because I have to be married or because I'm going to be the king. I want you to marry me because you need to start every day like this with me just as much as I need that."

He paused, his hooded gaze now fully captivating me. "I want you to be my queen, Jessica, but I want you to be my wife first. I promise you no matter what I'm supposed to do, I will always put you first, before myself, before my people, before my duties."

"You're serious," I finally said, my voice cracking.

"I am," he said, kissing me gently. "Jessica let me love you the rest of my life. Let me protect you and honor you every day from here on out. Please be my wife."

I blinked, struggling against the tears trickling past my eyelashes. "Yes, Aiden. I'll marry you."

He stared at me a moment, his smile widening. "Really?"

I giggled. "Yes, really."

Aiden kissed me again, this time pulling me against him as he rolled onto his back. We kissed until our lips were numb, and I couldn't stop smiling from the realization that I could do this every morning for the rest of my life.

"Was that really how you'd planned to ask me?" I asked him when we finally paused to catch our breath.

Aiden breathed a laugh, shaking his head. "No. I was going to propose later today when we were at the student union where we first got to know each other during our tutoring sessions."

I pictured that, and decided that, too, would have been romantic, then he continued.

"But you looked so beautiful right now that it actually scared me to think there was any chance at all that I wouldn't get to wake up beside you every day for the rest of my life. I had to know your answer. I couldn't wait six more hours."

"That's kind of sweet," I agreed. "I'm just trying to figure out what to say if people ask how you proposed." My grandma especially might not understand the romance of a proposal included in foreplay.

"You could just tell them my beautifully poetic words and say we were alone."

"What if someone asks what I was wearing when you proposed?" That would be one of Claire's questions for sure.

"Just be honest. Tell them you were wearing me," Aiden said with a smirk.

I giggled and pulled him close for another kiss. When we finally came up for air, Aiden spoke again.

"My marriage was supposed to be a business arrangement," he said. "Everything about it was supposed to be public and altogether impersonal. I don't want that. You know I don't. And this seemed more fitting for what we actually want. This way, I hope you see that I want to marry you for you, not because I'm supposed to marry someone soon. You'll always trust that I picked you because I love you and I want you to be my wife, not because I think you fit the description of the type of woman I need for a queen."

I started to reply, but before I found the words, Aiden cut me off with another kiss.

By the time we finally emerged from under the covers, I had less than a half hour until my first class of the day. I swore under my breath after glancing at the clock and scampered into the bathroom. Ten minutes later I emerged dressed, teeth and hair brushed, face washed, and minimal makeup applied. Aiden was seated on the edge of his bed, reading something on his phone, fully dressed in a business suit and completely dashing despite the fact that he had taken even less time than me to get ready.

"You won't have time to find parking," he said, standing and lifting my backpack. "I'll drop you off."

He was right about the parking since the closest lot was a ten minute walk to class. I shook my head. "I'm sure you have work to do."

Aiden frowned. "Yes. And I probably should start now since I'm taking off for lunch."

"We could do lunch another day," I said, starting down the hallway.

"No way," he protested. Aiden spotted Oliver at the bottom of the stairs. "Are you headed to campus now?" he called.

Oliver turned and nodded.

"Perfect. Will you drop Jessica at the history building? Her class is in fifteen minutes."

Oliver glanced at his watch and nodded.

"I love you," Aiden said softly to me, pulling me close for a kiss that really made me question my rationale in attending class.

"Going to be late," Oliver called.

We pulled apart and I scurried down the stairs. A guard outside the door held the door open for us and we were off in no time. I smiled, realizing I actually might make it on time. We rode in silence for the first few minutes, and then I noticed Oliver eying me warily.

"Do I even want to know why you're so smiley today?" he asked.

I wasn't sure how or when Aiden planned to tell his brother the news, so I just shook my head coyly. "Probably not. Thanks for the ride, though."

Oliver made a face, which I pretended not to see, then I scurried out to class, sliding into a chair just as the professor began. My first class was only fifty minutes, and then I had fifteen minutes before my next one, which was right down the hall. I was busy enough in the first class to stay focused, but in my second class, which was ninety minutes, my mind kept returning to the activities of the morning. When class ended, I popped out of my seat and zipped into the hall, eager to make my way to the union where I would meet up with my fiancé.

Instead, I rounded the corner of the classroom and slammed right into his statuesque body.

"Hurrying to get somewhere?" Aiden asked, biting back a grin. He relieved me of my backpack and gripped my hand tightly as we walked together.

We went through the cafeteria-style dining hall line at the union and then selected a table in the corner, by a window.

"I believe this is the exact spot where I first imparted my economics wisdom to you," Aiden said.

I felt my smile widen and then thought about what it would have been like if he had proposed there, in the middle of the student union dining hall. It was moderately busy now, with a mixture of students eating with friends and talking loudly along with students studying in silence while eating alone. It was not, from an objective point of view, a romantic spot, and yet I could totally see Aiden finding the charm in its appropriateness to our relationship.

"Kind of a boring lunch now that you rushed your plan, huh," I teased.

"Nothing is ever boring with you," he replied, in a tone that made the words more ominous than romantic. "Plus, this way I can actually eat because I'm not anxiously awaiting your response."

I rolled my eyes. "You know everything I'm thinking before I say it aloud, so I can't imagine you would have been too nervous. Besides, did you really have any doubt as to what I'd say?"

Aiden tilted his head curiously, gazing around the room at the other students milling about. "Yes, actually. I think you're crazy to want to marry me, and since I know you're a smart woman, I wasn't altogether sure what you'd say."

I considered that for a moment while picking at my bagel.

"I forgot something, though," Aiden said.

He slipped out of his seat as he spoke, so I thought he had said he dropped, rather than forgot, something, and I quickly looked under the table to see what could have fallen. When I glanced up, Aiden was kneeling in front of me. As I looked to him, he held out a large ring. It had a bright, shimmery princess cut diamond surrounded by smaller but equally sparkly round cut diamonds. The platinum band was lined with more princess cut diamonds along the middle with a row of round diamonds beneath and another row above. It was blindingly bright and so gorgeous it took my breath away.

Aiden smiled. "You agreed to be my wife without even seeing your ring. Will you accept this small token of my love?"

I nodded my head, suddenly feeling flushed and dizzy. Aiden slid the ring onto my finger and rose to his feet, pausing to kiss me before returning to his seat. I swallowed nervously and brought my hand to my lips, afraid to look around and see dozens of students gawking at Aiden's display of affection but equally concerned I was about to start crying at the sweet gesture.

Aiden scooted his chair closer, effectively blocking anyone's view of me, and squeezed my other hand.

"No one's watching," he said, surely lying. "I'm sorry if I embarrassed you."

I shook my head and tried to speak, but I couldn't formulate words.

Aiden patiently waited for me to regain my composure, smiling calmly. Finally, he spoke. "It looks good on you," he said.

I gazed down at the ring, barely recognizing my own hand. The ring fit perfectly, but nothing about it was subtle. It looked like it was suitable for royalty, not some regular old girl from a small Midwestern town.

"It's beautiful," I said. "And humongous. This must have cost a fortune. You didn't have…"

"Stop," Aiden interrupted. "I know I didn't have to, but I wanted to. I wanted a ring that was special for you and that reminded you how much I love you. And you should get used to it. You know I have money and I'm going to buy you nice things, whether you ask for them or not. You might as well just save yourself from losing multiple pointless arguments and learn to say thank you instead of protesting when I give you a gift."

"Thank you," I said, breaking my eyes away from the ring just long enough to make eye contact with the love of my life.

"You're welcome. Now finish your food so I don't make you late to your next class."

I groaned and scooted my tray to the side. "I lost my appetite."

"Well, you should eat something. You're going to need energy for what I have planned for tonight," Aiden said with a mischievous wink.

Of course that only made me blush more. I quickly tried to change the subject.

"Does Oliver know?"

Aiden shook his head. "Not unless you told him this morning."

"I didn't."

"I'm afraid we won't be able to keep it secret very long now that I've marked you as mine with precious jewels," he teased.

I laughed, but had to agree. This was not the sort of ring that people wouldn't notice. As I went to my final class of the day and multiple people commented on my new jewelry, my hunch certainly proved true. I was happy about my news and had no qualms about sharing it, but was surprised by the number of people who hadn't realized I was even in a serious relationship. And I was even more caught off guard by the three people who assumed my fiancé was Lucas.

I swallowed with dread at the awareness that I would have to tell Lucas the news soon, before he risked hearing it from anyone else. I didn't think it would truly come as a surprise to him, but since I'd worn his engagement ring for nearly a month over the summer, he had a right to be upset.

Lucas

Jessica called the week before Thanksgiving and asked if I could get her seats to my game in Chicago Tuesday night. Of course I agreed, no questions asked, but when she said she just needed one ticket, I was filled with relief. I knew she was dating Aiden again. As per my request, she'd been honest about that. But knowing she was dating him and seeing her flirt with him rinkside as I tried to focus on the game were two very different matters.

She had told me about Aiden back in October. I had just settled into my hotel room in New York when she called, and I'd known the second she spoke that something was different. I could hear it in her voice, the uncertainty, the concern. And I knew why, or rather who, before she told me.

She'd explained that she'd run into Oliver, Aiden's younger brother, on campus and that it turned out Aiden was going to be in town soon, so she was going to meet up with him to talk. "Just to talk," she had clarified. And then she'd quickly changed the subject, as if I'd be able to focus on her rants about her educational psychology professor when visions of her kissing Aiden were floating through my brain.

The next day, I missed an easy shot in our game. We still won, but it was the first time I'd screwed up. The coaches weren't hard on me, but I knew it couldn't happen again. That night, I went home with a redhead getting her MBA and made myself forget all about Jessica. I didn't miss another shot that month, even when Jessica told me she was officially dating Aiden again.

I spotted Jessica before my game that night, offering her a wide smile as she waved back, and then I played my heart out. I still wasn't getting as much time on the ice as I'd like, but I couldn't complain. For a first year rookie, I was enjoying more than my fair share of play. I dodged the press after the game and hit the showers quickly, eager to meet up with Jessica. I'd arranged for her to have a press pass so she could wait for me in the hall outside our locker room just like she had at all of my high school and college games.

When I met up with her, she was reading. I laughed at the absurdity of it all. As an actual hockey fan, I would've expected her to be more interested in the excitement surrounding her in the bustling hallway, filled with professional hockey players. But until she saw me, she actually looked bored.

Jeff walked out right behind me, so she chatted with him for a moment, then reached over to give me a hug. It was the first time I'd seen her since summer, and she was looking great. She'd regained the weight she'd lost at the start of summer, and her hair had more luster than before. She looked happy.

"You look good," I told her. "How have you been?"

"Good," she said. "You were amazing out there. Seriously. I need to come to more of your games."

"That can be arranged," I agreed "So, dinner?"

She nodded and we walked to my car.

"Do you need a place to stay tonight?" I asked, suddenly realizing she couldn't possibly drive back from Chicago this late at night. Not to be a chauvinist pig, but it just wasn't safe for a cute, young girl to drive through the city alone. "I'm all moved in and there's a full-service guest room at your disposal."

"I'm staying at a hotel. I'll head home tomorrow to spend the holiday with Grandma."

"You didn't have to get a hotel. I promise not to make things awkward."

Jessica hesitated, blushing. "I'm not alone… Aiden's here."

"Oh." I tried to act casual, but it took me a while to figure out something else to say. I might be a nice guy, but I wasn't about to offer to let them both stay in my guest room. "He didn't want to come to the game?"

"I didn't invite him," she said. "I wanted to talk to you."

"Uh-oh," I said.

She made me wait until after we'd gotten to the restaurant and ordered before telling me anything serious. I'm not sure why, since I couldn't really focus on her updates about her classes when I was trying to guess what big news she had.

"Aiden asked me to marry him," she blurted out as the waitress left with our menus.

"Oh." I waited for her to say more, but she didn't. I glanced down and noticed there was no ring on her hand. "Are you wanting my blessing or something?"

She smiled. "I'm not completely insane, Lucas. I just wanted you to know."

"So you said yes?"

She nodded.

"Where's the ring?"

Jessica glanced down at her jeans. "My pocket," she said sheepishly. "I didn't want you to see it before I told you."

"Well, let's see it," I said, regretting the words as soon as they left my mouth. But I figured it would be easier to get it over with now.

Jessica slipped her hand into her pocket and slid her ring onto her finger.

"Jesus!" The ring was gigantic and shockingly bright. It probably would've blinded the guys trying to shoot a goal if she'd had it on at the game.

She sipped her drink.

"Congratulations," I said, sucking at sounding genuine.

Jessica laughed. "Thanks. So you're not drinking?"

"I think I'll get a beer now," I said. "But that's all I can do. We have practice tomorrow, starting with a post-mortem on tonight's game."

"Will you be home for Thanksgiving?"

"I'll be in Thursday through Friday."

"I think my grandma and I are headed to your house Thursday."

"Will Aiden be with you guys?"

Jessica shook her head quickly, much to my relief. "No. He's dropping me off tomorrow. We are going to tell my grandma the news, and then he's flying to Germany or someplace for the week."

We managed to keep the rest of the meal civil, and I decided to at least be thankful for the timing of Jessica's news. Had she told me this within a few days of a game, I would've thrown it for sure. This way, at least I could process it all before our Saturday game.

CHAPTER TWENTY-FOUR

I couldn't believe my luck. Jessica was back, she had forgiven me, and she was comfortably in my arms with my sparkling diamond on her finger. I recognized it as that mythical moment where I had literally everything I wanted. I wasn't going to do anything to ruin it. She'd told Lucas and her grandma the news, and she claimed they'd both reacted well. I told Oliver, and Elgin obviously knew since he followed me around everywhere, but I'd left him in the precarious position of keeping his knowledge from his wife for the time being. I wasn't eager to share the happy news with the rest of my family.

"I love you," I said, peppering Jessica's forehead with kisses. "I just love you so much." I squeezed her tighter, then released, nervous I would hurt her.

"You're not going to break me," she said, gazing up at me with her brown eyes wide as saucers.

I resisted the urge to remind her that I had already broken her multiple times. From this point onward, I was going to leave the past behind us. If she could forgive me, I could attempt to forgive myself too, I supposed.

"I'm just so happy," I said.

Jessica smiled sleepily. "Me too."

Her eyes started to drift shut but I was still wide awake, my mind racing with the multitude of ways things could go wrong. My father would disapprove. My uncle would forbid the marriage. My people could launch an uprising. The sensible thing to do would be to accept a lengthy engagement, to give everyone plenty of time to come to terms with the fact that I was going to wed Jessica Grove. Hopefully, by the wedding day, they'd all be used to it—maybe even happy for us. Once it was a done deal, they would have to accept it, as divorce was not a common occurrence in the elf world.

And then it came to me. I sat abruptly, amused that I hadn't realized this sooner.

"We should get married!" I said.

"Mmm hmm," Jessica agreed, her eyes still shut.

I roused her gently. "No, really. I think we should get married now."

"Aiden, I said yes."

"You're not understanding. I don't want to wait." I observed her half-sleeping form and remembered Jessica needed rest. "Well, we could wait until morning."

Jessica frowned and opened her eyes a slit. "You're talking about eloping?"

I didn't love her terminology, but I supposed that was what I meant. "Yes. Only it doesn't have to be a secret. We could bring your grandmother."

"Aiden I just told her about the engagement last week. She'll think I'm pregnant if we surprise her with an impromptu wedding."

"Well, you can tell her you're not, and she'll see that anyway in a few months."

Jessica pulled away and shook her head. "Aiden, why do you want to rush things?"

"Because so much can go wrong, Jessica. Don't you see—I finally have you back, and I want this to be official so we don't have to worry anymore about anything keeping us apart."

She sighed. "I've already agreed to marry you, Aiden. Nothing could keep us apart now anyway. Are you worried you'll change your mind?"

I felt my eyes widen. How could she even think that? "No, Jessica, no! I will never change my mind. I just want to start our future together now. We've waited long enough. I don't want to deal with all the disapproval from my family and my people. I don't want anyone to feel like they have a say in what we decide to do. I just want this to be about you and I agreeing to spend the rest of our lives together. What does the wedding matter anyway?"

"It matters to me," she said softly.

I wasn't sure what to say to that. She was already giving up so much that she had planned for her life, just to be with me. It was clearly unfair for me to expect her to sacrifice her dream wedding, too. I pulled Jessica back against my chest.

"I'm sorry," I whispered, pressing my lips into her forehead. "I wasn't thinking. I'm just so scared something will go wrong. I can't stand the thought of losing you again."

"I know. You won't," she agreed.

"I want you to have the wedding you've always pictured," I said. "Will you tell me about it?"

She inhaled slowly and shut her eyes, smiling. "I've always wanted the traditional white dress, with a sequined train, and a lacy veil, and, of course, a cute tiara. I don't want a huge wedding, but I've always imagined the ceremony would be outside, with maybe a covered tent for the dinner."

"Will there be dancing?"

"Of course."

"And kissing?"

Jessica giggled. "Obviously."

We were silent for a moment. "I regret not asking for your grandma's blessing before proposing."

"You could ask her now. It's not too late." Jessica settled down beside me. "Now let me sleep or I'll be grumpy tomorrow."

"I love you," I whispered one last time.

JESSICA

My last final exam was a breeze. Somehow, that was a letdown. It was like all of my years of studying had finally culminated in this, my last semester of actual classes before student teaching. And for my last test ever to be a joke, well, it just felt wrong. I didn't dwell on it, though. Aiden had been gone for over a week and was due back any minute now. I headed directly to his house to wait for him. I had less than two weeks with him before heading home to spend Christmas with my grandma.

The house was quiet when I arrived, with no sign of life aside from the guard stationed just outside the front door. I made myself at home, dumped my backpack in the corner of the room, and fixed myself a quick snack in the kitchen before returning to the living room to veg out by the TV until Aiden returned home.

It wasn't long before I heard a commotion outside and switched off the TV, excitedly hopping up to greet Aiden. But when the front door opened, it wasn't Aiden who entered.

It was his father.

My breath hitched in my throat. He was taller and colder than I remembered him, not to mention completely forbidden from coming here. Whatever the reason for his visit, it couldn't be good. I took a cautious step backwards, about to shout for the guard when I realized Ivar had walked right in the door where the guard had been stationed. Either the guard was gone or he was on Ivar's side.

Ivar gazed around the room slowly before acknowledging me.

"I'm not going to hurt you," he said as though I were ridiculous for even considering the possibility. "I'm here to speak with Aiden."

"He's not here."

Ivar cocked his head to the side. "Yes, that explains why the guard let me in. You heard Aiden kicked me out of my own home, I suppose?"

I nodded.

"Well, I suppose it's convenient that you're here. The news I came to share with Aiden actually pertains to you, so I'll just tell you and you can pass it along to my son."

Ivar froze suddenly, his gaze locked on me. I glanced down and realized he was staring at my ring. His eyes widened, and even with all of his composure, he was unable to hide his surprise.

"So, it's official," he said, his voice even and calm.

"Yes," I replied, as softly as a whisper.

He inhaled deeply, paused, then exhaled, slowly releasing the air from his chest. "Well, I guess you'll have a lot to learn in the next few weeks then."

A noise from the back of the house startled both of us and I turned, relieved to see Aiden coming in through the kitchen with Elgin following quickly behind. Aiden looked to me first, confirming my well-being, then turned to his father, his stare hardening.

"You shouldn't be here," Aiden said, quickly approaching his father. Elgin remained in the corner of the room, unmoving, but his posture reminded me of a cat, ready to pounce.

Ivar turned and gestured to me. "Your fiancée and I were just discussing the happy news. Congratulations," he said, his tone anything but cheery. "I'm sure I don't need to remind you that Marius should be notified about this... development... immediately."

"My personal life isn't a matter of his concern. If he is unable to accept my relationship with Jessica, he is welcome to select a new king to succeed him."

Ivar's expression changed then to something best described as pride. I glanced at Aiden for some reassurance or explanation, but he was still staring angrily at his father.

"Tell me why I shouldn't have the guards escort you out now," Aiden said.

Ivar chuckled. "As head of the royal guard, I am technically still their boss. In that vein, I suspect they're more inclined to listen to me over you. Regardless, don't bother. I'll be on my way in a moment. I was reviewing some of our private history records and came across something interesting yesterday."

Aiden stepped closer to me, pulling me to his side and grasping my hand with his without breaking eye contact with his father. "Well?" he prompted.

"I just thought you'd both be interested to know that Jessica's parents did not die in an accident. Her mother was murdered. By elves." Ivar added, turning from Aiden to gaze directly at me.

His piercing stare locked on mine, he continued. "And your father is still alive, Jessica."

I heard myself gasp as I released Aiden's hand. And then the room went black.

THE END

Hollywood Endings

Is happily ever after only in the movies?

When Courtney Robbins moves to California, she isn't looking for love, fame, or fortune. She's focused on earning her law degree and advocating for victims of domestic violence. After a chance encounter with actor Justin Erikson, Courtney decides to spice up her life with a steamy fling. The chemistry between them is undeniable, but Courtney quickly learns there is more to Justin than his perfectly chiseled body, piercing blue eyes and adorable dimples. He's sensitive, thoughtful, and generous. Still, Courtney is hesitant to ponder a future with a Hollywood heartthrob.

As Courtney graduates law school and begins her dream job, Justin's career thrives. But as the passion between Justin and Courtney intensifies, Justin struggles to shelter Courtney from the paparazzi and is haunted by his own reputation as a womanizer. Just when Courtney starts to think that she can have it all—an idyllic romance and the perfect job—a tabloid rumor threatens both of their careers. As their two worlds continue to clash, they must decide what price they are willing to pay to stay together.

Available for purchase through Amazon, Google Play, Barnes & Noble, Apple Books and Kobo.

Hollywood Endings

The Brothers' Band

Two brothers, one band, one woman...what could possibly go wrong?

Lily Mitchell vowed never to date another musician, but Dylan Parker is nothing like the stereotype. Sure, he's mysterious and sexy, with a flashy car and serious bedroom skills, but he's also smart, hardworking, and humble. He shares Lily's passion for classic literature and constantly surprises her with romantic gestures. Their steamy relationship moves at whirlwind pace, and Lily has never been happier.

It's all so perfect that at first, Lily wills herself to ignore the emerging red flags. As her worries about Dylan increase, she finds friendship and comfort in his brother and bandmate, Thomas. But Lily soon discovers that as much as Thomas cares for his brother, he's also fallen hard for her.

As Dylan spirals further out of control, Lily must decide what she really wants, and whom she is willing to hurt.

Available for purchase through Amazon, Google Play, Barnes & Noble, Apple Books and Kobo.

The Brothers' Band

Sixty Days for Love

She's on the clock to win him back!

Chelsea Craig's life is perfect, until her husband David runs off with his paralegal. During the mandatory sixty-day waiting period before the divorce is finalized, Chelsea decides to transform herself into a woman David can't resist. Revamping her life isn't easy, though, and Chelsea lands in one embarrassing predicament after another. Luckily, Nick, a smoldering local cop, happily rushes to her rescue. Convinced that a fling with Nick couldn't hurt, Chelsea embraces the sizzling chemistry they share. But when the separation period draws to a close, Chelsea begins to question whether she's been working all this time to salvage a relationship with the wrong man.

Available for purchase through Amazon, Google Play, Barnes & Noble, Apple Books and Kobo.

Sixty Days for Love

For Love and Italian

An education in amore? Yes, please, Professore

Undergrad Bridget is no stranger to romantic advances from men. But when she meets Owen, an instant friendship forms, even though Owen happens to be Bridget's Italian teacher. Neither of them intends to cross that line, but once they do, they can't deny the passion and chemistry between them. Aware that their tryst is taboo, they keep their relationship clandestine. But like all juicy secrets, this one doesn't stay hidden for long. And once it's out, Owen and Bridget must decide what they're willing to risk in the name of love.

Available for purchase through Amazon, Google Play, Barnes & Noble, Apple Books and Kobo.

For Love and Italian

Forbidden Ink

Loving the bad boy never felt so good!

Ashley Kensington has it all—affluence, status, and the perfect boyfriend. Sheltered by her exclusive southern island community and overprotective father and brothers, Ashley has never strayed from the path her parents chose for her.

Until now.

When Adam Bricker rolls into town with no money, no family, and no ambition for the future, there's no reason that Ashley Kensington should be attracted to him; yet she is. Adam doesn't mind that the locals can't see past his collection of tattoos and his New England accent. Everyone assumes Adam isn't good enough for Ashley, but he's certain he can make her happy and he's ready to fight for what he wants.

For a while, Ashley believes nothing can shatter their epic romance. But when the unexpected happens, Adam is forced to accept that maybe everyone else was right about him from the start.

Available for purchase through Amazon, Google Play, Barnes & Noble,

Apple Books and Kobo.

Forbidden Ink

ACKNOWLEDGMENTS

As always with such a large endeavor, there are so many people who've helped me reach this point. Kimberly, I can't thank you enough for your editing services. JD Book Designs, thank you for your patience with this cover and with my inability to make up my mind about where Lucas should appear on the cover. Thank you to everyone who read early drafts of this book or gave me feedback on the initial cover. Finally, thank you to all my readers and reviewers. You are what truly brings my books to life.

Praise for *Hollywood Endings*:

5 stars for this "refreshing" "lifelike story of [a] normal girl dating a celebrity."

- I Like Books Best book blogger

www.ILikebooksbest.com

Praise for *The Brothers' Band*:

"Liza Malloy weaves together music, great works of literature, family relationships, and romantic relationships into this page turner."

- Verified Amazon Review

"Fun romance book, I couldn't put it down! Steamy love scenes and a great back story."

- Verified Amazon Review

Reviews of *For Love and Italian:*

"A fun, lighthearted and steamy romance, *For Love and Italian* is sweet, romantic, and naughty in the best ways. I was entertained the entire time and was quite sad when it was over. Liza Malloy knows how to write addictive and satisfyingly charming romance stories that will surely give you plenty of swoons and feels…I can't wait to see what she writes next."

- Karen Jo Custodio, Book Blogger.

www.SincerelyKarenJo.com

Praise for *Legacy: The Awakening*:

It is "so easy to get lost in the story and the characters" and "hard to put [] down"

- Verified Amazon Review

Praise for *Forbidden Ink*:

"Get comfortable, you won't be able to put the book down!"

- Amazon Customer Review

Praise for *Sixty Days for Love*:

"A perfect late-at-night after the kids are in bed escape. The heroine is fun and likeable and the hero is sexy and loveable. What more could you want?"

- Verified Amazon Review

ABOUT THE AUTHOR

Liza Malloy writes contemporary romance, new adult romance, women's fiction, and fantasy romance. She's a sucker for alpha males, bad boys, dimples, and muscles, and she can't resist a man in uniform. Liza loves creating worlds where her heroine discovers her own strength and finds her Happily Ever After. When Liza isn't reading or writing torrid love stories, she's a practicing attorney. Her other passions include gummy bears, jelly beans, and the occasional marathon. She lives in the Midwest with her four daughters and her own Prince Charming. *The Revelation* is her seventh published novel.

Visit her website at www.LizaMalloy.com

Join her email list for access to exclusive bonus content at http://bit.ly/34FrD71